To Jen—

Have an amazing read!

Hidden Presences

Book 1 of the Hidden Strength Series

Enjoy.

Jenna O'del

Jenna O'del

ISBN: 151734462X
ISBN-13: 978-1517344627

The Land

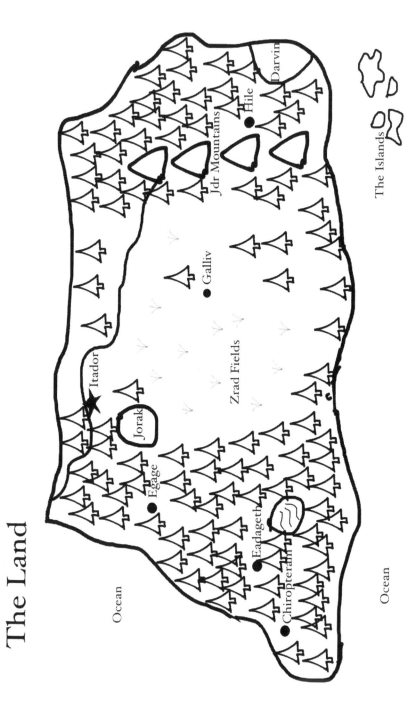

Author's Note:
All anthropomorphic, humanoid characters are referred to as 'a/the fur,' or 'furs' if not called by their actual name or species. 'The fur' is equivalent to 'the individual,' and 'the furs' is to 'many individuals.' 'Fur' is singular, and 'furs' refers to one or more anthropomorphic characters, regardless of whether or not the character has fur. It is unknown why these characters are referred to as 'furs;' perhaps it is because so many of them have fur, less have feathers, and those with scales are even fewer in number. An 'ancestor' is a non-anthropomorphic animal.

Furs
Adamar—(Add-Ah-Mahr) Fox, Miro's father, mate of Avaha, Eadageth archer
Avaha—(Ah-vah-ha) Fox, Miro's mother, mate of Adamar
Azoth—(A-zahth), Timber Wolf
Badr—(Bad-er), Possum, Eadageth archer
Briscoe—(Brisk-oh), Wildcat, Hile weapons maker
Cazy—(Cah-zee) Juvenile Blue Jay from Eadageth
Chenl—(Sha-nehl), Mouse, Eadageth healer
Chilo—(Chill-oh), Jackal, Girbindon's assistant
Ecetal—(Ehk-eih-tal), Dragon
Edgier—(Ehd-gee-er), Beaver, Eadageth archer
Fen—(Fen), Ferret, of Darvin
Girbindon—(Grr-bin-dohn), Bear, Darvin King
Hmo—(Huh-mo) Bat, Eadageth archer
Isun—(Iss-uhn), White-tailed Deer, Darvin worker
Jek—(Jhk) Deer, helper to Chenl
Kalina—(Kah-lean-a), Mink, Eadageth archer
Laurel—(Lawr-el), Skunk from Fride
Leona—(Lee-ohn-ah), Bobcat, Eadageth archer
Maln—(Mall-in) Squirrel, helper to Chenl
Miro—(Meero) Juvenile Fox, kit of Adamar and Avaha
Mosity—(Moss-it-e) Pine Marten, Eadageth archer
Norm—(Norm) Black-footed ferret, Eadageth archer
Ohanzee—(O-hahn-zee) Coyote, Eadageth archer
Osima—(O-see-mah), Mountain Lion from the Jdr Mountains
Rowena—(Rohw-ehn-ah), Jackal, Hile healer
Skyor—(Sky-or), Juvenile Gray Wolf from Hile
Slai—(Sli) Robin, helper to Chenl

Thayn—(Tahn), Red Wolf, Eadageth archer

Ancestors
Enki—(En-kee), Horse
Galene—(Gay-leene), Horse
Dakr—(Dahk-er), Horse
Olie—(Ohl-e), Horse

Locations
Chiropteram—(Cheer-oop-tehr-am)
Galliv—(Gal-iv)
Darvin—(Daarv-in)
Eadageth—(Eed-gah-deth)
Hile—(Hill)
Fride—(Freed)
Jdr Mountains—(Jah-der)
Kleak—(Kleek)

Hidden Presences

Prologue

Miro tossed in his crib, sleep snatched away by confused, terrified anxiety. His nose twitched as a strange scent filled the air. Somebody was coming. Someone he didn't know. The humanoid fox opened his eyes, rubbing at them with small furred, five-fingered fists. He caught sight of a dark figure coming closer to his bed, sneaking as if it shouldn't be here. Miro's nose told him it was some canine-like creature reaching down.

The fox kit refocused his gaze, and blinked at the sleep that still clouded his young eyes. When equally-furred strange hands brushed his sides, he immediately turned and twisted away. Where was his mother or father? He didn't like this new creature. It was unfamiliar and scary.

The canine-imitation quickly reached and scooped him up, cradling him to its chest. Miro squirmed in the unfamiliar grip, whining until two fingers circled his small muzzle, signaling silence. A hand yanked on his tail as the canine-imitation growled.

"Quiet, or you won't get any breakfast, you little pup."

A formidable threat to the young fox kit, Miro stayed quiet, gripping the folds of the canine-imitation's cloak with his tiny hands, digging his thumbs into the fabric. His eyes grew wide as the canine-imitation tripped when turning, and dug his claws into the stone wall above Miro's crib for balance. The sound screeched painfully in the kit's ears. Miro couldn't help a whimper. He then yelped as a slap on his back drove the wind out of him.

The canine-imitation growled at seeing the scratches in the wall. He smelled of annoyance.

"Now, hold on tight." He whispered, wrapping one arm around the fox kit. Miro dug his small nails even deeper into the cloak as the canine-imitation bolted. His flat, five-toed feet hit the ground softly, nails clacking whenever they passed over a stone road. Miro watched his home grow smaller. Then the whole village disappeared behind them.

The fox kit whined with an ache he didn't know and buried his face into the canine-imitation's chest.

One

Adamar notched his arrow and pulled back the bowstring, aiming at the target across the field. When the arrow was properly set, he released the string and let it fly. The arrow whistled through the air and landed in one of the inner rings crudely drawn on the hay and canvas target.

Sighing, Adamar picked up his now empty quiver and padded over to the target, retrieving his arrows quietly as the sun beat down against the orange fox fur on his back. He could smell the many furs that had passed by here before, getting their own arrows. His ears were up and alert, listening for any warnings to get out of the way before a stray arrow went through his back.

Once all his arrows had been retrieved, Adamar walked off the range and stowed his full quiver and bow in the weapons shed. He worked out a few knots in his muscles. His tongue poked out of his mouth in a pant.

"Hey, Adamar, you hungry?" A voice caught the tall fox's attention and he looked up to see a possum advancing, also clothed in only pants, in an effort of modesty while beating the heat of the sunny day. Adamar nodded and straightened.

"What's for lunch?" Adamar followed the possum to where the other archers were gathering, making his way past the range and toward a small building, which shadowed a long outdoor table.

"Bread and meat?" The possum and fox sniffed the air briefly, and the possum shook his head. "It was made quickly. Something's up in the village. I don't know what could've happened."

"No one here would, Badr. We all stayed the night here to practice our dusk archery. Remember? Or did that already leave your possum head?" Adamar grinned and elbowed Badr jokingly.

The possum narrowed his squinty eyes. He paused, looking at the fox over his shoulder. His gaze settled on something on Adamar's chest for a moment before he stalked off.

Adamar cocked his head, confused at the possum's sudden uptight manner. Badr had always been a little stiffer than the rest of the village, possibly due to his mysterious upbringing, but he could always, at the least, manage a smile for a joke. And what was so interesting on his chest? It was just fur.

The fox pushed the thought from his mind and sat down at the table. He tensed in embarrassment as his stomach let loose a roar, but couldn't keep a smile from his muzzle when the others laughed.

"Starving again, Adamar?" A ferret next to him teased. "Was the kit keeping you up all night and day yesterday? Forgot to pack a lunch?"

Adamar rolled his eyes. "Luckily I don't need to pack any lunch." he retorted. One of his ears swiveled toward a banging door and a vole who wore a stained apron carrying a couple trays of food outside.

Eager for food, Adamar sat up and placed his forearms on the wooden table, eyeing one of the trays filled with meat. The other had a non-meat option for vegetarian furs, made of fruits and vegetables that he would avoid if he could. He felt Badr's eyes on him, but managed to ignore them as the vole set down both platters of food.

"Sorry everyone." The vole apologized. "We only had time for cold leftovers made into sandwiches. We know you're working hard, training and all.

Hope your food's good." The vole disappeared back inside the food house.

Adamar grabbed one of the sandwiches. He didn't bother to glance at it curiously, instead stuffing half of it into his muzzle. His thoughts drifted to Miro, his young kit, as he ate, at the thought of Miro one day learning how to use a bow and arrow.

Everyone except Badr also wolfed down their food. The possum sat across from Adamar, nibbling at the bread while keeping his gaze glued on the fox.

Adamar met eyes with Badr for a moment, not understanding what he wanted.

"I got word of what happened yesterday. Really, last night." A wolf at the other end of the table mentioned as he finished one sandwich and reached for another.

"Something happened? What was it?" The mink next to him asked, halfway through her own lunch. "How'd you find out?"

"One of my arrows went awry and flew towards the village. As I was retrieving it, I heard some of the pups playing deep in the woods and talking about a 'canine intruder.' Supposedly some furs found tracks and weird scents in the village." he said, referring to the other villagers. "The pups had been sent out to play, to stay away from the adults' business."

Adamar looked at the wolf. "Whose pups?"

"I'm not sure. I think yours, Kalina." The wolf glanced at the mink next to him.

The squeaky voice of Badr cut off the next question. "What's that on your chest, Adamar?" His black eyes drilled through the fox.

Adamar glanced down at his white-furred torso. A splotch of brown fur decorated the white space next to where his heart lay. "I don't know." The fox shrugged and looked back up, giving the possum a look of wariness. "It's been there for years, at least since I was a young teenager. Probably some sort of birthmark. Why?"

Badr ignored the others that were watching him and went back to eating his food. "No reason."

Strange. But Adamar returned to his food and joined in on the endless drone of conversation. Soon the food was gone.

As everyone dispersed, Adamar retrieved his quiver from the shed and began mending a bent arrow. He bent over the task, sweat gathering between his toes. He only sweat on his muzzle, and on the underside of his feet and palms. The sun was warm for an autumn month.

Adamar's ears pricked as he heard his name. He looked up and turned, taking sight of a mouse rushing toward him, her small feet slapping the ground. "Adamar!" she squeaked, out of breath. "You have to come quickly. Something's happened."

The fox stood, smelling urgency on the rodent. "What happened?"

"Your mate is hysterical." The mouse drew closer, smelling of his home and his family. She swished her tail and glanced at the other archers stopping to watch. "I've only just now been able to get away and tell you."

Recalling Badr's odd actions, a tone of protectiveness crept into Adamar's words. "Chenl, what happened? Why is Avaha upset? Is Miro okay?"

Chenl shook her head. "That's the problem, Adamar. Miro's missing. We think he was stolen."

Two

Adamar bolted ahead of Chenl, leaving behind everything he'd taken to the range in his hurry to get home. The hardened pads of his flat, black-colored feet scraped at stones as he dashed through the woods. The range was just over a mile from the very edges of the village, well far enough to keep any arrows from accidentally hitting someone walking around in the town.

Thoughts swirled through the fox's mind as he ran. He had no idea who would've taken his pup, and why they would do so was an even more puzzling question. Adamar worried for his mate, for she loved the kit dearly. Just as much as he did. The fox had a concerning sense that the rumors of the intruder had to do with his kit going missing.

For a few seconds Adamar heard the sounds of the other archers wanting to help, but Chenl ushered them back enough so they resumed their training. Except Badr had stared at Adamar as he left, which Adamar didn't notice.

The fox leapt over a fallen branch and onto the outskirts of the village. A few farmhouses decorated the edge of the woods, but Adamar kept going. His own house was on the other side of the village.

The fox slowed his pace as he got to a stone house. The window in the side of the house allowed a glimpse of an empty room. Adamar continued to the front of the home, where a crowd had gathered and soft whimpers could be heard from inside. His ears lowered in wariness and fear. Furs turned toward him, offering sympathy as they watched him pass by.

Adamar took in the scene quickly, worry filling him. He smelled the cold, heavy smell of loss and of fear, as well as other scents he didn't recognize. His mate sat by the fireplace, her muzzle in her hands and furs clustered around her.

"Avaha." Adamar cried and went to his mate, kneeling down and pulling her into his arms.

She sniffed, burying her orange muzzle against his furred chest. "Miro..." she whimpered in her soft voice. Her dress was wrinkled, as if put on in a haste and picked from the filthy pile of laundry collected in their bedroom.

Adamar smelled only a lingering of Miro's young kit scent, and his body went nearly limp for a moment. His kit was truly gone.

Trying to keep himself together, the fox rubbed his mate's back. "I know. I know. I'm sorry that I couldn't have been here sooner." He searched for her gaze. "How long has he been missing?"

Avaha drew in a few shuddering breaths. "I'm not too sure. I woke to feed him, and he was just...gone." She stopped her weeping.

Rocking with her for a few moments, Adamar felt the world slow as he fully took in that his kit was gone. It just couldn't be. Miro was such a sweet pup. There would be no reason to take him. He never did anything to stand out. He was just a youngling. He was barely a year old. Just a young pup, his fur still the soft brown of a fox kit's.

But he couldn't be gone...they were all just playing a trick. It was some big, elaborate, cruel prank. Miro was just outside playing with the other village pups. Someone would bring him in any minute as he cried to be fed.

"Avaha," Adamar steeled himself and managed to catch her gaze. "I'm going to go see if I can tell who took him. I won't be long."

He stood, gently easing his mate off of himself so she wouldn't fall, and went over to the ajar door of Miro's room.

Adamar put his hand on the wood of the door, nose straining for any scent that confirmed the odd, hopeless chance that his pup would be there.

He pushed on the wood, ears twitching at the hinges scraping. His ears were pricked and alert, still checking to see if Miro's little squeal of joy would greet him.

When he looked inside at an empty room, his heart sank. The crib where his pup had slept was empty, the sheets mussed and unmade. The rocking chair sat still, as if death had put a stop to its movements. A glass window at the far wall looked too cloudy, like it wanted to weep just as much as Adamar did.

The fox stood there, trembling as his hands clenched into fists. He could smell the scent of his young kit and Avaha's frantic discovery, but near it was another...strange smell. Something like a canine's, unfamiliar to the wooded village of Eadageth. Adamar couldn't place it in the wave of emotions that crashed over him.

Who would dare take his pup? Why would they? They had no right to. Miro hadn't done anything wrong.

Adamar snarled with anger and made his way to Miro's crib, which he gripped the side of for support until his claws dug gouges in the hand-carved wood. He dipped his head, tears streaking down his grimy face. His ears laid flat, daring anyone to come close.

His tail lashed as fear became prominent. What did they want with young Miro? What were they going to do to him? Who were they? Were they cruel? Would they harm his little kit?

A growl came from his throat. If they, whoever they were, dared lay a claw on his kit, he would personally kill them. He would get Miro back. He knew he would.

His orange shoulders slumped as another realization came. He would find his pup, yes, but he just didn't know how. Or where to start. He couldn't even place the scent of who had supposedly taken Miro.

The fox whimpered with frustration and collapsed into the rocking chair, burying his muzzle in his hands. Warm tears dripped between his fingers.

The door creaked open again, and a figure slipped inside. Avaha knelt by her mate, switching roles as she rubbed his shoulder. "I know, honey. I know it hurts. But the furs of the village are helping. They're looking for clues as to who might have taken Miro."

Adamar shook his head, knowing words wouldn't obey him now. The village furs wouldn't be helpful. He needed furs who could track, like foxes could. Who knew Miro, like he and Avaha did.

The fox leaned into his mate, trembling as he struggled to contain the endless torment of emotions. She was right; his heart did ache. His kit was gone. Missing. Stolen. It felt like someone had ripped out every muscle in his body and sewn them back in all the wrong spots.

Adamar cried for a few minutes longer, getting it out before it overwhelmed him later on. He then stood, wiping at his soaked face and feeling the despair try to come back. He let the emotions charge him on.

"They won't find our kit." Adamar turned to Avaha, looking as determined as he could in his hurting and saddened state. "I will. I don't care what it takes." He said it more to remind himself that he would.

Avaha's eyes shined with worry. "You cannot, dear. You don't know who's out there. I don't want to see you as a corpse the next time I do."

Adamar drew in a shuddering breath. He looked his mate dead in the eye. "You've got to believe me."

"You just thought of this crazy idea a minute ago." Avaha retorted.

Adamar glanced back at his mate, except that his gaze again flashed to Miro's crib. The fox's eyes narrowed and he stepped closer, ignoring a protest from Avaha to leave the search alone.

Adamar traced three claw marks in the wall above his kit's crib. They were gouged in and rough, but the ends of the lines were lighter, as if whoever had made them had been in a hurry. They smelled like they were from whoever took Miro, but he had to check.

"Avaha." The fox beckoned his mate closer. "Did you make these marks?" When she shook her head no, Adamar pressed on. "Were these here when you put Miro to bed last night?"

His mate stared at the wall for a moment, then shook her head again. "No. They just appeared."

Acknowledging her words with a slow nod, Adamar caught again the scent of the unknown canine drifting from the crib. The scent mixed with Miro's young foxy smell.

The town's residential mystery solver, a wolf, walked in with his strong and knowledgable nose, even though Adamar believed him to be a little lazy. The wolf worked to decipher who might have taken Miro and which town they came from. He could only figure out that the canine-like scent was probably a jackal, whose family Adamar guessed had migrated here years ago during the Far-reaching

War. The wolf, Lan, made note of how he thought he smelled the slightest scent of bear, and then he went into how interesting the marks above Miro's crib were. How they looked accidental. He also commented on the pawprints that had been found in the village by Kalina's pups, how they might be connected. But that was the extent of his search.

Fighting hopeless tears, Adamar thanked him and sent him off. His sorrow soon turned into rising frustration, which he worked to hide from Avaha. She'd just think he was being rash about finding Miro. The sooner he left to find Miro, the better his chances of finding him safe and sound and in one piece.

As Lan walked outside, Avaha whimpered and put the soggy cloth clutched in her hands to her nose. "My kit. Stolen." She turned her ears out in sadness as Adamar came over and wrapped his arms about her.

"Avaha." he whispered, pressing his muzzle close to her pointed ear. He had to get right to the point. It wasn't worth it wasting time on formalities. "Did you ever learn about those marks?" Avaha had grown up outside of Eadageth, getting her education elsewhcre, like Badr had. "The gouges in the wall don't completely look like an accident." The depth of the gouges made them seem almost intentional.

His mate stilled and raised her red eyes to meet Adamar's. "I might've." she sniffed. "But please don't do what you're thinking. These furs that have taken Miro...they're..." She shook her head, as if fighting with herself to get the words out. "I believe...They're dangerous, especially if they're willing to steal someone's little kit."

A slight smirk crossed the fox's muzzle, despite the mood of the situation. "Everything and nothing is dangerous, Avaha."

Avaha tilted her head back to peer at her mate, her voice growing solemn. "We need to talk about this."

Adamar stepped back while his mate closed the shutters of the one window in Miro's room. She seemed almost anxious while she moved about, making sure prying ears wouldn't hear. Adamar had no idea what was so important to be kept secret. She had him settle in the empty rocking chair.

By sitting, the fox was shorter than his mate. It gave Avaha the sense of dominance, so she could conquer this talk more easily.

Avaha stood with her ears back, gazing down at her mate as if he was a kit who needed some reprimanding.

"Adamar," her voice was lowered, quiet. "I don't know where this jackal came from, who he came from. But I have a feeling that they're a very dangerous group. Who else would take a fox kit? And why else would they dare leave an intentional clue as to their identity?"

His gaze found the floor as he attempted to bring words to his tongue. She was right. Most thieves, unless arrogant of their power, wouldn't leave any intentional mark. So leaving a mark would mean they were from a strong group at least, whatever it was. Yet...she did not know of anyone that would make three simple claw gouges their signature. That was odd in its own right. As she'd told him before, her education had been very thorough and had covered nearly everywhere of the land, everywhere important.

Except, why would they put the marks there? Unless those marks weren't intentional...Why would they leave the marks? It was almost like...

"They want us to find them." Adamar looked at her, face grave, the dirt in his fur giving him a further ashen look.

"What?" Avaha paused the pacing she'd begun, looking at her mate. Fear jumped onto her expression for a moment before it faded. "Why would they do so? We don't have anything anyone could want."

Adamar nodded, gaze flicking to the ground for a moment. "I know. That doesn't make sense. I'm just a simple archer with a lovely mate and a lovely kit, not some wealthy fur. What could we give in ransom, if there was one?"

Shaking her head, Avaha sighed. "I don't know. I wish I did. I'm just really worried about Miro."

"I know." Adamar sighed. "But if they put a mark, that means they want us to find them, so what're they planning?" His mind started firing. "What if they don't want us to find them? What if it was an accident? Why would they take Miro? What skills, other than being a cute kit, does he have?" He had to get out of here before they did anything else to his kit, whatever it may be. He stood.

"No!" she protested, smelling what he was going to do. "I told you before, it's dangerous. Adamar, you can't go! I don't want you hurt."

Adamar looked at his mate. "Avaha, I won't just sit here waiting for someone to find him. You know me. I have to do something. I'll figure out where that mark comes from and go and get Miro. Besides, I'm a fox. So are you. We both know the quicker the better."

"Please, don't. You might get hurt. We don't know who those furs that took him are, other than that they're dangerous." Avaha's sad eyes bored into his own.

Adamar shook his head. "I can't just sit here. And anyways, also by being a fox, I'm elusive. They'll have to work hard to get at me before I get Miro back."

"Still. I'll worry if you're gone. And what if you don't come back? Adamar, you're too important to me. I don't want to lose my mate too."

Why was she so adamant against looking for Miro? He took in a breath. Maybe there was some way to compromise with her. "I'm aware of that. But I will. I'll come back. I won't be dead."

"Does that mean you won't be hurt either?" When he did not reply, Avaha went on. "Exactly. You can't know. Neither can I."

Shaking his head, Adamar picked at a grimy spot in his fur. "Avaha, I'm going to go find Miro. But before that, I just have to get this itchy and stiff dirt off me. I need to figure out how I'll start the search for Miro. Please think about what I said, so I can leave knowing you'll be alright."

Adamar ran through the village, a bar of soap in hand. Villagers called out more sympathy as he passed. They wouldn't leave him alone. Just when he wanted to be by himself. Be with himself, be with no one. His kit wasn't there. Why should he care?

Adamar shook his head to clear the vicious thoughts and continued on his way, passing through the village and turning down a path that led into the forest.

The fox relaxed as soon as he thought he was alone, seeing nothing but trees on all sides and feeling the dirt squish beneath his pawpads. Scents drifted in and out of Adamar's nose, the soft air of pine mixing with the heavier musk of small forest creatures who didn't bother to hide in the piles of fallen leaves.

A small four-legged ancestor mouse scurried along the side of the woods and the edge of his vision as he ran. Other ancestors moved about. As simmering anger drove him to get to the water quickly, bathe, figure out where to go, and get on the trail after Miro, a small four-legged fox started following him.

He tilted his head and growled softly to the small fox. Though they had a different body structure, furs and their ancestors could somewhat understand each other. The language was rough, often broken, but it was manageable. And when an ancestor contacted a fur, it was a rare, important experience.

What? Adamar growled again, though keeping his tone as gentle as possible. Even though Adamar was in a hurry, the four-legged ancestors of the furs enjoyed being talked to with the utmost respect.

The fox pointed its muzzle down the path then back at Adamar. *Go clean. I come. Wolf will search. Wolf will help.*

Adamar laid back an ear. *Wolf?* he repeated, wary. Another wolf would look for Miro? Why? *Your kind wolf?*

No. The fox shook its head and growled. *Tall kind wolf.*

A fellow fur? Lan had just looked. But the ancestor probably wasn't talking about him.

Why wolf? Adamar asked, but the ancestor fox ran ahead.

The thought that it was good luck to see a blood ancestor eased some of Adamar's churning emotions.

Having not noticed the sound of falling water while running, Adamar's ears pricked at the crash of a waterfall, and the scent of the clear water moving through the stream tantalized his nose.

Adamar stepped through an archway of oaks that had grown oddly to reach toward one another, their branches entwining as they turned to the sky. The clearing smelled gently of the forest, of the fresh cool water and of the joy from the furs that had been here a few hours ago, playing and splashing in the river.

A waterfall far to the side tumbled over eroded rocks and dumped into an expanding, near circular pool. The water then slowly drifted toward a smaller, foot high edge, where it gathered and slimmed down into a cool stream.

The ancestor fox loped around the side of the pool and sat on the opposite bank. It rested its head on its forepaws, watching Adamar curiously.

Adamar turned his attention to getting clean as quickly as possible as he peeled off his clothes and waded into the water. He headed to the waterfall. If he couldn't figure out what village that Miro may have been taken to, with or without someone else's help, he would just follow his nose. But he could smell a thunderstorm coming. If he didn't leave soon, he'd be stuck until after the rain.

He stepped into the middle of the waterfall and allowed himself to get fully soaked. He shook out his fur in the first few seconds of being beneath the pounding shower, and took the bar of soap to his fur before turning to his filthy pants.

As he washed, he felt the water wash away his conflicting emotions, cleaning the inhibiting ones of wanting to listen to Avaha and drawing focus to the main determination that had been lingering ever since word of Miro's disappearance.

Adamar also felt the fox's eyes on him, and he glanced through the rushing water at the orange creature, head laid upon its paws as it quietly watched. Other ancestors moved about around it, but it barely stirred. Odd.

He rolled his shoulders back as he glanced at the brown spot on his white chest, the one Badr had questioned earlier.

"Things going well there?"

Adamar jumped, and quickly moved behind the

curtain of falling water as he searched for the voice's owner. Scolding thoughts and fear rolled into his mind as he realized how unfocused thinking about finding Miro had made him. He hadn't even paid attention to his own nose.

"I'm over here, you goose."

Adamar flicked his ears and desperately slipped under the water in an attempt to pull on his pants while retaining dignity. He surfaced in soaked trousers. His gaze settled on a two-legged wolf squatting next to the resting ancestor fox, stroking it between the ears as it emitted a content sound, almost like a feline's purring.

The wolf's fur was scraggly, growing longer in patches and looking like it'd been ripped from his body in others. His ears, though, were perfect specimens of a wolf ear, rounded with a soft point at the top, while his muzzle was spotted with the whiter grays of an aging fur. His eyes were oddly colored, not the usual humanoid differing colors of brown, green, and blue, but the yellow of wolf ancestors.

A jumble of colors decorated the wolf's clothes, fading from the darkest brown to a lighter tan. The stitches binding separate pieces of cloth stood out.

As the wolf spoke, his voice shifted and changed, like the many colored leaves drifting off their trees. His eyes shined of intelligence.

"Doing well?" he asked. "Yes, it looks like you've some problems on your hands. Word has reached mine too of the present issue. You doing anything about it?" The wolf sat on the bank of the moving water, dipping his legs in the river.

Wary, Adamar took in a deep breath of the wolf's scent, smelling joyful and mischievous emotions. The wolf could have also used a bath a month ago. "Who're you?" he scrutinized the wolf for a moment, a brief flash of recognition churning. "Wait a second..."

The wolf nodded and crossed his legs beneath himself, yellow eyes never straying from Adamar's face. "That's it. I'm the village crazy. That's what they name me, at least. That fur just living on the edge of the woods. Or in the woods..." The wolf shrugged. "The name's Azoth. You're Adamar."

Adamar spoke carefully. "You listen around a lot, don't you?"

"Yeah, that, but I do sniff the news now and then. The arrow-archers mention it from time to time."

"I see." Adamar stood his ground, even though he probably looked like a drowned wildcat. "Why are you here? And why did you decide to talk to me when I'm bathing...?" He didn't mention that if Azoth knew what had happened, why was he stalling Adamar? Could he help find Miro?

The ancestor fox raised its head and looked at Adamar. It shook its muzzle slightly. *Trust wolf.*

"I'm here like all the furs. I was just here." A laugh poured itself from the wolf's muzzle. "I'm here, standing in this spot where I'm actually resting," he grinned, "Because I came to talk to you. Obviously. Why wouldn't that be obvious? You don't believe I'd come to peer at your bathing, do you?"

When Adamar didn't respond, Azoth continued. "Well now, I should be on before it's off. Your pup isn't in his crib anymore. You note anything about the scene?"

"Scene?" Adamar repeated. A dark thought crossed his mind: Did Azoth have something to do with it...?

Azoth rolled his yellow eyes. "Yes, scene, you bumbledraft. What do you remember about the problems?" he sighed. "You fool. That sniffer put some words to air and told about it. I heard of what was scalded into stone."

Adamar nodded slowly. 'Scalded into stone...'

The claw marks.

"Why're you asking?" Adamar watched him carefully. He moved towards the riverbank, ready to leave. This was a waste of time.

"You're asking for aid, right? You couldn't figure it out? I could tell you what's going on." Azoth smiled, a puppy's goofy grin falling upon his muzzle. "But...I want you take a look at the words first."

Adamar stilled. "They're not words. They're claw marks."

"Ah, that may be, Adamar, but now always are they. E'er heard that phrase that a scent tells a thousand words? Same goes with the claw marks in crime scenes. Crime...such an interesting word. They don't like to use that often. They considering stealing or harming better. Though a crime is a crime." He giggled. "Take a look at those marks, then come and talk to me. Observe them. Smell them. Capture them. When you're done, meet me around your house. I will tell you what you need to know. I know what you know not and you know what I know not."

The wolf turned and faded into the trees.

Three

After clambering onto the bank and shaking out his fur, Adamar sniffed the air to see if the wolf was nearby. But he realized, as he grabbed the bar of soap, that the air was blowing downwind, making it a challenge for him to catch any sort of scent that signified Azoth's presence.

Adamar ran back home, his wet footsteps marking up the path. He focused mainly on Azoth's words. For as long as Adamar knew, Azoth had been living on the outskirts of Eadageth and occasionally in the forest surrounding the archery range. He'd been marked as crazy ever since a small act in his puphood. Adamar didn't know what the event had been.

The village had then after regarded Azoth with an air of annoyance. Azoth had gone into hiding, and some time later he'd emerged from the forest, scraggly and half-starved. He'd been lightly accepted back if he lived on the edge of Eadageth. He'd then begun speaking in ways that many had a problem defining. The village again called him crazy.

Yet he appears smarter than he looks...Adamar sighed as a cool wind blew through his drying fur. A glance up showed the angry clouds gathering in the sky above.

The air smelled of the burnt, swirling scents of the storm. Too late to leave. He should have been faster. He would've gotten on some sort of scent trail for a little while at least.

Rain began to trickle down. Any furs on the road went inside to their homes, some clutching goods to their chests as they tucked their heads against the steadily falling rain.

A squawk caught Adamar's attention, and he turned his head to see a young blue jay fur curled into a ball on the ground, sobbing quietly to itself. The fox stopped, paternal instinct taking over.

Adamar's ears strained for a sound of the bird's parent, but when he heard none, he sighed and dropped to a crouch beside the chick. He didn't have time to do this. But how could he leave now, anyways? Rain washed away scents and made his nose blind to the world.

"Hey," he said. "Where's your mother or father?"

The bird shook its head and pulled its knees closer, blue and gray-feathered arms hugging them tightly to its trembling body.

Adamar gently touched the bird's shoulder. "Why're you out here?"

The chick flinched at Adamar's touch, then realized a hand was there to comfort, and leaned into him.

Warily, Adamar rubbed the bird's feathery back as it leaned against his sopping chest, sniffling. "I...I don't know...I saw this fur that was performing a magic trick, and, and when I turned around, father and brother were gone."

Adamar nodded; the fake-magic tricks were popular with young kits. And their fathers, Adamar had to admit. "Do you know where father may be?"

The bird shivered. "I'm not sure. He's..." The chick shook its head and started sobbing again as thunder rumbled off in the distance.

While the rain grew heavier, Adamar managed to get the information about which house he could go to give the chick back to its family.

After placing the soap beneath a dry barrel, Adamar stood, shivering in his already soaked fur. He clutched the young bird to his chest, soothing it while he jogged down the street and onto a road marked with homes in the trees. The avian furs liked to live in places similar to where their ancestors nested, making it rare to find a tree-dwelling bird fur tending a farm.

He ran down the lane until a large tree-home was in front of him. He hoped it was the right home, but he couldn't smell the house to be sure.

The bird clung to him, weeping, unaware that Adamar had stopped. The fox glanced at the house.

A winding staircase made its way up a thick oak tree, the wood of the stairs nearly the same colors as the tree it surrounded. The stairs led up to a rounded house perched in the tree's thick branches. The house looked worn, its wood nearly tan by the elements that had dashed it over the years, making it stand out against the darker forest. Glass-less windows dotted themselves over the house.

Adamar gently squeezed the bird and asked, "That's your home, right?"

The bird stopped its crying long enough to glance up through bleary eyes, and nodded its small beak.

Adamar started up the wooden stairs, his claws catching in the oddly shaped gouges caused by avian talons. The fox picked up his furred feet a bit more and made his way to the house's door. There he held the chick with one arm and knocked on the wood, nose twitching at the scents that emanated from the dry house. He was grateful for the tree's branches hanging over the entryway, stopping the rain and letting him smell something.

The door swung open to show an adult jay standing there in simple black clothes that rested against his blue color. Like many furs with winged ancestors, no sleeves covered the bird's arms, allowing the longer feathers protruding from the undersides of his arms to remain uncrushed.

"Are you missing your kit?" Adamar glanced at the jay, whose gaze went to the chick Adamar held. The adult jay squawked with joy and leapt forward.

"Cazy!" The bird reached for his chick.

Adamar found himself tightening a grip around the young bird, almost protectively, as if it was Miro and not an avian kit. He briefly turned out his ears in guilt as he released the chick.

"Thank you! Thank you!" The bird hugged his chick, who buried its beak in the adult jay's clothes and made his father equally soaked. The adult grinned at Adamar. "Where was he? I couldn't find him anywhere."

"In the middle of town, sitting next to the blacksmith's shop." Adamar shifted his weight. "Well, I must be going. It's good you've got him back."

The bird nodded, smiled at Cazy and then Adamar, and stepped into his home.
"Right. You should; get out of this pouring rain. Hey, I'm sorry about your chick. Have you gotten anywhere?"

Adamar found great interest in the staircase, having not glanced back at the bird. "I don't know." he said sadly. He raised his gaze to look out over the rained-upon world. With each second that the rain fell, more scents dissipated and more trails faded.

Four

"Where were you?" Avaha snarled when he walked in. "Adamar, you..." her eyes grew wet, her scent starting to carry the smells of despair. "I...I was worried you weren't coming home. I was worried you'd gone off already on that idea of yours."

Adamar lowered his wet ears and crossed his arms. "I wouldn't go without telling you...but you know that I will go on it. I have to get Miro back."

"And get killed!" Avaha's face streaked with tears as she moved closer to her mate, who began backing away, backing himself unintentionally into a corner.

Adamar didn't change his words. "I have to get Miro back."

"You're going to go off with no plan in mind, nowhere to go, no idea of anything to do?" Avaha stuck her muzzle near Adamar's. "Do you want to get killed?"

"No..." Adamar's eyes narrowed. "I'm not going to. I'll find him. I've got some ideas of where I can go." He could go away from Eadageth.

Avaha growled in frustration and glanced at her mate's fur. "You're sopping wet." she observed, turning to leave Adamar staring oddly after her as she disappeared. When she came back clutching a towel, her expression was softer, her smell kinder. She seemed to have entirely dropped the issue of missing Miro.

She handed the towel to him. "You took a long time. What happened?"

Adamar rubbed at his head. "I met an ancestor." He didn't mention Azoth for fear of inciting her rage again.

Avaha paused. "You did? Where? What'd they say?"

The ancestor fox's image and Azoth's words were dancing in his mind. Adamar shivered. "Could we talk later about it? I'm freezing."

Once Adamar had shook out his fur and put on dry pants, he sat on the ground in front of a slowly crackling fire, a blanket covering his furred body. His wet pants rested on the ground near the snapping warmth, drying as Avaha brought her mate a drink of warmed cider.

"Here," she said and sat down in the chair next to him. Adamar had agreed to stray from furniture until his fur dried, even though sitting where he was made him feel as a subordinate; not an equal. Like he was a kit being scolded.

Adamar voiced his appreciation and raised the cup to his muzzle. He tipped the cider down. It went over his long tongue and down his throat; making its way to warm his stomach.

Pulling the blanket tighter around himself, Adamar glanced up at his mate, and flinched when thunder smashed outside.

"You know the storm won't hurt you." Avaha met his fearful gaze.

"I know." Adamar nevertheless remained tense, and nearly jumped out of his skin when a roll of booms from the sky shook the house.

Avaha smiled down at him, attempting to reassure her mate. But his gaze had gone into the fire, watching its leaping flames and the acrobatics of its energy. He tried to turn his mind away from the storm, towards how he would get Avaha to agree with him and he could go get Miro without a guilty conscience.

He wondered if he should go with other furs, who could help in tracking.

Adamar started to relax, holding the blanket tight as if it would protect him. A slight wariness crept up, warning him the thunderstorm in the clouds wasn't the only storm that was going on.

"Why do you think you'll find Miro? We don't even know who took him, or why." Avaha rested her hand on one of the arms of the chair.

"I just know. And we do know it was a jackal. Why do you think I'll get killed?" A growing resentment of sitting on the floor flamed suddenly as Adamar looked up at his mate.

"Because...because it's dangerous, Adamar. I'm worried. You know that. Miro is gone, and I don't want you to be gone too. That's just not...I can't."

"You can't?"

"I can't stand you leaving. Please don't go."

Adamar sighed. "I...I have a way to find him. Avaha, I can and will come back. It's not like I'm leaving right now." Maybe he would set off after the sun rose. Get a good night's rest before heading out. Not that he wanted to wait any longer, but he couldn't start with this storm. And Azoth might be of some help. "It's just going to find him. It's not hard. I know you can fend for yourself when I'm not here."

Avaha's shoulders rose and fell. "Still, though. I don't want you to."

"You've said that a hundred times now. Why not? Because I'll get killed. You won't listen to me. I'll be careful." Thunder crashed and Adamar jumped. He would leave in the morning when the storm was over.

With silence being her only response, Avaha got up and went to their bedroom through the door branching off to the left, leaving Adamar alone by the fire. Adamar wallowed in anger and conflicting feelings for a moment before he recalled what Azoth had told him to do about the claw marks. He crept into Miro's room.

His ears lowered at the sight of not seeing his kit giggling in his crib, but he made himself focus. If he paid attention, he'd figure out what Azoth meant about the gouges quicker; he'd find Miro quicker. And the faster he had his kit back, the better.

Adamar went over and placed a hand on the wall next to the marks. His eyes traced over them, and then his fingers did.

They were three claw marks, the tops of them deep into the stone. They stayed mostly parallel with each other as they continued down. The ends of the lines fanned out a bit and weren't as heavily gouged into the stone as the beginning. They smelled like the jackal, a scent he was getting used to. And, if he smelled closely enough, he thought he could detect a slight smell of bear in the room. Lan was right. Another sharp smell entered his nose and he crouched to get to its source, by the bottom of Miro's crib. Miro had simply been lifted out of his crib and taken.

Anger. The harsh smell of severe anger filled his nose. Adamar narrowed his eyes. Whoever had taken Miro had been furious when they'd taken him. The fox hoped that they hadn't touched any fur on Miro's head, because if they had, he would kill them.

Again. After he'd killed them the first time, for stealing Miro.

Adamar looked back up at the claw marks and realized that it would've taken a fair amount of force to even scratch the rock, and so whoever had made the marks in it must've had a lot of strength behind them. How would they have made those marks so hastily?

As the rain fell, Adamar took in as many of details of the gouges as he could; measuring them with his thumb and index finger, noticing that there were only three claws instead of four minus the thumb from a usually five-fingered hand, attempting to recognize any specific scent of where the canine had come from. Any scent that would give him a better clue as to where Miro went. But he didn't recognize the scents left behind.

Once Adamar felt he'd examined the marks as best as he could, he went into the main room and was about to exit his home when he smelled his mate standing near the front door, glaring at the world outside the window and keeping her ears pressed to her skull.

Adamar turned. He went to his and Avaha's room, moving past the bed to a trunk pushed up against a wall. Adamar grabbed hold of the trunk's handle and pulled it back, wincing as the sounds of the trunk against the floor became loud in the near silence.

A glance and a sniff showed that Avaha hadn't moved from her position, and he turned back to where he'd removed the large piece of furniture. A small door stood in its place, maybe two feet tall and a little bit wider. It was barely visible in the stone.

Out of a hunch when he'd first been living with Avaha, he'd chipped out a small square in the wall, and managed to create an escape door out of it. He had shown it to his mate, explaining that if there was a need to not go through the front door, they had the back exit to leave, using the excuse of a rare possible raid from a nearby village. It had never been used.

Adamar's claws sought out the small indent for a grip in the door. Dust had gathered around the wall, tickling Adamar's nose and coating his hand in a layer of the years the door had been hidden. He traced the outline and cleaned out the hinges before the door decided to swing outward into the darkened world.

The storm had gratefully faded to just heavy rain. Adamar squeezed his way through the gap, and nearly went tumbling into the mud before he caught himself. He went over to the open door. His hand reached inside to pull it shut, but he was forced to leave the trunk out of place. He hoped that Avaha wouldn't notice its empty spot.

He turned and studied the woods near his home. A shadow moved. He blinked, watching the shadow start to make its way closer to him, then suddenly stop, turn, and dash into the forest.

"Who's there?" Adamar shouted, fur raising to intimidate any intruders. This couldn't be Azoth, unless the wolf was that strange. Could the fur that took Miro have come back for more? But why would they? What else was there to take?

The shadow paused at Adamar's voice, and seemed to glance his way. It stared for a moment before running off again, fading into nothingness.

"Who're you?" Adamar moved to the edge of the woods, his gaze searching out any forms as his nose sat, idle and unable to smell anything in the rain. With the shadow unresponsive, Adamar decided to go into the forest to confront it.

He stepped cautiously into the forest, his feet crushing soggy leaves as he pricked both ears, keeping them upright and alert. He looked around, eyes searching for the shadow.

An arm wrapped itself around his neck.

The fox clawed at the arm in surprise as it tightened its hold and pulled him back against a sopping body. The fur's other arm grabbed at Adamar's own arms and dug claws into them as the fur dragged Adamar backwards.

Thrashing, Adamar briefly hated having a long muzzle, as he was unable to bite the flesh of his captor. His own claws worked against those of the fur's, but made no progress compared to the red streaks the strong fur was causing.

A brief thought coated Adamar's mind as the fox kicked out. This was the jackal. It was coming back for him, to use Miro to get to him...to do whatever it had in mind. The timing was helpful—Adamar had a minimized sense of smell and muted vision in the rain, though his ears were sharp as ever. How had the fur managed to sneak up on him?

Maybe it was the storm...

The fur continued to drag him backwards, silent until it dragged Adamar to a point it deemed suitable, and released him.

The fox jumped away, snarling, ears pinned back against his skull, his body tense. His narrowed eyes immediately found the fur who'd gotten hold of him, and Adamar's words came out as a growl.

"Azoth."

The wolf smiled lopsidedly, standing beneath a pair of trees. "Greetings."

"Why'd you do that?" Adamar snarled, keeping a glare on the grinning wolf.

"I had to talk to you somehow. You wouldn't have just kept pace behind me in the death of night, now would you?"

Adamar scrutinized Azoth for a moment. "I suppose not."

"So..." Azoth's yellow eyes sparked. "Did you take a look at the claw marks?"

With a slow nod, Adamar confirmed the wolf's question. "Why?" The gouges in his arm burned. Blood mixed with the rain.

Azoth threw his hands up in the air. "Can you just describe what they looked like? Like I asked."

With his voice betraying his wariness, Adamar detailed the traits of the claw marks. Azoth listened intently while the fox listed what he found odd about the gouges and what he'd smelled from them.

Azoth's smile fell and he dropped to the ground, folding both legs beneath himself as he let his tail trail lazily away from his body. Adamar remained standing.

The wolf began thinking aloud, tracing the marks Adamar had described in the dirt. He refused to let Adamar get close to his drawing. "That canine was falling when the marks were gouged, he was tripping...it would make sense. But why would he be tripping? Was he thinking of the punishment he'd get? But no...he wouldn't get a punishment for acting out well. How come his fingers...Ah."

Azoth smiled and dashed a hand over the sketch in the dirt, obscuring its image completely. "Your perpetrator was making the mark of a kingdom. It was out of habit, an unconscious act. An act I think might be influenced by some strong power, like magic or something. Yet it appears that he might've just tripped. That's why the marks would be so deep at the beginning. The pressure he was pushing down, pushing down to catch himself so he wouldn't make a loud clamor."

Adamar furrowed his brow. "Wouldn't the sound of claws going through stone still make a noise?"

"It would...your mate was home when this event supposedly happened?" Azoth met the fox's gaze.

"She was."

"Then, that's odd as a donkey's beak."

"So whose kingdom was the canine from?" Adamar attempted a step forward, but at just the lifting of his foot, the wolf snarled at him.

Azoth let his hands rest in his lap, saying nothing, then lifted a hand and began to inspect his black claws, ears relaxed. Adamar wished he could smell and understand Azoth's emotions right now. The wolf contemplated his thoughts for a few moments. "I believe that's the mark of the Darvin kingdom."

"Darvin?" Adamar repeated, pricking his ears. Someone knew where Miro might be. "Who're they?"

"Oh, just a horse's butt's annoyance that wallows in the red mud of the land and came from a speck of dirt." Azoth shrugged as if this was common knowledge. When Adamar asked him to clarify, the wolf huffed in irritation, but went on.

"The Darvin kingdom's is this place from down, up, right. Southeast, maybe, if you go by the point of the stars." He listed the names of a few stars. "It's located maybe in the forest, or near the ocean. Roundabout ways you'll go to get there, though—"

"Are they strong? Cruel? Why would they take Miro?" Adamar couldn't help the questions from jumping off his tongue. He could not wait for Azoth to take so long to get to the point.

Azoth glanced at him. "Impatient, fox. I guess they could be harming, but who wouldn't be? Everyone harms others in their own way. It's kind of interesting to think about, you know? Well, maybe I don't know why they'd want a little orange cub. Of course I can't read inside their minds..." The wolf trailed off and looked toward an ancestor mink that had crept up to the edge of a nearby tree and was watching him intently.

Adamar crossed his arms as the mink stepped forward, ambling to Azoth. The mink emitted a few soft growls and squeaks; tail swiping slowly across the wet forest floor.

Azoth dipped his muzzle closer to the mink and responded in a canine's fashion. Growls, squeaks, and whimpers flowed back and forth between the two for several minutes as they spoke, leaving Adamar absolutely amazed.

And a little annoyed. He was not here to watch Azoth have an entire unrelated conversation.

When the communication ceased a minute later, Adamar glanced at Azoth. "How'd you do that?"

"Do what?" Azoth began stroking the mink's tiny head with a couple fingers. "Talk? You know how to do that, Adamar. Really. Must your questions be so absolutely brainless?"

"Yeah...but..." Adamar felt the growing sense of viewing Azoth as a half-crazy teacher. "Furs can only speak to their species' ancestors. You're a wolf. How were you able to speak to the mink?"

Azoth shrugged, a mischievous look shadowing his yellow eyes. "Reasons that may or may not be known by any or by none." he laughed. "Have you figured out who the Darvin kingdom is ruled by?"

Adamar let a growl touch his words. "You never asked me to do that. And what did the mink say? Ancestors don't come over to talk to you unless they have a good reason to. Did it have anything to do with Miro?"

"Things, Adamar. If they were for your ears, you would've understood them. Isn't that why I wasn't able to hear you and that fox ancestor speaking of lupine canines?" Azoth sighed and shook his head, continuing to pet the content mink by his side.

"The Darvin kingdom is a smaller group that became prominent in the past century. Their motive may be as clear as a sheep's tail, but they're known to be dangerous."

"Dangerous?" Adamar repeated. Azoth's answer half terrified and half motivated him. "Dangerous to...Miro?

Azoth nodded again. "Cruel as anything, they are. I think there's a bear that runs them. Ha. Runs them. Forces. Causes. Creates. Funny." A giggle passed out of the wolf's muzzle. "Those three marks. The marks of their warriors...to tell they've been here...possibly...but that wasn't intentional." Azoth glanced at Adamar. "Three gouges, right?"

Adamar nodded. "Three."

"The fur that took Miro probably lost a finger when he didn't do something right for the leader. The ruler of the kingdom's supposed to be cruel as chicken claws. One mistake, a finger goes." Azoth's ears turned out sadly as the mink got up and dashed back into the shadows of the forest.

Worried for his kit's safety, Adamar felt an even greater impulse to leave immediately and go find him. As soon as the rain let up. But he had to know one thing.

"What's the ruler's name? Do you know?" Now he could know exactly whom to target.

Azoth narrowed his eyes, thinking. "Girbindon."

Adamar nearly found himself making nervous little whimpers that seemed to unconsciously emerge from his throat. He struggled to swallow the degrading whines. "So...my kit...he's being held by a cruel fur?"

"Girbindon's claimed to be the harshest in the land." Azoth glanced at the treetops for a moment, but when he looked back down, Adamar was off and running into the forest.

Anxiety boiled throughout Adamar's body as he ran. He'd go mad if he didn't do something to get the worry out. He couldn't keep running. But his feet wouldn't stop chasing the trees.

Eventually Adamar forced himself to stop moving, nearly colliding with an oak tree in the process.

As tears streamed down his already wet face, Adamar raised his muzzle to the dark sky, and let loose a howl of anguish.

Five

"Adamar, you're getting the bed wet again."

Adamar groaned and blinked open his eyes, letting his sleepy gaze track Avaha, who calmly folded clothes near him and smelled of content emotions. She looked like she'd been awake for hours. He jerked up, worried he wouldn't have enough time to get Miro before the Darvin kingdom did whatever they were going to do to him. But a glance at the window in the corner and a draw of fresh scents showed it was just the beginning of the morning. Many furs didn't stay up through the entire night, even if their ancestors were nocturnal.

Adamar noticed the great splotch darkening the sheets on which he'd slept. After being informed of where Miro probably was, and howling into the night, he'd stumbled home and collapsed into bed, not caring about his soaked fur or equally drenched clothing. He'd been hit by a wall of no energy as he came home, and the rain wouldn't have helped him leave anyways.

Besides, he had to properly say goodbye to Avaha. He owed that much to her.

Avaha shook her head at him and sighed. "Come on, get up, so you can hang the bed sheets out to dry." As Adamar began to do so, Avaha joined in to help. "You know," she said, not looking at him as she pulled at a blanket, "You really have to stop falling into bed when you're sopping wet."

Adamar smiled weakly in a form of apology. His mate always criticized him for doing just so, especially after a particularly long day of archery testing. He would bathe the grime from his body, but would be so exhausted that he wouldn't notice he had fallen asleep still soaked until he awoke the next morning.

They worked in silence for a while, Adamar's mind racing. Did Avaha still want him to stay home, not look for Miro? When Adamar was bringing out the damp sheets and hanging them off a tree branch, he nearly fell the ten feet to the ground as Avaha startled him.

"Are you still thinking of going to find Miro?"

Gripping the thicker end of the branch with both hands, Adamar hoisted himself up over the tree limb and climbed down the trunk before he responded.

"Of course I am. Even though you don't still agree with it." Adamar crossed his arms and glanced at his mate, who was observing the small yard and woods their house looked out on.

The smell of anger started to drift from Avaha. "You're not listening to me. How can you just go, not even a day after Miro was stolen?"

"That's the thing. Not even a day. I have a better chance of following his scent, even though it probably got washed away by the rain." Adamar sighed. "I know where to go. Well..." he shifted his weight. "An idea of it, at least."

"Oh?" One of Avaha's ears pricked somewhat. "Was it a dangerous kingdom like I suspected it might be?"

Adamar narrowed his eyes. "Yes, but, I'm still going after him." He told her its name, and she seemed to have no idea of the Darvin kingdom. She only smelled of surprise and fear for her kit.

A brief argument ensued, both foxes trying to convince the other that what they were thinking was best. Adamar was mostly glad that emotions didn't boil over, but a small part of him was worried when Avaha remained calm throughout the discussion, until the end.

A growl surfaced from her throat and her fists clenched as she glared at Adamar. They'd moved inside for more privacy after a few minutes, but that didn't mean anything now.

"You cannot go! You are too important to me for you to just leave!" Avaha shouted, her upper lip curling back to bare her canines.

Adamar winced as the sound ricocheted off the walls and into his orange ears. Out of the corner of his eye he noticed the window had been left open, and that the furs that were passing by outside had paused in their walk.

Lowering his voice, Adamar stepped closer to his mate. "Avaha, you're attracting attention. We don't need the whole village splitting up and taking sides because we can't agree on something."

"We don't?" Avaha's claws twitched, but she forced her hand to relax as tears wet her cheeks. She shook her head, gaze falling to the ground. "No, you're right." She exhaled. "But—" she glanced outside, and her eyes flashed with what looked like resentment. "But since my voice was so loud, the furs now know what we're talking about. At least, a little."

And of course, Adamar heard a knock at the door and a voice calling in.

"Adamar? Avaha? What's going on? Why're you talking about leaving?" Chenl's voice and smell came through the door, and at Avaha's permission, the mouse walked in, followed by a few other of the villagers.

Adamar's ears turned out as he noticed a robin, a young squirrel, and a teenage buck crowd around the mouse. He had already smelled their presence before they came in, but it was still a surprise.

"Slai, Maln, Jek, what're you all doing here?" Adamar's gaze flicked to each fur.

Chenl glanced at her followers and then back at the fox. "They're following me. They've decided to apprentice in health. We were on a small tour of the village to reaffirm their knowledge of its layout when we heard Avaha say something." She looked between the two foxes. "What's happening?"

The robin, Slai, stepped forward. "Is everything alright?"

Adamar looked at his mate, who attempted a small smile.

"Yeah, everything's okay. We're just having a light argument." Avaha said.

"Then why did you yell?" Chenl pressed.

Avaha shrugged. "Just emotions getting the better of me. I'm not pleased about Adamar's decision to go after the fur that stole Miro."

Adamar shot his mate a look, but tensed when the attention turned on him. The buck, Jek, in particular, seemed to be intently interested on why he was deciding to go off on this ridiculous idea.

"You know that there's a possibility of casualty while trying to get your fawn?" Jek's growing antlers nearly rose to the height of Adamar's pricked ears. "You're one of the archers of this village; our defense system. While there are others that are trained in weaponry, they do not have as much skill as you do.

"Are you aware that if you do go off to find your fawn, you'll have to leave behind everything you know for an unknown time? Including not seeing Avaha for a while, not practicing your favorite sport?"

Adamar glanced elsewhere. The buck was right; he wouldn't be able to practice archery for a while. The fox loved that, enjoyed it almost as much as he was fond of his small family. Of course he wouldn't admit it; but others could see it in his gaze, in his scent, when he pulled back on the bowstring, when he saw the arrow fly through the air.

Adamar leveled his gaze. "I'm aware. I'm willing to do so. I just want my pup back." He insisted. "Miro's very important to me."

"I understand that," Jek said. "So you say you're willing to risk your life to find him?"

"Of course." Adamar nodded, eyes narrowing slightly.

"Hmm."

The three apprentices and Chenl began discussing quietly, their heads bowed together and eyes glancing at Adamar on occasion, as if he was insane. Adamar could feel anger start to rise.

Avaha looked at her mate, and grabbed Adamar's hands in her own. He turned to her, his expression a mix between wariness, annoyance, and sadness.

"Adamar, please don't. I didn't mean for other furs to get involved, but...they're only supporting my point." A fleeting smile decorated Avaha's muzzle as she briefly paused. "What if I let you have some time to yourself? Time to think this over and realize the right thing to do in awareness of your safety. Maybe you can go see the rest of the archers? That..."

Adamar didn't hear his mate's words as he debated the idea of venturing outside, knowing that the ears of many furs in the village were strong, strong enough to have at least caught one of Avaha's shouted words. But maybe he could go gather supplies at the archery range.

"Alright." Exhaling, Adamar shook himself from Avaha's grip and stepped back, causing the four to stop their discussion and look up. "I'll..." he looked at them all. "I'll be back later."

As Adamar walked outside, he found more eyes on him. His ears flattened while he crossed his arms, but the eyes continued to track him. Furs stood quietly, pausing in their conversations when he passed by, as if he'd just killed someone.

It was a big deal for someone to leave the small village. Even though the village wasn't that small. Maybe over two hundred furs resided here, but that was nothing compared to the larger towns and cities in other places in the Land.

"Hey, Adamar, what's happening?"

"What're you leaving for?"

"Why?"

At first with each question, Adamar rolled his eyes, but soon found himself resisting the urge to growl in annoyance.

Adamar broke into a run to get away from the constant questions. The weak thoughts in his mind of doubt, of not leaving and actually listening to what the others were saying, fled his brain.

He just wanted to go find Miro. But he felt guilty about leaving Avaha like this. Like Miro, she was so important to him. He'd loved her from the start, when they'd been just getting to know each other a few years ago. She had helped support him as he got better at archery and being a warrior. She had gotten on well with everyone in Eadageth, even though she'd been new to the village. She was one of the nicest furs he knew, helping him through thunderstorms that he was terrified of.

And as much he didn't want to admit it, she was partially right: he didn't really know where to go. Azoth had told him the direction to follow, and a few stars to look out for, but that was it.

And tracking Miro was now nearly lost. The rain had washed away most scents. And, even though foxes could track older smells, the day that had passed since Miro had been stolen didn't help.

The smells of arrows and working furs drifted into Adamar's nose before he saw the expanse of the archery range. A few archers walked over to him as he emerged from the woods. His mind was frazzled. It was weird, knowing what he wanted to do but for some reason holding himself back until he'd had enough of the advice.

A pine marten and a bobcat approached him. Adamar noticed the worn-smooth leather guards on the marten's forearms, a darker tanned breastplate across the weasel's chest, and a worn brown visor covering the marten's upper muzzle and head, leaving just the tip of his nose, lower jaw, eyes and ears poking through large openings in the mask. The bobcat was similarly dressed, except that her sparring attire, which was what all the archers wore in rare moments of battle, was fitted to a feline's form.

Adamar glanced at the marten. "Mosity, why are you and Leona wearing armor? You smell like you were sparring. We don't have the trials coming up soon."

Annually, the warriors of the various towns and cities in the land, both small and large, would travel to the monarchy's head city, Itador, named promptly after the first queen following the Far-reaching war: Queen Itidoria. She'd been a wise alpha wolf to rule, but had had a few problems, mainly her being quite egotistical. The naming of the city would've been the one for the entire kingdom, but everyone had protested against it, and luckily Queen Itidoria had backed down.

Itidoria had started a tradition of cycling in and out the main army for her city through a series of trials. The trials had been in use, with some changes, since Queen Itidoria had established her rule. The rulers following her had made it acceptable for all of the furs—those that weren't mammals—to compete in the tournament.

Leona glanced at Adamar. Leona's smell of fatigue that preceded her smell of energy confused the fox. "We were narrowing down who are our two best warriors, who can both shoot an arrow and fight."

"Why?" Adamar glanced at the faces of each of his fellow archers, but was unable to clearly pick out an emotion from any of them through either sight or scent.

"Avaha." Mosity replied. "Your mate's louder than thought. Hmo had lost an arrow in the woods, and as he was retrieving it—"

A bat, clothed in a brown shirt that faded against his body, folded his sleeveless arms. There was a space in the shirt cut out for the thin, black membranes stretching from the underside of the bat's arms to the sides of his torso. The bat's eyes—working and not as blind as those of his ancestors—watched Adamar carefully as he interrupted Mosity.

"While I was getting my arrow," A deeper tone than expected to come from the bat resonated through his chest, "I faintly heard your mate's cry, Adamar. I then heard other village furs talking about it. I didn't make much sense of it until they—" One of his arms swept out to indicate the rest of the archers. "Until they showed me. You know I have no pups of my own. I do not understand the great emotions felt toward one's own pups."

There was always an air of formality around Hmo, with whatever he was doing. Though, he was often reserved and quiet, leaving much of himself up to mystery.

"She said she didn't intend that. It was just an accident. Sometimes things get overwhelming. It did for Avaha, with my wanting to leave and with Miro already having disappeared."

Leona twitched her small tail. "But still, that's why Mosity and I were sparring. We decided to test each other to see who would be best to go with you on your expedition to find your kit."

Adamar's eyes widened. "You mean you're not against me, like many in the village are."

A soft smile stretched across Leona's small muzzle. She chuckled. "Of course not, Adamar. We're fighters too. Well...primarily archers, but we get the passion you feel for your kitten and how you're willing to risk a lot to find him." She paused for a minute. "What did Avaha say, exactly?"

As Adamar summarized the content of her protests, he noticed, for a moment, Badr standing at the back, face solemn while his tail seemed to be almost twitching with glee. Adamar stared at him.

Kalina's mink tail swished. "Mosity was right," she acknowledged, drawing Adamar's attention. The mink switched her gaze to him. "Mosity thought that Avaha didn't want you to go for selfish reasons. That she didn't understand how important getting Miro back is to you, and doing it as quick as possible."

Adamar let an ear back. "Avaha's not selfish." He glared at Kalina. "She's just..." he paused, searching for the right word, and when he said it, he bit his tongue in annoyance. "Worried." At the moment, he didn't know how to describe her better.

"Worried!" A wolf exclaimed. "She's not worried. She's selfish, wanting just the fame of having you as a mate, Adamar."

"I'm not famous." Adamar growled in return. "Just a fox that likes to fire arrows through the air. Nothing else to it." This criticism of his mate drove a worrisome thought into Adamar's mind: Foxes were naturally protective of their young. So why was Avaha stopping him from going?

"Please, Adamar." The wolf rolled his eyes. "You know you're more than that. And besides, if Avaha was extremely worried, she would be trying to have a better argument. One that's better than repeating the same phrase over and over."

Adamar scowled. "Maybe."

Six

After hearing that he wouldn't go alone, Adamar objected immediately, centering his brief argument around their safety and that it wasn't their kits missing—Miro was his.

Everyone then reasoned that it was better for him to have companions for this quest, using Adamar's own explanations against him. The mention of safety for all and that wherever they were going would be dangerous mostly won Adamar over, but he agreed to the idea when Kalina mentioned that if it was anyone else's pup going missing, Adamar would be doing the very same thing in offering his services to find the lost cub.

Once that had been settled, Adamar had been questioned on what he knew about the kingdom that took Miro. He told what he knew about Darvin: where it was, and that it was ruled by a fur named Girbindon, who was supposed to be extremely cruel and dangerous.

One of the archers, Rachi the raccoon, offered to spar with Adamar if he wanted to get some energy out. A moment of indecision passed and Adamar fought the raccoon, only to end up flat on the ground after a few minutes. But, as Rachi playfully smirked and told him he did well nonetheless, the fox did feel stronger. He had new bruises. But the fight had kicked up more than just mental energy to go find Miro. Now he really had to get out of Eadageth. He was itching for it.

As the final fight started, Adamar's mind wandered lightly, eventually settling on the image of Miro. Adamar pictured him smiling, cooing and giggling, just as he had before he'd been stolen. The joyful images gave Adamar's muzzle a soft smile, but the pictures only lasted a short time before they contorted into scenes of horror; Miro getting beaten, Miro bloodied, crying and alone; Miro's dead body.

Adamar shook his head and growled inwardly, clearing the images from his mind. He'd find Miro. Alive.

Hmo stood in the center of a fighting circle, the brown leather of his armor contrasting the black of his skin and fur. His arms were folded across his chest as he looked on, expression calm, but his passive features gave him a menacing presence.

A black footed ferret was standing nearby, dressed in the armor Mosity had been wearing. The dark shade of fur that usually surrounded the ferret's eyes was covered by the leather mask.

Mosity had moved to stand in a patch of shade, where he announced the names and accomplishments of the furs about to spar.

"Today," he said as he had for all the other trials, "We have gathered to watch a spar between Hmo of Chriopteram and Norm of Eadageth."

Adamar saw Hmo stiffen as his hometown was mentioned. The bat had moved to Eadageth a few years before Miro was born, saying that he did not want to be living in a village that consisted of just bat furs living there. He'd wanted something different, he had mentioned.

The fight was long, with neither fur getting the upper hand. Eventually Mosity stepped in and declared both Norm and Hmo triumphant in a tie. The two left the circle, only to be replaced by two more archers.

The beaver's legs were shorter than that of other furs, but they weren't as stumpy as his four legged ancestors. The shortness of the legs was made up by claws that extended from the toes on both the beaver's feet, and as he absentmindedly flexed a foot, his claws dug into dirt. But the beaver wasn't as harmful as he looked. Edgier was a good fur, always ready to help.

A coyote stood across from Edgier, as gray as his ancestors and short like them. All coyote furs were shorter than other canine furs, making them appear like pups if they talked to a wolf. Foxes were affected similarly, but all furs, regardless of species had an average, standard height. Adamar was glad that he'd grown much taller than normal--over the height of some wolves, so he didn't have to look up at anyone.

Mosity announced the names and hometowns of the two furs fighting, and the two set off.

Adamar was surprised when Ohanzee won. Edgier was known for using his thick tail as a disabling weapon, yet the coyote had managed to duck away from it.

The four furs that had been in the final rounds lined up to stand next to one another, all facing Adamar.

"Alright, Adamar," Mosity said. "Four candidates for the furs that will be accompanying you on finding Miro are standing here. Hmo, Norm, Edgier, and Ohanzee. Which two will go with you?"

Adamar gazed over the four.

Hmo stood as he usually did, his arms crossed over his chest. His archery was pretty good, but he was also quite familiar with the Land as a whole.

Norm's hands twisted together, fingers interlocking and separating as he waited for Adamar to say something. Norm's slender tail lay out behind him, curling gently at the end to point back to the deciding fox. Norm had done well in the fight, using his thin and flexible body to his advantage. He'd be good for twisting out of an enemy's grasp, if it ever came to that.

Feeling all eyes on him, Adamar looked at Edgier. The beaver had performed well in the spar, but hadn't been able to conquer a small, quick-moving coyote. Nevertheless, Edgier's large body and two pointed teeth that jutted over his bottom lip gave him an intimidating stance. It made some sense that Edgier hadn't achieved catching Ohanzee, given that his bigger form caused problems when trying to turn, swiftly and slyly. Luckily, that didn't affect his skill with shooting arrows.

Adamar's ears pricked to the scuffling of the coyote's foot. Ohanzee was shifting his weight back and forth, as if he was nervous. His tail waved occasionally. Ohanzee might be helpful in combat, considering how he eluded Edgier's frame and thick tail, and considering that he did well with archery specifically on horseback.

"Well, Adamar?" Mosity asked.

Adamar nodded and glanced at the four furs in turn again. "I believe that Ohanzee and Hmo will do well in helping me find Miro."

Seven

The archers sent Adamar, Ohanzee, and Hmo away to go plan their quest, while the rest of the archers collected some basic supplies for the trip. The three were surprised when another archer appeared behind Hmo, offering his help and saying that whomever they were fighting, to get Miro back, greater numbers were probably better to have. More noses to track Miro.

Even though the rain had basically washed away that option.

The third fur, a red wolf named Thayn, tall as Adamar, stood next to the fox's chosen comrades. He didn't say much, other than that he was here with more knowledge on Darvin.

Adamar repeated everything Azoth had shared about Darvin. "Azoth said that the fur that took him was probably from the Darvin kingdom. A small group that's supposed to be very cruel. They're in the southeast. Apparently they came to power after the Far-reaching war."

The four began discussing strategies to find Miro, mostly looking to Hmo and Thayn for information. The bat had traveled a lot before coming to Eadageth.

Thayn spoke about Girbindon. "He would like to have his empire grow stronger. He's been able to contact certain furs in subtle ways, so he can have his empire grow."

Adamar was surprised at how far information about Darvin had traveled. Thayn was on the other side of the country from Darvin, but he knew about it, like Azoth had.

"Has the kingdom gotten any stronger?" Ohanzee asked.

"Not too much."

"How do you even know of this? I've never heard of him until now."

"Azoth knew of Girbindon," Adamar reminded the coyote.

"He's Azoth. No one knows what he learned when he was encouraged away from here." Ohanzee held a slight smile.

"Why was he pushed away?" Adamar asked Ohanzee out of curiosity. "I know his eyes were different, but that's all." The fox had been a young kit when Azoth was pushed out of the town. Then, Azoth had been in his teens. Now Azoth was around forty.

"He was also very odd. As a pup, I believe, he'd just do odd things. Things that made sense to him and not to anyone else." Ohanzee shrugged. "I'm not too sure. Some older furs might know. Luckily, they've stopped pushing furs out."

Adamar nodded, and the discussion turned back toward Girbindon and Miro. The discussion lasted for an hour with the help of an old map of the Land, the only map the archers had. Eadageth's army was not the most well-funded army.

The four emerged around lunch, and were greeted by full saddlebags being fixed onto waiting horses. Hmo, Ohanzee, and Thayn, went over to their rides, Hmo taking a black horse, Thayn hopping up onto a palomino, while Ohanzee found comfort in one of the horses that he cared for in his spare time: a flea-bitten coated mare fondly named Galene—from the ancient language of the ancestors where it meant "calm seas."

Adamar was just about to take the reins of a roan horse when a bucket of water was dumped over his head.

The fox spat out the liquid and smelled for who had soaked him. His gaze settled on the laughing Mosity and Kalina. They had an empty bucket in their hands, the rest of the archers smirking behind them.

"What was that for?" Adamar snorted, trying to keep up a menacing face, but his muzzle soon gave way to a lopsided smile.

"Your good-luck present for your trip." Mosity grinned.

"Very funny." In return, Adamar shook out his sopping fur, making sure that he sprayed those around him.

Adamar felt the wind blow against his wet clothes, and the fox sighed. "I keep getting soaked." He turned and thanked a badger, who handed him a pile of dry clothes. The fox disappeared back inside to change and get dry, hurrying as fast as he could to get on the trail after Miro.

In case of emergency, some simple living supplies were left at the range, including a set of clothes for each fur that frequented there. Adamar suspected that was where most of the supplies had been gotten for the four packs kindly prepared for him, Hmo, Thayn, and Ohanzee.

Adamar stepped back out onto the grass, dressed in a long riding robe that was often used for traveling. But to keep some modesty, brown pants clothed Adamar's legs, and a sleeveless t-shirt covered his chest beneath the robe.

The fox felt the weight of a hood on the back of his cloak. Wind blew against his ears, removing the last of the water that clung to Adamar's fur. He noticed that Hmo and Ohanzee and Thayn were also wearing robes, but a space had been cut out for the leathery skin that was attached to Hmo's arms and sides.

"Good luck, Adamar." Leona said as she handed him the reins of the roan horse. Adamar nodded and put his foot into the stirrup, hoisting himself up into the worn seat of the saddle, his tail trailing off to one side. The horse looked at Leona, who put her furred hand on the horse's nose and stroked its face.

"It's alright," she murmured, comforting her horse. She looked up at Adamar, her expression stern. "Be good with Dakr. If you come back with Miro, and Dakr is somehow missing, I'll beat you to the other side of town."

Adamar chuckled, but nodded and turned in his seat to check the saddlebags. He glanced quickly over the contents inside, and confirmed that his quiver was strung across his back. He wrapped a hand around the grip of his bow, holding the reins in his other hand.

He moved Dakr up to stand next to Thayn's, Hmo's, and Ohanzee's horses. He took a breath, feeling his heart start to race. "Well, I guess it's time to be off on the search for Miro. Thanks for the help." This he directed at no one. Adamar set his ears forward, his gaze traveling the trail that went through the woods to the village.

As the four went to the forest, a chorus of good lucks and words of wishing well sounded. Adamar smiled briefly, Ohanzee doing the same, while Hmo's and Thayn's faces were placid as ever.

Adamar's ears twitched as he heard a possum's voice rise above the other tones.

"Bye, Adamar!" Badr called, waving his hand enthusiastically. "Have fun on your trip!"

Adamar's flicked back for a moment at the oddness of Badr. But he let the feeling fade.

The horses picked their way through the small stretch of trees, leaves crunching beneath their hooves as their riders guided them on. When they got to the village, Ohanzee turned toward his family's home, wanting to give his mate and pups a hug and kiss and tell them he was leaving. Hmo and Thayn stayed with Adamar as the fox traveled to his own home. Adamar felt a slight pang of sadness for why the coyote had disappeared, because Ohanzee had a chance to see his pups, while Adamar had to go find small Miro.

The fox asked Hmo and Thayn to hang back as the three got closer to the fox's house, and the scent of his family flooded Adamar's nostrils. Miro's faded smell drifting from underneath the front door. Avaha's strong, anguished and angry scent. The smells of Chenl and Jek, still not welcomed by Adamar.

Anxiety flashed over Adamar as he stopped a few feet from his front door. He could already imagine the shrieks of Avaha as she protested his leaving, and the thought had him cringe. But Adamar swung down from Dakr. He slipped the reins over the horse's head, and had the horse walk next to him while he mulled over the best way to explain to his mate that he was leaving.

Adamar raised a fist to knock against the unlatched door, even though he could hear and smell Avaha's weeping. "Avaha?" Adamar called, hesitating.

The door opened to reveal his mate with eyes bloodshot and her soft face dirtied by the trails of tears. She clutched a handkerchief.

Adamar felt a sharp pain in his chest at his mate's sadness, his ears turning out and to the sides. He watched her unhappy expression stay while she glanced at Adamar's traveling gear. Avaha's bottom lip stuck out. She choked down a sob, which was soon replaced by the quiet, "So you're going now?"

Chenl appeared behind her, and farther back

Adamar saw one of her apprentices: the buck, Jek, holding a cup of tea, to apparently comfort Avaha.

"I am." Adamar responded, looking at his mate with a solemn nod. "I know you don't like the idea, but I'll be as quick as I can about it. Leona's letting me ride Dakr. You know he's a fast horse." Adamar found himself starting to ramble on, and was grateful when his mate stopped him, but her whining voice hurt his ears.

"You know I'll worry about you never coming back. Please, Adamar. Just rethink this." Avaha ignored Chenl and Jek; her gaze never left her mate.

Adamar shook his head. "No, Avaha. I won't. I know this is right. I...I worry that the furs that took Miro want to hurt him. If we just wait for him to come back, if he does come back, too much damage could have already been done." Adamar twisted the excess of Dakr's reins in his hands. "I've not come to argue, but to say goodbye, of course for some time."

A soft whimper came from Avaha's throat. Her eyes shone with new tears. "Adamar...please..." When Adamar saw her tense, he stepped back in alarm, not wanting to be tackled again. He glanced at the furs behind his mate, who moved closer.

"Don't go." Avaha's words were no heavier than a whisper, but her ears flattened and she lunged at Adamar. Dakr reared in alarm. Adamar dug his feet into the ground and guided the horse back down, keeping hold of the reins while he looked at Avaha almost desperately.

"Adamar! Please! Stay with me!" Avaha reached out for her mate, held back only by the frantic arms of Chenl wrapped about her waist. "Please!" His mate cried again, smelling of heavy anguish, sadness, and fear. Her anger had dissipated. "Please, Adamar, don't go!"

Fighting the ache that was pulling him back to her, Adamar moved away, gathered the reins, and swung himself up into Dakr's saddle. He looked at his mate, and met her gaze for a moment.

"I'll miss you." She said at last, sadness saturating her voice.

"I'll come back." At that, Adamar gathered his comrades and went to the edges of Eadageth, where a trading route traveled away from the town. He nodded to the couple archers who patrolled this road.

Every archer was required to be on patrol duty a couple nights a week, whether it was here, or in the woods near and surrounding the archery range and on the edges of the town. Patrol was a grueling, twelve-hour shift, day or night. And it was only to guard against Eadageth's few, minor enemies of years past. When Miro had been born, Adamar hadn't been allowed to go out on patrol for a few months. The archers had told him that he would not go, he had his pup to take care of.

As they left, Adamar saw that Ohanzee's riding robe looked somewhat rumpled, as if four pairs of arms had hugged the small coyote, all at once and then individually again.

"You ready?" Hmo asked, his deep voice breaking Adamar from a ruminating stupor. Adamar nodded and questioned the same of his comrades, getting the same response.

"Let's go." Adamar checked his grip on his bow, pulled in a little of the reins, and voiced for Dakr to start cantering down the old path. His heart raced with the anxiety, fear, and energy of his quest. He would do this. He would get Miro.

The sound of hooves striking the dirt confirmed that Ohanzee, Thayn, and Hmo were following.

Eight

A hand nudged the fox kit, shaking Miro until the kit opened his eyes and yawned. Miro looked up, searching for what had woken him, but his gaze fell, amazed, on his surroundings.

Still clinging to the canine's chest, Miro looked around at the great hall he was in. The walls climbed up into what seemed like forever, but Miro could see the small hints of rafters stretching from wall to wall, crisscrossing and doubling back over another, much like the spider webs, shining with morning water, that his father had once showed him.

Where was his father, anyways?

Over the canine's shoulder Miro saw a set of double, heavy wooden doors with a bar strewn across them, blocking anyone from entering the room. The walls next to the main entryway were bare of any decoration, but the rest of the walls were covered in long pieces of fabric, which he later learned were called tapestries, depicting differing scenes, some hanging down nearly to the floor, others falling only a few feet below where they had been hung up. Miro saw that the tops of the woven stories all started at the same height, close to the ceiling.

The room's two windows let the beginnings of morning light into the room. The faint beams of yellow streamed by the panes set in the glass, and cast themselves across the middle of the stone floor.

Miro yelped when he was roughly turned around, facing the front of the chamber, where even more tapestries warmed the walls. The focus of each tapestry was the same as before: a bear in the middle of the image, opening his great maw in a wicked grin, or when his mouth was closed, the bear's gaze would be smiling.

The tapestries framed a large throne lavishly colored in gold, which gave off a strange scent. The entire place did smell strange, mainly because Miro's range of recognizable scents was limited at best, but he nonetheless tried to distinguish one scent from another.

The fox kit scrunched up his nose at an unpleasant smell drifting into his nostrils, one that seemed to come simultaneously from all the around the room and only from one figure in the chamber.

A bear sat in the great chair, watching Miro from where the throne had been raised up. The bear's claws tapped the edges of the chair, making a clacking sound echo off the stonewalls, as he gazed at Miro almost lazily. The bear's gaze shifted to the canine that was holding Miro. In a guttural, unkind tone, the bear commanded: "Speak."

Miro cocked his head at the order, unsure of what to do, but the jackal had an idea.

Panting from his journey, the canine eased himself down onto one knee, holding out Miro as if he was offering the kit to the bear. The jackal bowed his head and began his report.

"I have done what you asked, Great King Girbindon. I have gone to the village to the west, and with your hints, I have stolen the pup. I came back as quick as I could, using your generous share of magic to get here quicker, and stopping only by your equally generous offering of one half of a rest night, where I made sure that the pup was fed. And now I have brought him here. My King, have I done well?"

The bear glanced at Miro, who squirmed in the dog's grip until the canine squeezed his ribs. Miro cried out, then settled with whining unhappily.

Girbindon raised his gaze to peer at the doors behind the jackal. "Did you leave any visible traces behind?" The canine flinched, but didn't respond and continued to stare shamefully at the ground. "Chilo," Girbindon sighed in annoyance, but Miro saw a flash of glee in the bear's eyes. "Do I have to cut off yet another of your fingers? If you tell me what happened, I will take off only one of your fingers, not two. And do not leave out details. You know I can tell if you're speaking the full truth. I've known you long enough. And I have other methods to smell if you're lying, if I need."

Miro paused his whimpers, and again tried to get free of the canine's, Chilo's, grip. He pressed his small hands against the jackal's fingers, clawing at the furred flesh with tiny black nails.

"Hold on, Chilo." A smile carved Girbindon's face. "Tell me your wrongful deeds later. It appears that our little guest wants to come to me. A smart fox already. He senses your wrongs."

Chilo's ears turned out and his tail went between his legs as Girbindon got up from his throne. "I'm sorry, King Girbindon." His voice was so soft in its despair.

"As you should be." The bear's muzzle grew a small smile, one that looked like it was trying to be kind, but Miro guessed that Girbindon was unable to even look kind.

Torches stood on either side of the throne. They cast their light against the bear as he went down the few stone steps.

Chilo released Miro, and the fox fell the short distance to the hard floor, where he started crying. The stone hurt. It was cold. And his father wasn't in sight. Where'd he go? Miro couldn't smell him. All his nose captured was the stench of the bear standing closely in front of him. His mother would do, as well, but he liked his father better. His mother didn't give him as much attention, just set him off to the side while she talked with strange furs.

After he made sure Chilo hadn't moved, the jackal's palms braced against the stone and his sandy-colored muzzle still pointing to the ground, Girbindon crouched in front of Miro. The bear's gaze tracked Miro, and he reached out a massive hand toward the kit. "Come here, Miro. Come to the King."

Miro looked at Girbindon. His huge, dark form took up most of Miro's vision, and the teeth that peeked at the edges of Girbindon's mouth looked like murderous monsters to the cub.

With a yelp, Miro pushed himself to his feet, and though he was still somewhat wobbly, ran off as fast as his legs could carry him. The kit whimpered while he crossed the room, which seemed to grow larger in his pursuit to find a place to hide.

Miro stumbled the last few inches to a darkened corner, and went tumbling into one of the longer tapestries that stretched down to the floor. Miro grabbed the edge of the woven fabric and hid behind it, balling it up in his clumsy hands as tears soaked his fur.

Miro's ears twitched when he heard the faint scuffling of the bear standing and walking closer to Miro's hiding spot.

"Young Miro, come out, do come out from beneath the tapestry. Come to me. I am the Great King." Girbindon cooed, chuckling, his claws clacking against the stone as he pretended to take a while searching for Miro.

The terrified fox kit began to wail louder, his hands fisting the fabric to the point of starting to tear. Miro whimpered and buried his snot-leaking nose into the wall hanging, while his thoughts waited anxiously for his father or mother to appear and save him from the scary Girbindon.

Miro cried when the fabric was torn away and he was left naked, except for cloth wrapped around his bottom, cornered by the massive bear. Girbindon leaned in for a second, his features and smell sliding into a brief expression of sadness.

"Oh, Miro, come here. Don't ruin the tapestry." Girbindon reached his brown-furred hands out to Miro, who tried to turn and get away, run in any direction, as long as he could be far from the bear. But Girbindon's form filled up all the space Miro could use for escape. Miro squirmed when the bear picked him up.

Cries drifted from the kit's throat, only increasing in volume when the bear squeezed him.

"Hush, oh, hush now." Girbindon shuffled over to his throne, where he placed down the sniveling fox. The bear's hand disappeared inside the folds of his extravagant clothes for a moment as he smiled at Miro. "Do you want a sweet treat? You'll get a sweet if you stop crying."

Miro sniffled and rubbed at his teary eyes. A sweet? He liked sweets. Sweets were tasty.

The fox's small tail began wagging. Miro nodded eagerly, his mouth opening in a small smile.

Girbindon grinned and held out a sweet cookie to Miro, but before the kit could grab it, the bear drew his hand back. "You'll be quiet after this? You won't get the treat if you are loud and crying." The bear's teeth revealed themselves in an expression of wicked joy. "Good fox. Here you go."

Miro's small hands nabbed the sweet, and the fox cub jammed the treat into his mouth, still-developing canines sluicing through the tough parts of the cookie to get at the chocolate inside. Miro smiled as he munched on the treat, his tail waving in joy while his face lit up.

Maybe the bear wasn't so bad. Bad furs didn't give out tasty treats, did they?

As Miro ate, he watched Girbindon turn and face Chilo, who had not yet moved. Girbindon glanced at the jackal's hands, but his gaze focused on the one that was already missing a finger.

"Chilo." The bear growled, his voice dropping an octave and scaring Miro. "Stand up. Now, go call up the Unstable, and make sure it is in a good viewing position. Once that is done, you will go wait in your room, a knife placed out for my use."

Though Miro could see Chilo trembling, his tail tucked, and could smell his pure terror, the jackal bowed as he agreed to his King's orders, managing to keep fear out of his voice. "Yes, my King. Right away."

Miro's muzzle was covered in crumbs while he licked cookie off his hands with joy. The fox kit watched Chilo leave, the bear scowling after him. Girbindon turned back towards the fox, a grin on his face.

"Was that good?" Girbindon reached out a hand toward Miro, but stopped when he noticed the fox's tail curling in sudden fear.

"Oh, Miro, relax now. Very soon, you're going to see someone you know really well. I'm sure you'll like it."

Miro cocked his head. Who? Would it be his father? Was the bear that nice?

Girbindon stepped closer to the fox kit. "Come with me. I'll show you where you'll live while you're here. I'm sure you'll find the accommodations...wonderful." The bear's grin wavered. "Now, now. Don't hesitate. You'll see them soon. But for now, you should rest. You're probably tired from all that you had to do so you wouldn't fall off of Chilo."

Girbindon snatched up Miro, though he held the kit a little bit gentler than before, letting Miro rest against his chest as the bear walked into a hall that branched off from the room. The bear had to push a tapestry out of the way to reveal the corridor, which allowed dozens of strange scents to escape.

Miro's nose wrinkled in disgust. Why were they going into a place that reeked of...what was it...blood?

"This is where you'll be living, from now on." Girbindon's voice jolted the kit out of a short nap he'd taken while the bear walked down the hallway.

Miro yawned and raised his head, smelling the cold stone and faint scents of furs that had been here long ago. His gaze settled on the rough stone wall in front of him, which was bare except for a sheet of fabric that covered a gap in the stone. A gust of wind blew the fabric in, revealing the bars that strode across the high-up window. Larger, thicker bars danced in front of the wall, only they were moved a few feet away from the wall. A piece of the bars were shortened, with hinges placed upon them to show a door's outline.

Miro looked up at Girbindon in confusion, who was smiling down at him. The light from the window and the sheets of weak candlelight from the hallway illuminated the bear's face.

The rest of the room was bare of anything except for a small, worn table that rested against one of the walls. Miro caught the scent of old and stale food that once sat on the wood.

"Hey. You look at me when I'm speaking to you." Girbindon snarled, his hand grabbing Miro by his scruff and lifting the kit up to eye level. Miro grunted and squirmed, pain shooting from his back when Girbindon twisted the loose skin.

"Stop struggling, Miro. Now." When the kit didn't comply, Girbindon growled and shook him. Miro whimpered before he hung limp in the bear's grasp.

"Good fox." Girbindon said. "Since you're so little, Miro, I would not have you kept in a place like this while you're staying here with me. But..." Wickedness flashed in the bear's gaze. "I can't be sure of your skills, even if you are just a cub. So you'll be residing here for the time being. I won't commit you to any tests today. You can rest and get acquainted with your living quarters. Tomorrow, however, will be different. You better get some sleep, you brat. For you'll learn that I'm being very generous."

The bear strode to the metal bars that separated half the room and reached at the door handle, yanking it open with a sharp creak. Miro flinched. Girbindon snarled at the fox's complaint roughly placed Miro into the cell.

As the door slammed shut, Miro landed on the hard dirt, gathering bruises on his side and back while tears streamed down his orange furred face, onto his orange-and-white muzzle. He whimpered, his young body radiating pain that his soul was not yet used to.

Nine

"Hey. Wake up."

Miro stirred, his small muzzle poking out of the ball he'd curled himself into before crying until sleep had taken him away. His fur was caked with dirt, and he snorted some dust from his nose.

He didn't sit up until he saw that it wasn't the cruel Girbindon, but Chilo, whose expression was twisted into one of agony and attempted coldness. Even though the jackal wasn't as frightening as Girbindon, Miro rolled over and crawled to a corner, where he tried to become invisible.

Ears lowering in sympathy, Chilo bent to the ground and slid a tin through a thin slot at the base of the bars. "It's food." He said quietly. The jackal rested back on his haunches, watching Miro. Miro could see that Chilo was cradling one hand. When the jackal realized where Miro's gaze was, Chilo sighed and let go of his wrist.

Miro cocked his head at the bandage he saw wrapping around Chilo's hand, covering the spot where the kit thought another finger had just been yesterday. Blood stained the white cloth.

Chilo raised his head to look at Miro once the kit was done scrutinizing his injured hand. "I didn't do well enough in getting you here, Miro." Cruelty tried to sneak into the jackal's gaze, but failed. "Now eat up. You won't get fed for another few hours. And be quick about it."

The kit looked tentatively at the tin Chilo had pushed beneath the bars, as if focusing on it, but his thoughts were elsewhere. He had heard howls as he drifted in and out of sleep; cries as if a fur was being tortured and in sheer agony.

"Eat, Miro. Time's wasting."

Miro crawled over to the tray of food, and his gaze remained unhappy at the sight of just stale-smelling scraps for food. It wasn't what his mother or father usually fed him. But his stomach was beginning to growl in hunger, and he grabbed at a hunk of bread.

At first, when the fox got a taste of the stale bread, he put it down in disgust and pushed the tray away, but Chilo snarled, ordering him to eat it or starve.

Once the plate was clear, Miro toddled over to the bars and tried to squeeze through them, a thought crossing his still-developing mind.

Chilo growled. "What're you doing? You can't leave. This was made to hold all but the smallest of prisoners." He watched Miro for a moment, then put his good hand between the bars and pushed the fox back. "If you keep doing that, the King will not be happy."

Miro stared at the jackal, falling flat on his bottom.

"What?" Chilo's ears perked at the same time as Miro's did, when the two heard something crash a few halls away and echo back.

Chilo sighed and stood, going over to a rusted chain that kept the cell door to the bars. He grunted as he undid the makeshift lock, the metal banging against his injured hand before he could push the door inward and step into the cell.

Miro squealed in fright. He tried to run away, but he was stuck in the small space, and so unable to get far before Chilo caught up with him. He picked him up by his scruff.

"Don't bother struggling." Chilo warned, bringing Miro over to a bucket that was placed behind the table. The jackal put Miro into the bucket, ignoring the kit's cries of protest as he lifted it to sit on top of the table.

Miro whined and tried to climb out of the bucket, the icy water flowing through his still-thin fur and striking against skin. Chilo pushed him down, growling, and the cub sat in the water, warms tears heating his face while he shivered.

"Get used to it." As Chilo began soaping up the fox kit, he explained: "Every time you visit the Great King, you must be as clean as you can be, for the Great King expects utter respect and cleanliness."

Throughout the process of being washed, Miro fought to get out of the ice water, his small claws lashing out at Chilo, catching the jackal on his injured hand. As Chilo cradled his wound, a smile grew on Miro's face, and the kit began to giggle in delight.

"Oh, shut your muzzle." Chilo scolded, his narrowed eyes trying to stare down the fox, but Miro thought he saw a glimmer of amusement in Chilo's gaze.

Miro clung to Chilo's robes, not wanting to fall out of the one-armed grasp and hit the floor. Once the jackal had finished bathing Miro, he'd dried and attempted to change him, but had had a difficult time when the fox kit ran off, naked except for his fur, and began streaking down the hallways. Miro had nearly made it to the great room where the bear's throne was, but Chilo caught up and lunged for him, grabbing Miro as he landed awkwardly, some of his weight going on the knuckles of his injured hand. Miro watched the jackal grit his teeth. While changing Miro in the second and successful try, Chilo had let his hand rest as often as possible.

Chilo had commanded the fox kit to hold on while he carried him, one-handed, so his bloodied fingers could not touch anything and the jackal could avoid more pain.

Miro watched their entrance into the great hall. The tapestry swung back behind Chilo as he exited it and moved toward another wall hanging, one on the wall behind the throne.

The one they headed to depicted a fur lying on an observation table, while a large bear stood over him.

The tapestry hid another hallway. Miro wondered as they passed beneath it if there were other rooms hidden in plain sight. But he did not have a chance to wonder for long.

Miro found himself in a small room after passing through the short corridor. Books lined shelves on one side of the room, where the walls were rough and the room's ceiling rounded, as if it had been carved from stone. Miro's eyes widened at the blue color of the rock, which shifted colors when one moved around.

Taking up most of the room was a large stone basin, covered by a lid of similar rocks fused together with a gray paste. Miro's nose told him that water filled the rocky tub. Standing on top of the covering was a metal platform, which held a large, octagonal mirror. Dark polished wood encircled part of the reflecting glass, and then branched off to the edges of the mirror, where the edge of the glass had been sawed down to a fine, smooth edge. Dust and scratches coated the separated border of the mirror, but the center glass was as clear and undisturbed as a rain puddle.

Girbindon stood by the mirror, the shadows casting an eerie look over his muzzle. His grin seemed to stretch, the teeth growing larger and larger as Miro's imagination explored frightening images.

It frightened the fox kit. Tears wet his eyes and he whimpered.

Almost immediately, Girbindon's smile wavered and his lip curled back to angrily bare the bright white teeth. A growl seemed to try and edge its way into the air, but Girbindon evidently held it back.

"Miro..." Chilo squeezed the crying kit. "There's no need to be sad in front of the Great King. He'll help you become the best of what you can be; what you should be." Chilo raised his gaze to meet Girbindon's, then quickly found interest in the wall.

"I have brought your prisoner, King Girbindon, per your request." Chilo briefly looked at the bear, uncertain. "Where should I put him?"

Girbindon smirked and walked to the bookshelves, passing Chilo on the way. His fist knocked into the jackal's injured hand. "Oh. You can just hold him the whole time. Have fun."

Miro sniffled and looked up at Chilo, watching pain fall over the jackal's eyes, but Chilo didn't say anything. He just smelled of hurt.

Girbindon stood on one side of the basin and placed both hands on its edge. Though he faced the mirror, his gaze had turned to intently observe Miro.

The bear looked back at the reflecting glass, and Miro watched with a cocked head, his fur still streaked with tears, as Girbindon's muzzle moved, silent words slithering from his tongue.

Miro perked his ears, fascinated. The center of the mirror began to change. Colors danced across it, swirling and circling before fading into a gray mist, slowly turning round and round. Girbindon spoke a few more words, then the mist seemed to flee, as if it couldn't wait to get away from the bear's presence. Miro could agree with the mist.

An image began to form in the center of the mirror, coming at first as a shapeless mass and then separating into four fast moving figures. The sight was from a bird's eye view.

Miro's father lead three furs the fox kit vaguely recognized, all four of them hunched over as they galloped their horses down an unfamiliar path. Trees flashed by on the edges of the image.

As Miro's eyes widened and he saw his father racing by on the glass, he began to cry again. He reached out to the image, his small hands grasping at air while he squirmed and kicked. His father was so close.

"No. Miro, no." Chilo tightened his hold on the fox, stepping back from the mirror until he bumped into a wall two steps behind him. "You can't..." The canine's words trailed off as a loud squeal of protest came from the struggling kit.

Miro, through his blurry eyes, saw the bear grin again and gesture to the image. "Yes, Miro. Good fox. That is your father. And he's coming to find you."

Pausing in his sniffling, Miro cocked his head. His father was coming? He was going to get away from this horrible bear? Miro's tail began to wag.

"Ah, but—" Something flashed in Girbindon's gaze. "I wouldn't be so happy if I were you. His path is going to be delayed. It is. That way, you and I can have more time for a long chat, and I can test you effectively and still get what your father may have."

As the image faded and Miro was taken back to the cell, his expanding mind was so full of despair, annoyance, and agony that he did not wonder what the bear could mean about talking, about how the mirror had even show his father.

Ten

"Have you smelled Miro's scent at all? I've been smelling some fox on the trail, but I might be wrong. I don't know Miro like you do, Adamar. And I don't know the smell of jackal." Ohanzee bit at the leg of deer he held in both hands.

The horses rested, tethered to separate trees as the four furs made camp in the forest that they'd ridden through for hours. They had ridden through the night and past the middle of the day, pausing twice to let the horses get a drink from the many streams and rivers they passed along the way.

They'd read the stars when darkness had fallen, traveling through the forest, before stopping to make camp for the night, leaving the horses to catch up on sleep while Adamar chose to go test his archery and shoot at a couple of four-legged animals. He'd managed to put an arrow in a deer's shoulder.

Once the deer was dragged back to camp, it had been skinned and set to roast over a fire Ohanzee had built. Adamar, Ohanzee, Thayn, and Hmo acknowledged that the animal had been killed only out of the means of providing nourishment, as they sank their teeth into the warm meat.

Across the Land, all furs knew that to kill an ancestor for sport was not only a great crime, but also a severe blow to one's honor. Many furs had been taught to leave the ancestors to their ways, and to never disturb them if it could be avoided.

The wind twisted tree branches, making their leaves flutter as a strong gust blew through, carrying with it a sound that seemed almost like furs were whispering. Adamar, Ohanzee, and Hmo raised their heads, glancing at each other and then the woods around before deciding it was just the wind shifting in the forest. None of them smelled anything abnormal, just the forest, the ancestors, each other, and their horses.

"Maybe." Adamar responded, twisting the deer thigh in his hands while he thought about Ohanzee's question. He wished he hadn't been so hasty to leave that he hadn't let his comrades smell the scent of his target. "But Miro was carried by this jackal, so not a lot of his scent would be on a trail. And it rained pretty heavily in this area. I'm also still working on being able to accurately identify the scent of a jackal. And, now that I recall, there was some other odd scent. Not the jackal's."

"What do you mean?" The coyote tilted his head.

"It wasn't something I could completely identify. It was subtle, but still sharp. I couldn't make sense of it." Adamar tore off a piece of the meat and dove into his thoughts.

The four ate in silence, filling their bellies and nourishing their demanding bodies. Furs had gotten the trait of being able to eat much at once from their ancestors, the four-legged animals that were often used to feasting and starving relatively frequently. Many could go for a while without food, but whenever it was possible to eat, furs wolfed down whatever was in front of them, as long as it wasn't a member of their ancestors. To eat the meat of one's direct ancestor was considered to be cannibalism.

After they buried the bones to honor the lost deer, and began to prepare the leftover meat for travel, Adamar took a breath and asked, "Are you sure you three want to do this?" he glanced up at his comrades. "This idea just came out of the blue. I'm not sure how dangerous this could possibly be, or how long it may take. You'll be separated from your family, Ohanzee, for until who knows when. We rode fast last night, but if we expect to get to the Darvin kingdom as quickly as possible, our horses will be so exhausted that riding them back home could take three times as the trek there.

"And we may need to be able to ride quickly away from the Darvin kingdom. They're not supposed to be friendly." Paranoia and anxiety guided Adamar's words. "Besides, you three are riding out on a mission with just a fellow archer, to find my kit so young that he probably won't remember being stolen when he grows to adulthood."

Ohanzee looked at him accusingly. "You're degrading yourself."

"You also sound like you don't think we can survive this." Hmo watched Adamar, arms crossed over his chest as always.

Adamar's ears turned out and he shook his head. "No. No. That's not what I meant at all...I just...I..." How could he explain how terrified he was that, now this mission had actually begun, it would never be near to successful?

"You are doubting yourself, and those with you, Adamar." Hmo chided, but his deep voice somehow calmed the fox's uncertain emotions. "You don't want to do that. You could be left alone. Some furs survive on their own, solitarily, without damage. Some don't."

"Ready, Adamar?"

After dampening the fire to reduce its attention-seeking glow and smell, the four agreed on practicing their sparring. They wanted to make sure that they would be ready for any possible hand-to-hand combat they would have to partake in. And, sparring would draw Adamar's mind away from his fear.

Adamar nodded. He glanced over at Ohanzee.

Thayn drew a ring in the dirt. He had barely spoken a word since they'd set out. Adamar and Ohanzee stood on opposing sides. Hmo voiced the start of the spar.

Adamar launched at the coyote with a snarl, allowing his anger of Miro's disappearance to flow out and energize his actions. While he'd been riding Dakr, his mind had been racing and anger had been boiling in his veins.

Eyes wide, Ohanzee tucked out of the way, twisting his small body as his hands reached out to grab onto Adamar's tail and yank the fox back. Adamar growled and kicked, catching the coyote in the back of his knee and pushing him to the ground. Minutes passed.

"Adamar is triumphant." Hmo went into the ring and grabbed at the fox's scruff, pulling him away from the coyote squirming beneath. The two had been sparring with neither able to get an advantage over another until Girbindon's name had come into Adamar's mind. The fox had felt a surge of strength, which surprised him for a moment before he realized how useful it would be in the spar. He was easily able to overpower Ohanzee, pinning him to the ground and baring teeth near the coyote's throat.

"Where'd that come from, Adamar?" Ohanzee panted, standing and shaking the dirt off of his fur. He glanced at the fox, who had gone to a nearby tree and sat against it to rest.

Adamar didn't respond as exhaustion draped a thick blanket across his shoulders. He hadn't expected the burst of vitality to take as much out of him as it had. His gaze felt like it was dancing. Spots clouded his peripheral vision. He could feel his heart beating quicker than it should have, even after a spar, and confirmed the rapid pulse by putting shaky fingers to the underside of his wrist.

"Hey, Adamar, are you alright?" Ohanzee moved closer to Adamar, watching him with a worried expression. "What's wrong?"

Adamar growled and turned his head away, trying to push out wicked thoughts that randomly stormed into his brain, chanting only one thing, over and over: *Kill him. Kill him.*

Thayn came to the coyote's side and gently put a hand on his arm. "Leave him alone, Ohanzee. He's just stricken with the pain of losing his pup. The fight took a lot out of him."

As Ohanzee was dragged away, he looked between the red wolf, Hmo over by the fire, and Adamar. To the fox, Ohanzee appeared as a stupid, unknowing pup. More questions flowed from Ohanzee's muzzle, but Adamar had stopped listening, pulling up against the tree and finding comfort in its bark. Sleep took him away.

Adamar's dreams created a picture he despised. Miro sat in a dark corner, where blackness surrounded the kit, while the edges of the image were a bright white, illuminating the tears that stained Miro's face. The kit cried out, hand swiping toward an unseen figure. Adamar's ears twitched in his sleep while he thought he heard the young voice of his kit asking for someone.

Yet that was impossible. Kits didn't begin speaking clear words until they were about a year and a half of age. Why would Miro be asking for his father? How could he?

Adamar shivered, an idea torturing his mind. He would find Miro soon, before he got older. This quest would not take years. He would hear Miro's first words. He would. He had to.

A hand touched Adamar's shoulder and jerked him from the nightmare. Adamar rolled onto his back, tired gaze looking up at the coyote that stood over him.

"We're getting ready to go." Ohanzee nudged Adamar in the ribs with his foot, unknowingly putting pressure against a bruise the fox had gotten in the previous night's spar.

The short jab of pain awakened Adamar's mind, and he turned, pushing off the ground and standing. The nightmare lingered at the edges of his thoughts, but he tried to shake them away as he rid his fur of the dirt that clung to it.

He made sure that the traces of the fire had been scattered. Adamar drew in a breath, catching the scents of himself, Ohanzee, Hmo, Thayn, and the horses. Last night's dinner was traceable, but the scent was masked by their movements as they'd sparred, and the ancestors that had walked into their camp overnight.

Adamar grabbed Dakr's saddle from the tree it had lain against, pulling on his robe. He saddled the horse. The robe threatened to make him overheat, unnecessary as autumn began to arrive but needed for the eventual trek over the Jdr Mountains. And there was no way he could fit it into Dakr's saddlebags.

While making a quick check on the supplies, Adamar pricked his ears, listening to the world around him. He heard just sounds of the forest: the ancestor squirrels chattering as they moved about, birds cheeping, feeding their young while the leaves rustled with a slight breeze blowing across the treetops. The faint scratching of rabbits in the bushes nearby.

Adamar took his offered bow from Ohanzee and swung onto Dakr as his comrades did the same. Once the four were settled, Hmo guided his black horse into the lead and the four started off.

Eleven

A couple days went by as the four rode, only light idle talk passing between them. The sound of the horses' hooves striking against the ever changing forest floor filled the air. By noon on the third day of the quest they had passed out of part of the forest that bordered Eadageth, and were trekking across the Lazus plains when they came upon a village.

"I think that's Fride, up ahead." Ohanzee pulled his horse up alongside Adamar and Dakr, ears pricking. The four archers looked at the buildings in front of them.

"Should we go around it?" Adamar looked at the coyote. He and the archers didn't look entirely friendly with their weapons. And it didn't help that Thayn and Hmo didn't really smell of any emotion, while Adamar's emotions were running all over the place. Friendly furs would smell...well, friendly. Happy. Content. Curious. Not emotionless or too full of emotions.

"It's not my decision." Ohanzee shrugged, gaze going to Hmo, who was still guiding them along.

"Fride's a peaceful place, Adamar. You've been there. You should have no problems there. It will take less time then going around it, considering it is near a few larger lakes." Hmo advised. As always, Adamar couldn't smell an emotion from him.

Adamar turned around in his saddle to see Thayn behind him. "What do you think, Thayn? You haven't really said a word since we left Eadageth."

The soft, reflective voice of the red wolf was carried forward by a gentle breeze. "How quickly do you want to find Miro?"

Adamar faced forward again, his thoughts flipping themselves over and over. The wolf was right; Adamar wanted to find Miro quickly. Going around Fride, even though it wasn't as big as other places were, would take some time. And why was he worrying like this? He was being paranoid.

"Let's go." Adamar encouraged Dakr forward. "We're just passing through, though. Okay, Ohanzee? No stopping for sweets."

The coyote grinned sheepishly. He had an addiction to anything saccharine.

Adamar rode alongside Hmo, while Ohanzee was next to Thayn as they walked onto a long, seemingly endless road that divided Fride down the middle. Like Eadageth, there was a single, main street where the furs practiced their trades and trained apprentices. Unlike Eadageth, few lived above their workplaces, instead choosing to live on the outskirts of the village, which were designated as anywhere that wasn't the main road.

Adamar's ears lowered as he noticed the apprehensive smell in the air, mixed with something foreign, and the absence of furs milling about the street. Once when the archers had gone up to partake in the trials, they had chosen the longer route back home, going through Fride, which Adamar now remembered as a loud, happy place filled with the kindest furs one could ever meet.

"It's...empty." The fox observed audibly, his gaze sweeping across the various buildings and shops as the four rode slowly down the street.

"Where could everyone have gone?" Ohanzee voiced.

Adamar narrowed his eyes as he saw furs looking at him through shuttered windows, muzzles peeking around the cracks of doors and ears pressed close to outside walls.

A skunk fur poked her head out from the side of a building, her gaze tracking the four moving bodies of her ancestors, and those that sat atop them.

"Hey, foreigners." She stepped fully into view, a brown dress nearly the same color as Thayn's horse covering most of her body. The slender sleeves made way to calloused black hands, but her voice was as gentle as her appearance. "I'll tell you what's going on."

Adamar smelled no ill will from her, and halted Dakr.

The fur stepped up next to Ohanzee's horse, putting a hand on the horse's shoulder. Galene turned to look at and nuzzle her.

The skunk patted Galene's long muzzle, her glee evident and smelling pleasant in the air even while four armed furs watched her apprehensively, defensively.

The skunk continued petting Galene for a while, long enough for Thayn's horse to stamp a hoof in impatience. Adamar thought he could sense a bit of jealousy radiating from the ancestor horse. Personally, he was also getting a little impatient. They had not walked through Fride so Galene could get a long grooming.

"My name's Laurel." The skunk looked up, first at Ohanzee, then to Adamar and the other two archers. "You smell like some bad event has happened. You, fox. What happened?"

Adamar twisted the surplus of Dakr's reins. She could be connected to the Darvin kingdom. It wasn't like she had just appeared in a town of frightened furs peering out across streets filled only with dust and dirt. And she was stalling them from getting to Miro faster.

"Why?" he questioned, feeling Hmo's gaze briefly on his shoulders.

"Curious." She looked up at Adamar. "But you don't have to say. I know you're on some mission and in a hurry." She exhaled. "There are prints on the ground from a fur that had dashed through here a couple of days ago. You can't really smell it because of the rain. And your horse's hooves have beaten over the ones further back. But if you look ahead of you, all the way down the road you'll see the spaced-out prints of a running canine.

"They're foreign. Not from around here. When you get close, they smell strange." Laurel explained. "No one knows who it was, or why they were running through here, but they stole some meat from our butcher. The furs of Fride aren't used to someone coming in and taking things. We're used to everyone being welcoming, not dashing around in the middle of the night. Stealing in any village is rare, as you know. This is just disturbing."

"Don't you have someone that could take a look at the prints and see if they knew the bandit's scent?" Adamar put a little trust into Laurel's words as he tried to ignore the eyes constantly watching from the shadows.

The skunk shook her head. "We've never needed one. And so everyone's scared into their homes whenever strangers come through."

Hmo's horse shifted, bored. The fox paused. "And yet, you're out here."

Laurel's nodded. "I am, but we've appointed furs to take watch for a few hours every day for the next few days, until these weird events die down. It's my watch right now."

"Ah, alright." Adamar nodded to her. "Well, we should be off. Time can't be stalled. Thanks for telling us what was going on."

She turned away, slipping back into the gloom that clung onto the sides of buildings.

Not wanting to be in Fride a moment longer, Adamar squeezed Dakr's sides and the horse shot off, pounding down the street, tailed by the other three archers and their rides.

Adamar watched the dirt road blur into a mass of brown, but as Dakr neared the end of the road and Fride, the fox did see a print with the toes dug deep into the dirt, as if the fur that had made the mark had been running. The print was spaced far from another, identical print. So she was right. He slowed his horse and sniffed the air around the print. Thayn did the same, and said that it smelled like Darvin.

The print smelled like the scent that had lingered near Miro's crib. That jackal had come this way.

Twelve

"What was that about?" Ohanzee asked as soon as they slowed down, letting the horses move at a quick walk after they were half a mile from Fride.

"I don't know." Adamar shook his head. "But it was strange. That wasn't the Fride I remember. It felt wrong." The fox turned in his saddle to look at Thayn, who met Adamar's gaze almost immediately. "You said it smelled like Darvin. How did you know?"

"My father was once in contact with Girbindon. I know the smell. And I won't discuss it further right now."

Adamar looked at the fields of grass that ended soon in another forest. "Do you think it was the fur that stole Miro?" Who else could it be?

"Who are you asking?" Ohanzee said.

"All of you." Adamar sighed, his mind dancing. "Do you mind if I ride ahead a little? I'll stay in sight." When permission was given, Adamar pushed Dakr into a canter.

As Dakr ran away from the group, Adamar gripped his bow tighter and comforted himself in the rhythm of the horse's movements, allowing his thoughts to wander. When he was out of earshot of his comrades, he let the horse walk. It was fine if they could still smell him.

He noticed that the sun was already beginning to dip, casting its shadowed rays back across him and illuminating a path that morphed into a forest trail.

What if, Adamar realized with a bit of dread, the bear that was keeping Miro had already killed him, if that was his goal? What if they got to the Darvin kingdom too late, and if they were lucky, were handed back Miro's slaughtered remains?

But why, then, would the jackal have not just killed Miro on the spot? It wouldn't be as efficient to take him all the way across the Land to the Darvin kingdom. Then again, how would the jackal be able to cross the entirety of the Land on foot in less than a few days? Even if he ran the entire time at a sprint, he still wouldn't be able to get far without a quicker-moving ancestor horse.

And he would be carrying a young kit that he should be careful with, not drag along on the ground and make his father quite angry. Furious, really.

Adamar pulled on Dakr's reins, sitting back with a soft vocal cue to halt the horse before the forest. Adamar turned to look at Ohanzee, Thayn, and Hmo still riding along the path, now urging their horses into a canter to catch up. Ohanzee led them closer.

"Let's go, Adamar!" With a whoop of joy Ohanzee pushed Galene into a gallop and set off down the trail.

"Let's set up." Adamar guided Dakr over to a smooth branch on the edge of the clearing, hung his bow by its head, and then dismounted, walking Dakr to another tree.

As Ohanzee and Thayn did the same, Adamar glanced at Hmo still sitting on his black horse, bow hanging on the branch next to Adamar's while the bat focused on a branch in his hands. Hmo dug a claw into the end of the green branch, and split it down its middle.

Adamar slid a leather sack from the saddlebags and submerged it in a stream rushing down into a small valley not too far from the clearing.

Adamar brought the filled sack up and let Dakr dip into his muzzle into it, drinking nosily. The fox watched Hmo continue to rip apart branches, then dropping them into a pile on the ground beside his patient and calm horse.

Once Hmo apparently deemed the pile substantial, he dismounted and tied his horse next to Dakr.

"Hmo," Adamar asked. "What are you doing with those branches?"

The bat didn't turn towards the fox as he took the saddle off his horse. "No rope was packed in those saddlebags, right?"

"No. Why?"

"I've learned how to create suitable rope from the flesh of trees. Once it's ready the line will be able to serve as a halter for the horses, so they won't have to constantly have a hard bit in their mouths."

Adamar perked his ears. "How?"

Hmo looked up. "First, you need to build a fire. I'll show you after."

Adamar nodded and turned to the tree the two horses were tethered to. He tied the sack to it in a way that the horses could drink but the water wouldn't fall.

The fox slowly built a fire to warm the meat from last night. Once the fire was strong enough, Hmo took the green flesh of his torn branches and tied it all together, dumping it onto the flames.

The bat explained the point of setting the branches on fire. "The fire will melt the branches a little. The heat will fuse them together, and after being left alone for a moment or so, there will be an improvised rope left in its place."

Adamar nodded and handed warmed meat to Ohanzee and Thayn, who had just sat down from tending to their horses and feeding all four horses. "How is that possible?" The fox asked. "I've not heard of any type of tree that can do that."

Hmo sat with his legs crossed beneath himself. "Yes you have. You just weren't taught some of its properties. Only the choom trees can do this." Hmo reached forward and snatched the burning line from the fire. He held it gingerly in his claws while the colder night air began to cool it. "I used this when I was coming to Eadageth and got caught in a snow storm. It was so cold and Olie's bridle was so worn that it cracked and tore."

"So I took the bridle off of him. I knew he wouldn't run off. I've had him since he was a colt. I only have him tied to trees now because, with other horses, he once in a while gets a bit spooked." Hmo looked at where Olie rested, his black coat blending into the night. "When Olie's bridle froze, I improvised. The halter held." The bat went to his horse.

When Hmo returned after stashing the bridle in Olie's saddlebags, Adamar asked if he could show the three of them how to create the rope from choom trees. The bat did so, and soon the coyote, red wolf, and fox had choom tree rope burning in the fire.

As it burned, the fox sat quietly, gaze on the trees ahead of him. They'd managed to finish crossing the Lazus plains only an hour before they'd stopped for the night. None of them had wanted to make camp in the middle of a giant field, in full view of everything and everyone.

Once they got past this last expanse of forest and over the Zrad fields, they had to cross the Jdr Mountains. That would take a few days. But after that they would eventually come across Darvin.

Adamar longed to be there now, to get rid of Girbindon, to grab Miro and turn around and go home. But that was days away. In truth, they weren't too close. The Zrad fields were massive.

Time was drifting away, the fox noticed. Moonless night had darkened the world. His nose twitched with the crispness of the air. They should move through the spars quickly if they wanted to get a good rest and still set out before the sun came halfway through the sky. If they did even do the spars, to save time.

"Hey, Adamar, your rope is going to burn to shreds." Ohanzee mentioned as he walked close to the fox, carrying his own choom tree halter in his hands.

"Right." Adamar returned to reality and went over to the fire, seizing the fused rope in two claws before the flames took it down to fuel the smoke.

As he waited for the rope to cool enough that it wouldn't burn Dakr, Adamar ran his furred fingers along the rope, feeling its rough ductile surface. Small ridges formed a pattern across it, as if the tree was attempting to imitate rope instead of just replacing it.

Adamar went back over to Dakr, tying the rope into a halter and removing the horse's bridle before replacing it with the halter. He placed the bridle in the bags, not wanting to risk losing it in the forest by some interested ancestor wandering about. Dakr nuzzled Adamar's hands, as if he had a treat with him.

"How about you stay and rest instead of sparring?" Ohanzee came up to Adamar. "It's late and you look and smell exhausted. Hmo and I will have a quick spar."

Adamar sighed, wanting to stretch his muscles after sitting on a horse the entire day. "Alright." He complied, then turned and glanced at the fire, seeing only Hmo. "Where's Thayn?" Adamar asked.

"He went down to the stream. He's fine. He said he just wants to think." Ohanzee shrugged. "Let him, I say. So just rest, Adamar. We'll be getting near to the Zrad fields hopefully soon."

While Hmo and Ohanzee began their spar, Adamar arranged the horses' saddles as pillows, in a way that there would be enough space between each so the four furs could sleep comfortably and not bang into each other.

Adamar shook the saddle blankets of horsehair and dust. He draped the blankets over the saddles, and then went to the now-empty sacks of water that were hanging for the four horses.

Adamar carried the sacks down to the stream, filling them next to where Thayn was sitting. The wolf appeared lost in thought, his eyes glazed over, and his arms wrapped around his knees. His ears were drooping, his smell faint. But the crunch of Adamar's feet smashing leaves made the wolf's ears prick and his gaze briefly go to Adamar.

Thayn looked over the fox for a moment, then back at the water, still in the same position as he had been, his gaze starting to fog over once more.

Adamar, not disturbing the wolf further, filled the water sacks and went quietly back up to the horses.

Leaving the thick robe by his side, Adamar reclined against Dakr's saddle, his legs stretched out in front of him and his back against the hard leather, gaze lazily following Ohanzee and Hmo as they finished up the spar.

Hmo tackled the coyote, managing to catch him quickly. He pressed his wrist up against Ohanzee's throat as he held him in a headlock. The coyote struggled for a moment, but Adamar could see the coyote wasn't really trying.

Adamar watched them dampen the fire, their movements sluggish.

Ohanzee sat down heavily next to Adamar, his eyes closing with exhaustion. He leaned back, and by the time Hmo had sat down, was asleep.

Adamar's mind strayed back home, wondering what Avaha was doing and how she was taking his disappearance. She had been hysterical, and he worried about her. Hopefully Chenl, or Jek, or someone was still taking care of her, even if he didn't particularly like Jek for going against him. Adamar knew she could hold her own, but no one can function as well as they might have been able to with a great blow to their emotions.

Maybe she was spending time with some of the furs from the village. She was never overly social, but did get around on occasion, little bits of talk filling her free hours.

Adamar began to close his eyes, feeling the heaviness of sleep on him, when a sound of an arrow flying cut through the air and a hand-fashioned dart landed in the fox's side. Adamar glanced at the weapon protruding from his flesh with alarm, but his eyes dropped closed and a soothing warmness overtook his body as a second dart went into Hmo beside him.

Thirteen

An aching spread throughout Adamar's side. His ribcage throbbed as if he'd been kicked. A line of fire seemed to radiate up and down his shoulder blades.

The only scent that entered his nostrils was the thick, merciless attack of smoke from a real fire. It masked the smell of the creatures that Adamar sensed were nearby him. His ears quickly filled with the sounds of pain and the crackling of the fire. The campfire seemed stronger than before, though. As if someone had fed it after it had been dampened.

He opened his eyes and when he caught sight of the scene, he shut his eyes again in disbelief.

Adamar looked about again, watching everything come into focus. Black smoke sat near the lowest branches of trees, and drifted up to the darkened sky. A fire roiled in the middle of the clearing, illuminating the faces of the archers and then two furs that Adamar couldn't recognize. Ohanzee's head was lowered. Both he and Hmo were tied to the same tree, but the bat was awake, watching with narrowed eyes. The horses were nowhere in sight. The fox wished he could smell something other than smoke, so he could smell what was happening.

He rolled his painful shoulders, trying to move his hands. His gaze rested on Thayn. The wolf was restrained against a choom tree like his comrades, but a cloaked fur, who looked like a canine, pressed a blade to his throat. Blood splattered the ground at Thayn's feet.

Working his hands against the ropes that bound them, Adamar focused his ears on the two. The fox looked at Hmo briefly, meeting the bat's unwavering, emotionless gaze. He hated not being able to smell anything. And he had no idea how much time had passed.

Or, what was going on.

Were these furs just typical bandits? Or were they with Girbindon?

"Which one of you is Adamar?" The canine in front of Thayn snarled.

When Thayn said nothing, the canine repeated his question and stepped closer. "Tell me or you'll die."

Thayn glared down at the canine, ears pressed flat. "Which one? Of what? Which one of the trees?"

"You know what I'm talking about, you stupid wolf."

Thayn watched the canine for a few moments, and as the canine got ready to throw his blade into Thayn's neck, the wolf leaned forward and grabbed the edge of the canine's cloak between his teeth.

With a growl, Thayn's pulled back on the fabric, yanking it hard enough to choke the canine. Adamar smirked at the sight.

A second cloaked figure stepped up behind the first one. It reached up a hand and wrapped it around Thayn's muzzle. The wolf quickly shook off the hand, not relaxing his grip.

The second figure moved its hand again, but, instead of going for Thayn's muzzle, the claws dove for his sensitive nose. As the claws pierced his nose, Thayn thrashed his head, not wanting to let go of the first figure, but the pain of his nose being pulled to shreds quickly caused him to loosen his grip.

Growling in pain and anger, Thayn ripped off the piece of fabric, blood dripping from his nose. The second fur let go and grinned at the red wolf.

"Pain. We will give you more pain, if you do not tell us which one of you is Adamar."

In response, Thayn spat out the slobbered piece of fabric and smiled when it hit the second fur in the eye.

While his accomplice was wiping the spit from his eye, the first fur moved forward and put the blade to Thayn's throat for a second time. "Tell us. You'll die."

"I haven't fallen to death yet." Thayn replied. "And how are you going to confirm that one of us is Adamar? You don't know what he smells like, do you?"

The two attackers scowled, annoyed by Thayn's wit. The fox focused on slicing the thick ropes that bound his wrists around the thin trunk of a choom tree. He worked a claw into the restraints, but the ropes didn't want to be cut in half. At least, now he knew that the ropes were strong enough to hold the horses.

"Your friend over here." The fur with the ripped cloak spat. "The one that told you to sit down and stay at the river. The one you've been traveling with for a couple days that always made you stay at the back of the pack. You never got to be in front." He was trying to anger the wolf.

Thayn bared his teeth, and his voice blended with a low growl. "Those choices were never forced upon me. Those are lies. I made the decisions myself."

The ripped-cloak fur laughed. "You really think you're so smart, don't you? If you are so smart, tell us which of you is Adamar!"

Thayn said nothing.

The fur growled and grabbed Thayn by his snout. "Do we need to beat you into submission? You were hard enough to drag up the river. Killing you is easier."

Adamar paused as he heard the new line of information, and his gaze ran over Thayn. The fox knew one's fur would hide any bruises, so he looked for scrapes and cuts. Cruel gashes covered Thayn's legs and tail.

Thayn's expression revealed no feelings of pain. "Then, are you going to kill me now?"

Thayn jerked his head to surprise the two, and bit the cloaked wolf on the muzzle, sinking his teeth in. His jaws locked as he thrashed his head again, blood rolling down and off the two struggling canines.

A loud snap seemed to extinguish the fire's sound for a moment, and Thayn let go of the other wolf, letting its body drop to the ground. The red wolf spat out blood and looked at the other fur, their gazes meeting for a fraction of a second before the fur roared in fury and ran Thayn's throat through with the knife. The blade tip protruded through the back of Thayn's neck and stuck in the tree.

Alarm shot through Adamar, and he worked even more feverishly to get free. Thayn was hurt. He had to help, even though it looked too late.

Sadness coated Thayn's gaze, and pain finally leaked onto his features. His breath grew more and more watery. His tongue lolled out the side of his mouth. A minute passed.

With a weak growl, Thayn closed his eyes.

The remaining fur turned toward Adamar with enough speed to blow his hood off his head, revealing the brown and white face of an unhappy ferret.

As Adamar's gaze met the ferret's, the ferret smiled and grabbed a knife from his dead comrade, then moved toward Adamar.

The ferret came close enough for their noses to nearly touch. Adamar leveled his gaze and growled with flat ears. "You killed my friend." He again tried to smell something, but only the smoke scent burned his nose. It was getting into his lungs.

"Does it make you sad?" The ferret responded, his twisted smile never leaving his face. "Do you want to do something about it?"

"How about killing you?" Adamar offered. "If you just let me go, I could shot you through with an arrow, easy. I can show you."

The ferret snorted. "Like that'll happen, fox. Think again." The ferret ran a finger along the edge of his curved knife. "So, tell me now, where is Adamar? Are you him? Do you want what happened to your friend happen to you?"

Adamar's thoughts immediately drifted to an image of Miro seeing his father's grave, and never seeing him in the flesh and fur.

Adamar narrowed his eyes at the ferret, keeping quiet for a brief moment. Then he said, "No."

"Good." The ferret swished his tail happily. "So you'll tell me where Adamar is."

Adamar worked at the bindings on his wrists, and ignored the weasel's stupidity. "What kind of rope did you use?"

The ferret's ears flicked back. "Why?"

"Curious."

"Rope. Though, my friend and I were thinking of thanking you for supplying extra rope for us. If it was good enough to hold your horses, we thought it would be able to hold you and your non-cooperating friends." The ferret shrugged. "But enough of chat. Tell me where he is." He dragged the knife down

Adamar's arm, slitting the fabric of his sleeve and creating a thin line of blood to rise from beneath the fur. The knife caught on the scabs from Adamar's rainy meeting with Azoth.

Adamar growled. "Why do you need to know? What are you doing here?" He glanced across the clearing, noticing with relief that Ohanzee had woken up. Ohanzee shook his head and tugged at the ropes groggily. He paused when he met Adamar's gaze and tilted his head questioningly at the ferret. Hmo leaned over to speak to him.

"Hey!" The ferret yelled, grabbing the end of Adamar's muzzle and enclosing it in his surprisingly strong grip. "You look at me, and no one else. Not until you tell me where he is."

Angered, Adamar snarled and tore his snout away from the ferret. He opened his mouth to reveal teeth that were happy to bite down on a few fingers.

The ferret took the opportunity and put the tip of his knife blade into Adamar's canine mouth, the sharper end point up toward Adamar's palate. "I will impale you if you try to bite me like your friend did."

Adamar narrowed his eyes, waiting for the ferret to slide the knife away before he closed his mouth, but only after snapping teeth close to the weasel. "And what if I tell you what you want to know?"

Revealing that he hadn't thought of such an idea, the ferret hesitated. "I...just tell me who is Adamar."

"No." When the ferret placed the blade against his throat, he immediately tensed in worry.

"Tell me. Fine, then, don't. But tell me this: What will his kit do anything for?"

Adamar's heart skipped a beat. What did they want with Miro? He wouldn't tell them about Miro's favorite food: chocolate. Whatever it meant to the ferret, it couldn't mean something good.

He growled. "Take the knife away from my neck." He felt the blade press harder against his flesh.

He shouldn't be worried. He'd sensed the ferret didn't intend to kill him. The ferret was hesitating too much. But he couldn't be sure. And no one had ever held up a weapon against him, not in something other than a spar or a fight at the trials.

"Where...Where are you from?" Adamar asked, forcing his voice to relax.

"Where is he?" The ferret countered, pressing the knife edge against Adamar's unguarded throat. "What does his kit like?

When silence became the only response the weasel would get, the ferret scowled and removed his knife from Adamar's neck, only to stick his face right up in Adamar's. The fox bared his teeth. He knew the weasel couldn't kill him. He also knew that the ferret was lacking in intelligence.

"You'll tell me the answer. You will eventually. Don't deny it." The ferret smashed a fist into Adamar's chest and stepped away, going to the middle of the clearing, where he stood with the fire snapping behind him.

"You all will get punished for this!" The ferret snatched a stick from the ground and began scattering the rocks that kept the fire at bay. "You'll get punished for killing the wolf, my partner. Your friend deserved to die. You should've told us where he is. Have fun getting out of this. You'll never get to your precious kit."

Then the weasel tipped over one of the logs of the fire and set flame to the forest floor. He bolted before the burning tongues could reach him. "Girbindon will have his revenge! He will conquer!"

Fourteen

The black vapor destroyed Adamar's vision for a few moments. He shut his eyes against the stinging smoke, focusing intently on slicing through the restraints. He worried that if he didn't get free, he wouldn't ever get to Miro. The worry made his movements almost frantic.

A darkened hand appeared on Adamar's shoulder. The fox startled and emitted a low growl in warning, if the ferret had decided to come back.

To Adamar's relief he saw Ohanzee's head pop up, covered in soot and offering a faint smile before the coyote went behind Adamar's back. Adamar relaxed his muscles when Ohanzee began untying the ropes.

Hmo appeared out of the smoke, his black form nearly blending into the gray smog. The bat's expression had changed, for once, and irritation was prominent. Adamar noticed the burn of rope branding the delicate membrane beneath Hmo's arms.

"I'll look for the horses." The bat turned, grabbing the discarded horses' bridles and reins from the ground, and disappeared into the forest.

"Alright." Adamar looked at Ohanzee. "How'd you get out?"

"I'm small. Underestimated."

The fox nodded. "Let's try to put out this fire."

Adamar coughed and moved closer to the smoke wall, letting the wind push at his back as he searched for the tree where the horses had been tethered. His senses were useless, the smoke disorienting his vision and clogging his nose, while the sound of the fire filled his ears. The fox reached blindly through the black vapor, glad when he felt his hand touch the bark of a tree that was still waiting for the murderous flames. He ran his hand along the tree, and crouched, nose straining for clearer air as his fingers brushed the lip of the leather sack. Unaware if it was full of water or not, Adamar grabbed hold of the leather and stood, turning back toward the fire.

He tossed what water was left in the bag at the flames, not pausing to listen to the flames hiss in protest as he ran down towards the stream.

Adamar breathed in as much of the smokeless air as he could while he filled the sack, and ran back up to the flames. Ohanzee quickly found the other water bag and joined in. The two of them worked for panicky minutes, until the smoke began to clear and the fire died to a small spark that Ohanzee stomped out.

Adamar poured the last bag of water onto the ground, and watched mud run down the hill.

Ohanzee coughed. "I think that's the last of it. We just need to wash off..." The coyote smirked. "You're kind of covered in soot, Adamar."

Adamar rolled his eyes, barely glancing down at his ash-covered body. "Same with you." He stilled as the smell of blood stung the air.

Adamar went over to where Thayn's body stood, still tied against the tree with the knife pinning his throat, head back against the bark. Blood had flowed down the front of the wolf, soaking his fur and giving him an even more red appearance. Adamar stepped close and gently removed the reddened blade from Thayn's neck.

Ohanzee untied the wolf. Once his body was free, Thayn's body fell forward. Adamar caught him and laid his body along the ground.

The fox bent down next to the dead wolf, his ears turned out. He felt for a pulse under Thayn's chin, even though he knew full well that no beat would respond to his touch. The fox sat back on his heels, tail limp. He watched Thayn's body not stir, barely noticing that Ohanzee had sat down across from him and Hmo had returned, trailed by horses and with a hand clutching four sets of reins. The bat tied the horses to a tree, and walked over.

"We should bury him." Adamar tried for Thayn's pulse again. All that answered his touch was cold, bloody flesh beneath the wolf's fur.

Silence ensued for a few moments.

Adamar hadn't known Thayn all too well, but his death was nonetheless disturbing. No one had really known who Thayn was. All everyone knew was that Thayn had been young when he became an archer for Eadageth. And quickly, he'd fallen into the background, shooting the arrows that no one could understand where they'd come from until he presented himself.

That had seemed to be where Thayn had been most comfortable. None could guess why the wolf was so quiet. Thayn always rode at the back. If he wasn't at the archery range, he would be near water. A stream, a pond, occasionally even a puddle if he was too tired to travel far. Thayn had a home, but no one could never figure out where it was.

Adamar rose and went over to where the bows were still hanging, side by side, on an untouched tree.

"Let's find a place to bury him." Ohanzee said, voice quiet.

Adamar pushed the last pile of dirt away from the seven-foot long hole he and Ohanzee had dug.

While the fox and coyote had scooped out soil, Hmo cleaned up Thayn's body as best as possible. He'd removed the blood, giving Thayn a look that had less agony. The wolf's expression was the same as it had been a few hours he died, calm, one of the two expressions Adamar had ever seen Thayn wearing.

The other had been the slight indication of a smile at the corner of his mouth, as if Thayn had just conquered something the others knew nothing about.

The three solemn furs lowered Thayn's body carefully into the grave. Adamar then went to the bows. Thayn's bow was next to his own, a beautiful bow made out of a bright cherry wood, carved and sanded down by Thayn himself. The wolf had worked on his bow for days, adding the sinew and increasing its flexibility, instead of going to Edgier's father, Eadageth's wood carver, for a bow.

"Thayn was a great archer. He died with honor, and so he shall be buried with the same honor he presented, and has deserved for years, years unknown to all. You protected your comrades even in the face of death. We will miss you, Thayn." Ohanzee looked at Adamar, who bent at the edge of the grave and placed the bow on top of Thayn's chest. The three stood for a few quiet moments.

As Hmo started to saddle the horses, Adamar and Ohanzee filled in the grave of the red wolf that had lived for only twenty-three years.

Fifteen

"Maybe I should go home."

Adamar looked up at Ohanzee, and tilted his head. "What made you say that?"

The coyote shrugged, watching Adamar rub a poultice on the burns of the membranes between Hmo's chest and outstretched arms.

"I probably just got in the way, when those furs caught us. Thayn died and I did nothing." Ohanzee dabbed a finger into the small jar of medicine they'd brought from Eadageth, and smoothed it across burns on his tail.

"None of us could do anything." Adamar's voice grew quieter. The three hadn't gotten over Thayn's death, even after a few hours of calm, quiet riding. They'd stopped in the woods to treat the gashes and burns gotten from the fire before they set off. Any coughing from the smoke had faded.

"Still. How am I going to help in finding your pup, Adamar? I don't want to be someone who drags along, doing nothing helpful."

Adamar focused his gaze again on Hmo's burns. "I picked you two for a reason. You each have skills that will greatly help with combating the head of the Darvin kingdom. I don't think that we'll be able to get Miro back without at least a small fight. And three is better than one. More noses and ears. More strength."

"How? How do I help?" Ohanzee asked.

"Just a few hours ago, you were agile enough to get out of those ropes and free us before the whole forest burned. Ohanzee, why are you doubting yourself?"

Ohanzee shrugged for a second time. "Just am."

"You shouldn't."

The coyote didn't say anything. But beneath the smell of fire that lingered on all of them, Adamar could smell the cool scent of his sadness.

As soon as Adamar finished tending to Hmo's burns, the bat thanked him and stood to check on his horse. They would have to be riding soon, and without much food left, the three were worried how fast and far the horses would be able to go. There was only so much edible food on the forest floor.

"What was that about, Ohanzee?" Adamar asked as the coyote wound a torn piece of cloth around the now-clean cut on Adamar's arm.

"I don't know. That just suddenly came into my mind." The coyote was quiet for a few moments. "Are you scared?"

"Of?"

"Of the possibility that your pup won't be found. That Azoth was wrong about where he is. Or that...horrid things have happened to Miro." Ohanzee tied the cloth in place, and checked to make sure it was wrapped snugly.

Adamar's ears lowered. "Yes. But I won't let that get in my way. I can't let it." He paused, emotions coming over him. "He's too important." He couldn't let anything stop him. He just couldn't.

Adamar sat on Dakr, holding the reins of Thayn's horse. The palomino horse looked fairly peaceful, but considering his longtime rider was nowhere to be found, Adamar was keeping himself as alert as possible in case the horse spooked easily.

The three furs and four ancestor horses headed out, moving at a slower pace than before. They watched the sun rise and then sink in the sky, falling with their energy. Adamar estimated, as he nearly swayed in the saddle, that they'd gotten less than a few hours of rest.

An inn was found as a place to rest for the night. No one felt safe out in the open, on the edge of the Zrad fields and after last night.

They asked as vaguely as possible at the bar about strange furs coming in and out of the village near the inn. The boar tending the front room had shaken his head, grisly tusks coming dangerously near Adamar's muzzle.

The inn's owners had been kind enough to allow them to stable their horses in an old, five-stall barn that sagged next to the inn. Adamar pulled a trough full of grain over to Dakr, Galene, and Olie. The fox turned to Hmo, who held Thayn's horse. The horse still wore its tack.

"What should we do with her?" The fox asked, laying a hand on the horse's shoulder. The horse glanced briefly at him, and then went back to grazing.

Hmo shifted the thick cloak he wore as a cold wind blew, pulling the fabric tighter around his body. "What would Thayn have wanted?"

Ohanzee spoke, his gaze on the ground. "Thayn never told anyone much of anything, but I did talk to him sometimes. He responded on occasion." The coyote began taking the tack off of Thayn's horse.

"Thayn would want his horse to be free. Now that he's gone, the horse doesn't have a fur to care for. I don't believe that Thayn would want his horse to be sold and sold again to owners of varying skills and kindness. That's a fate none would want to endure. So—" Ohanzee removed the horse's last piece of tack, and set its bridle on top of the saddle.

The coyote smiled sadly. He briefly stroked the horse's mane, then guided the horse out into the field. He combed a burr from the horse's mane, and nudged it gently toward the woods that bordered the Zrad fields.

The horse looked at Ohanzee curiously for a moment. Its ears flicked, focusing toward the coyote. Then it seemed to get the idea, looked back at the woods, and it galloped across the field. With a joyful whinny it disappeared among the trees.

The three gathered their horses' and Thayns' tack.

The fox and coyote discussed what to do with the extra tack as they moved up the stairs, climbing to the rooms that rested above the tavern's loud main floor. Adamar unlocked one of the doors and pushed it in, smelling the furs that had been here before and glancing over the two thin beds, an open closet, a simple round table, and a large window that made up the surprisingly spacious room.

Adamar set down the tack and crossed the floor, his paw pads scraping against the rough and splintered wood. The fox let himself become lost in thought about Miro. About how Avaha was faring with him and her kit gone.

After a quick dinner downstairs, Adamar was seated with Hmo and Ohanzee at the small table.

"You said you talked to Thayn. How'd you get him to answer your questions with more than just vague answers? You couldn't have derived your knowledge from just a simple yes or no." Adamar looked at Ohanzee.

The coyote shrugged. "I just talked to him. But I never went too far in the amount of questions I asked, or how personal they would have been to him."

"Did you ask about his past?"

Ohanzee nodded. "I did. That's why he was so quiet." The coyote hesitated.

Hmo chose a different conversation topic. "Why do you think we were attacked earlier this morning, by furs of the Darvin kingdom?"

"Those furs didn't seem to know what they were after." Adamar recalled. "They kept asking Thayn about me, and where I was, but they didn't know that I was a fox. I'd think if Girbindon knew about and took my kit, he'd know that I'd be his father. And then, that ferret wanted to know Miro's favorite thing. I'm not sure I want to know why he did." Anger snaked its way around Adamar's words.

"And even without that, they just seemed like they were sent to stall us. Didn't the ferret mention something about a delay?" Ohanzee looked at Hmo and Adamar. "He and the other one he was with, the wolf, they just seemed like they wanted nothing other than to stall us."

"But they were asking about me and Miro." Adamar countered gently.

"Still, though." Ohanzee shook his head. "They did not seem too organized. They just killed Thayn, tried to set the forest on the fire, let loose our horses, and left."

"They wanted to push us back." Adamar offered. "Maybe they knew that Thayn knew information about Darvin, and didn't want him helping. And maybe they didn't want him to help us on this mission to find Miro. With one less nose and set of ears to help us look, and one less fur to help fight Girbindon, we're weaker."

"That makes sense." Ohanzee acknowledged. He exhaled, smelling and looking fatigued.

"But then, Adamar, why were they asking about you?" Hmo's voice was solemn, thought-provoking.

"I don't know. Maybe I have something they want?" Adamar tried. Despair started to rise. "Maybe they wanted to take me to Darvin, to see my reactions as they hurt my kit?" He tried to keep the despair from overwhelming him. He was too tired and worn after this morning to talk about this.

"Maybe." Hmo said. "Or maybe they want to torture you in some other way, maybe tell you awful stories about Miro while you are halfway across the land from him."

"Your mind is dark, Hmo." Ohanzee admonished.

Hurtful, terrifying images swirled into Adamar's mind. "Can we just not discuss this? I don't want to lose time. It's already late." The fox stood and decided to grab the floor for rest. Ohanzee and Hmo took the only two beds.

Gratefully, sleep was quick to come.

"Avaha?" Adamar's eyes went wide as he rose from the table on the edge of the inn's main room, where the owners served breakfast. His ears pricked beneath his hood. The fox's gaze was on a fur relaxing at another table, her cloak's hood down and her scent drifting with the rest of the inn's customers. The scent smelled like Avaha's sweet scent. Adamar stepped to go over and check to see if he was looking at his mate, his thoughts not on the odd possibility that she'd be able to travel so fast.

A hand grabbed Adamar's elbow, pulling him back down.

"No, Adamar." Hmo chided. "Even if that is Avaha, you shouldn't go up to her."

"Why not?" The fox protested, his gaze on the other fox.

"Because we're in an inn somewhere. How would she know where we are? Her presence here couldn't be just a coincidence." Hmo picked at the food on his plate. "Just don't go up to her. What if that's not Avaha, but someone else you've never met? Maybe someone that likes to kill and works for Girbindon?" The bat raised his gaze to meet Adamar's. "Adamar, you and Ohanzee haven't really been outside of Eadageth, unless it was for the trials. You've never needed to really worry about trusting strangers not from your own town.

"Furs have to learn about trust. Some learn it the hard way, others don't. Whichever way you do is up to you."

Adamar looked at the unknown fur, his ears lowered unhappily. He ached to see Avaha again, to be able to talk to her, hug her. He wanted to be near her.

Adamar nearly whined like a pup, but turned back to his breakfast. A few minutes passed, and the other fox's smell faded. He looked up to find the other fox gone.

Sixteen

Miro opened his eyes and curled into a ball, whimpering pathetically as a nightmare superimposed itself on reality for a moment before it faded away. Girbindon appeared.

The bear grinned at Miro, never unsmiling, and waved at him almost manically from where he sat outside Miro's cell. Wind blew in through the open window and dove down toward the kit. He shivered, while Girbindon didn't even acknowledge the strong breeze.

Miro whimpered. He crawled to a corner away from the window, burying himself in the windless space while his stomach growled in anguish.

"Miro, why're you running? You can't get anywhere." Girbindon chided, his voice sounding like it wanted to be kind, but was unable to. "Come here, Miro. I have some food. I know you're hungry."

Miro shook his head and made a grunting noise in response, despite the pain that clawed at his belly, clambering up his throat.

Girbindon watched Miro for a second. "Miro, do come here. I'll show you something if you do." When the kit didn't answer, Girbindon continued on. "How about a nice little bug? You're a cub. You like bugs, don't you? Aren't they cool?"

Closing one hand into a fist, Girbindon's smile seemed to grow. "Show me your magical strength, Miro. I know you have it. Come here, and you can see a nice insect. Then you can do just what I did."

Something landed near Miro, and the kit opened an eye to glance at the bread that was sitting in the dirt less than a foot away. He didn't want to eat it; the bread didn't taste good.

But his stomach won over.

Miro tentatively snatched the bread and tore off a chunk, stuffing it into his muzzle with joy. Once the bread had vanished down his throat, Miro watched Girbindon curiously.

"Miro, you idiot, over here." Girbindon growled, the faux kindness gone. "You've eaten, now, what more do you want?"

Miro sniffled. He wanted his father.

The kit whined. Girbindon picked up a coiled leather cord. The bear reached through the bars and cracked the whip. A snap shot through the air, and the burning tip landed on Miro.

Blood welled from the cut on Miro's side. He began crying relentlessly, pain overtaking his mind.

"Now come here before I sear this whip into your neck!" Girbindon shouted. Miro began crawling over, desperate to avoid any more pain. The bear grinned.

Girbindon's massive hand reached out and grabbed Miro by the scruff, pulling him forward. He unlocked the door and dragged Miro through, setting him down on the ground and giving him a small cookie.

Miro's cries stifled themselves as he bit down on the treat. His gaze tracked Girbindon's every move.

"Now, Miro," The bear said, the opposite of the monster he'd been a moment ago. "I'm going to show you something very secret. I know your side hurts and is sticky, but you have to be quiet. Otherwise I won't be able to show you the pretty secret."

Miro perked his ears. He'd always seen his mother talking to some fur, leaning over the washbasin with her nose nearly touching the water, and when he would make a sound of boredom from his play area, she'd look over. A smile would jump on her face and she'd whisper, "Don't tell your father, Miro. It's a secret."

Miro had learned well to keep secrets, even if the idea of pronouncing language was still mysterious to him. He understood a few words, but his tongue couldn't repeat clearly any words, instead sounding out only cries and tasting possibly edible things.

Miro looked at the bear, his head tilted curiously.

Girbindon laughed, one hand closed into a tight fist. "Alright, Miro. Now you be a good fox and stay quiet." The bear spoke a few indistinguishable words, his gaze on his closed fist and unaware that Miro had jabbed a few fingers into the wound in his side.

The kit held back a whine of pain as agony flooded up through where his touch connected with the bloody mess. Miro removed his fingers from the gash and held them up, looking at the red that coated his fur before swiping it off along his opposite arm.

Miro's tail thumped at the ground as he saw, with delight, three little bands of red that had made cool patterns in his fur. The blood just rested on top of the orange fur, but as Miro tried to rub it out, the red stuck and didn't move.

Not about to drop an opportunity, however, Miro began drawing marks on himself with the blood until Girbindon noticed him. His side hurt less the more he focused on drawing.

"Look at me!" The bear shouted.

Miro paused his bloody doodling and looked up at Girbindon, his gaze catching on the insect that rested in Girbindon's palm.

A butterfly lazily flapped its wings, wings bordered with purple and black. Green splashed itself inside the border's boundaries. It flapped its wings again and the wings began to glow, as if light was pouring through them.

Miro watched with awe. His puppy mind told him to try and touch the pretty butterfly, and so he attempted to do so.

Just as Miro's fingers were about to connect with the insect's wings, Girbindon's hand closed into a fist, a glow briefly streaming between his fingers before it died all together.

Miro's ears lowered, tears in his eyes as he stared at where the butterfly had been. He stood up and teetered over to Girbindon, placing bloody fingers on the bear's fist. Miro tried to pry open Girbindon's grasp, wanting to see where the butterfly had gone, but the bear pushed him back and said calmly, "Now you must show me the same."

A minute passed by, Miro not understanding what the bear was talking about and Girbindon becoming frustrated.

For the past few days, Girbindon had been asking Miro to show him an unclarified skill, sometimes mentioning magic. Each morning and evening Girbindon the bear and fox would meet, whether here at Miro's cell or in the throne room. Girbindon would occasionally give Miro a piece of food, and start asking him questions that the kit barely understood.

Girbindon, persistent in finding whatever he was looking for, never budged on how long he would interrogate Miro. The kit would grow hungry and tired but that didn't matter to Girbindon.

The bear had hurt Miro enough that the kit had learned to keep quiet when he was told to. Miro wasn't a learning prodigy; he just didn't enjoy the thought of feeling pain.

"Miro." Girbindon repeated. "Show me your own magic. I know you have it." Girbindon bared his teeth. "Show me! Now! You cannot disobey me, you little idiot of a cub. You must show me what you can do. Show me now, show me, show me before I slice off your head and hang it on the wall!"

Miro smiled and soiled his diaper.

"Miro, Miro..." A hen clucked as she changed the fox kit. Miro squirmed against her, giggling when a stream of yellow hit the hen in the beak, which only made her angry.

The hen worked quickly on the kit, unhappy with her job of being a caretaker. Miro didn't learn her name, but he really didn't care. His young mind had made up a different title for the hen.

Stupid.

Stupid jabbed a finger at Miro's chest. Her large form moved around to gather supplies from the basket next to the table.

"Can you just listen for once, Miro?" Stupid grabbed Miro's muzzle in her hand and shook his snout, jarring his head to the point of Miro reaching up with his small hands and clawing at her grip. He blew his nose into her feathery hand when she didn't let go.

"Agh, Miro! That's bad!" The hen slapped him with her opposite, non snot-covered hand.

She handed the kit over to Girbindon immediately after she deemed Miro had been thoroughly cleansed of waste, blood, and dirt. The kit sat in front of Girbindon once again, though this time a small chair had been placed in front of the bear's throne, which Miro had been sat in and ordered not to leave.

Miro picked at the bandage on his side, cowering in front of Girbindon with his ears down and his form unconsciously submissive.

"Are you ready now, Miro?" Girbindon asked, resting both hands on the arms of his great chair while he looked passively at the kit. "Are you being serious? I'm aware much is being asked of you, more than that you're not even two yet, but you still must be listening. If you succeed with my simple, easy requests, you could be able to do well."

The bear did not seem to be cognizant of the fact that he was talking to someone who understood only half of what he was saying. In fact, the entire time Girbindon had been talking, Miro had been watching a spider scuttle across the floor before disappearing into one of the minuscule cracks that decorated the rough tile.

"It is quite easy, Miro. You have to show me your skill. Just think of what you want, imagine it, and concentrate. I've made using your magic easier for you, to help you. You just have to think of what you want. You may feel hungry, but don't start crying." The bear narrowed his eyes. "Miro. Are you even listening? I can kill you and avoid going through all this mess." When further attempts to get the kit to look up failed, Girbindon stood from his throne and grabbed Miro by his scruff, shaking him.

"Think of what you want! Think of it now!"

Miro fell limp as he tried, almost desperately, to understand and do what Girbindon said. He searched his expanding mind for an image that looked pleasing.

Miro's mind passed over his father and settled on a stream that had been in his nightmare, but this time it was calmer, just a simple brook that tumbled calmly over rocks jutting out from a miniature cliff.

He focused on the image. But only for a moment. He quickly looked back up at Girbindon, head cocked in confusion. The fun water wasn't appearing. It was just in his imagination.

"Do you know of the words you must speak to make the image appear? That may help."

Miro shook his head. Girbindon responded with a growl, lowering Miro to his chair. Feet scraped behind the kit.

The kit turned around, curious, and noticed Chilo standing just inside the room from behind a tapestry.

"What is it, Chilo?' The bear asked, but the growl finishing his words warned that it wasn't the best time to be interrupting.

Chilo, pausing, raised his gaze to meet Girbindon's.

Girbindon sighed. "Yes, you can speak."

A nod began Chilo's brief words. "Your workers have returned. They informed me that the four had been captured, and one was killed, as well as one of the two furs you sent out."

Girbindon narrowed his eyes. "Four? Miro's father is just the one. I only needed him captured and taken here. Or some information from him."

"Yes, but," Chilo added, "He has accomplices, as seen in the Unstable. He's serious about coming here to fight you and win. But I know that will not happen, My Great King, for you are too strong."

Girbindon nodded, sounding as if this was routine and he would like to just get on with it. "Yes, yes. What else were you told?"

The jackal looked behind himself. "Should I go...and get the fur you sent out?"

"Since when do I rely on them for accurate information? You're the highest ranked here, Chilo. You tell me what happened."

Chilo flattened his ears. "The ferret, Fen, that

came back reported that three of the four were drugged, while the fourth wasn't. The fourth was not because Fen stated that the fourth already appeared dazed. Apparently that wasn't true. As soon as they neared the fourth, a red wolf, he attacked them. They were able to drag the red wolf up from the stream where he'd been sitting. Like the other three, he was put against a tree, interrogated, and eventually killed because he wouldn't answer the question."

"The red wolf wouldn't tell Fen who Miro's father was, even though it was obvious?" Girbindon summarized. "What about the others? Did Fen ever get to Miro's father?"

"He was the only other one that Fen questioned. But Fen didn't know that at the time, not until I told him just now."

Miro glanced at Girbindon's grin. "Fen, that idiot, was supposed to capture Miro's father and take him here." The bear shook his head. "That shrewd fox. He'll pay." Girbindon looked back at Chilo. "Are the other three dead?"

Chilo looked and smelled terrified as he delivered his piece of news, cradling his healing hand against his chest. "Fen doesn't know. He set fire to the forest and ran off, believing that it was pointless to question them further, leaving the three still tied to trees. He hopes that they are dead, but he wasn't able to tell, since smoke likes to hang in the air even after the fire has died."

"So Fen ran away, and didn't complete his simple mission..." Girbindon mused. "Tell him he will be punished, Chilo."

The jackal nodded, tail tucked in fear. "I will. Is there anything else you wish to know about?"

Girbindon began to say something, but his gaze was caught on Miro. The kit appeared confused, as if everything that was being said was even stranger than the events he'd been through in the past few days.

The bear stared at Miro for a few moments, then seemed to get the idea of what the fox was wondering about. Girbindon leveled his gaze. "Chilo, why are we trying to kill them and get Miro's father?"

Smelling of fear, Chilo looked uneasy. "Because you want to stop them from getting Miro, and because his father may have something special that you want?"

"Yes, and?" Girbindon watched the jackal.

Chilo found great interest in the floor beneath his paw pads. "I—I'm not sure, Great King Girbindon."

Girbindon narrowed his eyes and stepped closer to Chilo, who shrank back, trying to look as small as possible. "And this is why I am in charge here, you idiot!" He knocked Chilo to the ground.

"You know nothing. Nothing." Girbindon scowled. "We want to kill them because we want to see if we can get a reaction from Miro; we want to see if emotions fuel his strength. Or, if his father knows something about Miro that will help us." The bear reached down and tugged Chilo up, squeezing his injured hand until the jackal cried out. "You're weak, Chilo." The bear snarled.

Miro watched the scene with his young gaze, his mind beginning to make connections. It was a bad thing to not know what one should know, the kit realized, watching the bear and canine. One got hurt for not knowing.

Miro stuck his thumb in his mouth as Girbindon turned back, leaving Chilo to scurry away as quick as he could.

One should never express pain. To do so was to show weakness.

Seventeen

"Since when do valleys get this steep?" Adamar grunted as he leaned forward, lying almost flat against Dakr's neck.

Days had passed by of continuous riding and brief conversations while working on strategies to fight Girbindon and rescue Miro when they arrived at Darvin.

The path had been as direct as possible, still based on Azoth's vague directions. The stars guided their way when it grew dark, before they took the night to rest.

"Are we near Galliv yet, Hmo?"

"Unless the town has transported itself away from this hill, then we should be close." Hmo said.

Galliv was a large village that had settled long ago on a hill with no name. The furs that had taken residence there had never decided to name it, but eventually it gathered a name in place of 'that town on the hill.'

Adamar wasn't all too sure of Galliv's history. He hadn't been listening to the lessons his father had tried to teach him as a kit. Instead, he had delighted in watching the ancestor birds soar across the sky.

"We're not staying in Galliv, are we?" Ohanzee asked.

"I don't see any reason to do so. We're just getting some fresh supplies and making sure our directions are correct. Let's be quick about it. I don't know exactly how much more time it'll take to get to Miro, and I'd like to see him as soon as possible." Adamar raised his gaze, seeing the town emerge in the distance. They would be there soon.

"Alright." Ohanzee said. "I'll probably just grab a few snacks for myself while we're there. Nothing much."

Adamar rolled his eyes. Ohanzee's sheepish smile could already be heard in his voice.

"Cease your movements in the name of Galliv!" A fur shouted from atop the hill.

Adamar halted Dakr and gazed up, craning his neck back to catch a glimpse of the fur that had stopped them.

Shaped similar to a mushroom, Galliv rose into the air on a wide, rough cylinder of dirt and soil which no one was sure how it had formed. An immense grassy top made up the ground of Galliv, foliage dripping over the edges of the base. Ground extended for multiple feet out in all directions over the top, and was devoid of nearly any buildings or life. Most furs didn't want to walk right off the edge of their town in the morning.

War tools and battlements had once been set up along the border of Galliv, creating gouges in the ground. Some gouges were deep enough to break through the turf and let a stream of sunlight through to the furs waiting below.

Adamar wasn't able to see anything inside the town, which was an important tactic that the town's various leaders had used in thwarting its enemies.

"State your name and your purpose of being here!" The fur growled.

Hmo replied. "I am Hmo of Chriopteram, and these are my comrades, Adamar and Ohanzee of Eadageth. We are here to replenish our supplies after a thunderstorm, and to ask for help in getting to our destination.

A powerful storm had rolled in last night, shutting the night into unrelenting darkness and striking down trees with quick bolts of lightning. The horses ad spooked when lightning had struck an oak near their campsite. Everything had gotten soaked.

The fur was silent for a moment, contemplating. "You may enter. Approach the center."

"Approach the center?" Adamar repeated, only to see Hmo instructing Olie to walk forward, beneath the shade of the overhanging ground. Adamar and Ohanzee followed, enjoying the cool air underneath the top of the mushroom village.

Hmo dismounted from Olie and went to the base, pressing a hand against the dirt trunk. He pushed in on something Adamar couldn't see and quickly stood up, hopping back on his horse. The base started rumbling.

Galene neighed uneasily. Ohanzee worked to calm her as soil began to crumble down the mushroom's trunk. Dust clogged the air.

The side of a large stone appeared. It jutted out above the ground, and was followed by more boulders appearing like an oversized staircase along the sides of the mushroom's trunk.

"They're steps to climb up into Galliv." Hmo said, answering a question before Adamar could ask it. The bat clicked his tongue, and Olie put a tentative hoof up a couple feet into the air, letting it come down on the first stone step. The horse snorted, stepped back, then jumped forward and landed on the step. Olie was ready to leap up to the second stone when Hmo twisted back to look down at Adamar and Ohanzee, who were watching warily. "Come on. They won't stay out forever. You don't want to get stuck near the top as the stones pull back in, and you're fifty feet off the ground."

Adamar and Ohanzee shared a glance, uneasy with the steps. Then Adamar shrugged and guided Dakr over to the first step. The roan horse whinnied uneasily when the fox urged him forward. Dakr snorted, trying to shy away and find anything else to do.

"Dakr..." Adamar gently chided, dismounting and slipping the reins over Dakr's head. He climbed up onto the first stone and guided the horse on. "Come here, Dakr. You're okay."

Adamar collapsed onto the soft grass, panting. He looked up at the sky, watching the delicate plumes of clouds drift by and change their shape as the wind stirred them. He despised heights, and hadn't enjoyed the view as he'd climbed into Galliv.

"Hey, Adamar!" Ohanzee called from a few yards away. "You might want to take a look at this."

Hearing the ominous tone in the coyote's voice, Adamar turned over and pushed himself up, averting his gaze from the edge of Galliv. Ohanzee stood next to a message board that, along with welcoming everyone to Galliv, announced recent events in and around the town.

Adamar walked over. "What's wrong?"

Ohanzee gestured to a scroll that was unrolling itself with no visual help. Adamar cocked his ears, watching, as the parchment flattened against the rest of the notices and an invisible hand began writing on the parchment.

Miro.

As soon as the name was finished the unseen hand paused for a second, then the name vanished only to be rewritten again and again. Adamar watched, his suspicion rising as the ink began to drip down the paper, fall off, but dematerialize before it hit the ground. The letters became distorted, the hand scrawling the name faster and faster. Miro's name became an image of the fox kit, crying, blood streaking his fur while his grimy hands rubbed at exhausted eyes.

Adamar watched the image, anger and despair growing. He lifted his upper lip in a snarl. The image disappeared.

The hand then scrawled a dozen lines on the parchment with blinding speed, apparently decided it didn't like the message, and erased the words.

"What is this?" Adamar asked, gaze never moving from the slowly forming words. Was this Girbindon? If it was, how did he know this quickly where Adamar was?

"No idea." Ohanzee responded. "It's strange, whatever it is." The coyote glanced at the buildings that lay beyond the board. He crossed his arms.

The hand scrawled out its last words, then made a jab toward Adamar; ink flew through the air and landed on the fox's muzzle. Adamar snorted, trying to wipe the black mess from his nose. He only managed to smear it further along his snout.

Miro's father, Miro's father. Adamar, right? I know you're coming for me. The letter began. *I have your cub, if you're wondering. I hope your trip has gone well.*

You want Miro desperately, don't you? You'd do anything for him? Would you kill for him? Well, don't worry about that. You can't kill me. I am stronger than you.

However, I'll be generous. If you want him, you have to prove yourself in a challenge. You have ten days to reach and enter my kingdom, as well as attempting to get Miro back into your hands. If you come after ten days, you will not see your cub alive again. Or...maybe he'll see you. Just see your dead body.

As another option, you can turn back now and risk no harm to your physical self. Miro will remain in my possession, and you will never have to worry about him from now on.

Whatever is decided, you have ten days. Enjoy finding my kingdom.

And, if you encounter my workers along the way, tell them I send greetings. They will be testing you.

Adamar flattened his ears as the unseen hand twisted the end of the last letter in Girbindon's name. The message stayed for a few brief moments, and disappeared. The scroll rolled itself back up.

Ohanzee unrolled the paper, only to see a notice about a recent birth in Galliv.

The coyote turned to Adamar. "What're you going to do, Adamar?" He turned out his ears. "You might lose your pup forever."

Adamar's narrowed gaze remained on the scroll where the message had just been. His thoughts weaved and writhed in agony. The choices Girbindon gave had an outcome good for only the bear and his vile kingdom. Which was probably Girbindon's point.

Adamar wanted to wring the life from the bear's neck.

"Maybe you should go to Itador. Tell them of your case and have them work it out. They could have a chance to get Miro back." Ohanzee suggested.

"Yeah, just get him back in pieces." Adamar replied, and shook his head. "I can't let that happen. Besides, I won't have time to do that. The capitol's far from here."

"Then will you go home, like Girbindon offered? You may not see Miro again...but at least you know he won't be killed..." Ohanzee attempted a sympathetic smile, but the expression dropped from his face as quickly as it had appeared. He had pups of his own. He was frightened, Adamar saw and smelled.

"No." Adamar shook his head. "We'll find him. If you want to, you can go home, if you're worried about your family. I'll go find Miro. I want to see my kit again, just not in pieces."

Ohanzee rolled his eyes, the fear slowly disappearing. "Like that's happening. Girbindon will probably be able to take you, maybe all of us in a fight against him alone. His army, even if it's small, has probably more tricks up their sleeves than we think. You need someone to travel with you."

"Besides," Hmo walked over from where he'd been talking with a fur about Darvin, "Traveling alone for a long period of time isn't always good for your mental state."

Adamar glanced at both of them and nodded, letting out a shaky breath. "Then, let's get something to eat, find somewhere to replace the arrows lost, and see if anyone knows anything more about Darvin." Without Thayn to help them, they couldn't know exactly where they were going in the search for Miro. Azoth's directions were only so helpful.

As Adamar walked away from a fur they'd just been asking about Darvin, Ohanzee rushed up to him. Hmo walked up.

"We should leave." Ohanzee panted, having run across the large town of Galliv to get to the other side, where the stables were and where Adamar had been asking for help.

"Why?" Adamar asked. He'd only been able to ask a few furs about Darvin. Hmo had just joined him from getting more supplies. They'd told him that Darvin was over there, at the end of the Zrad fields, beyond the Jdr Mountains, near Hile, and that whoever was ruling it kept sending their small, unskilled army to Galliv to bother the town.

"Someone's been following us. When I went to get some sweets, a fur was watching me as I went in and out of the bakery. I don't know who it was, but it smelled like another canine. Maybe from Girbindon."

"Are you sure they were watching you?"

Ohanzee nodded. "I can show you where they were standing, but—"

A form leapt out from the shadows and tackled Ohanzee to the ground. As Adamar and Hmo moved to help, two more furs jumped out and grabbed them too.

Adamar growled as his arms were wrenched back, and bucked, trying to throw the fur off. The fur's grip tightened in response, and he leaned forward to bite Adamar's jugular, digging his claws into the fox's wrists in an attempt to tear open his veins. Adamar tried to twist around, waiting to take the fur's muzzle between his jaws. He squirmed until his gaze met the canine forcing him down, who was surprised by an arrow that flew into his side.

Adamar threw the canine off and stood up. He pushed the canine to the ground, pinning his arms by his side. The fox bared his teeth close to the canine's snout.

"Who are you?" he growled. "Where're you coming from?"

The canine whimpered, his blood creating a puddle at his side. "Leave me alone. I was only doing what was asked of me."

"Who asked you to attack us?" Adamar dug his claws into the canine's wrists.

"Why do you want to know?" The canine glanced fearfully at Adamar. "Leave me alone, please." His terror hung heavily in the air.

Adamar's gaze swept over the canine's expression, watching him for a moment. He let go of the canine, only to grip him by his scruff as he stood, intent on not letting the canine attack again so soon. The canine whined in protest and put a hand on his wound.

Ohanzee and Hmo had their attackers in similar positions, and from a quick glance, Adamar saw that neither had gotten hurt. And that there were only three attackers.

"Where are you from?" Adamar asked the canine again, letting fury wrap around his voice.

"Why?"

"Where are you from?" The fox growled. He guessed Girbindon had sent him.

"Darvin. We were sent here to kill a fox, bat, and coyote that are traveling to Darvin to do harm to the kingdom."

Dozens of furs poured into the street, dressed in armor and wielding various weapons. Relief relaxed Adamar. Galliv's army was ready to help.

"You are not getting out of here alive!" One warrior shouted. "Girbindon will never allow it, and so it shall not be done. That arrow was meant for you, fox. I hope you were fooled by the citizens of Galliv that complained about the great Darvin kingdom."

What? Girbindon had control over this town? Alarm flashed in Adamar's mind. He wished his bow was not sitting next to Dakr's stall, out of reach. Why had he left it there, anyways?

"Attack!"

The army surged towards the three furs. Adamar, Ohanzee, and Hmo dropped their attackers and ran towards the stables.

Eighteen

Ohanzee reached the stables first, running down a narrow street. He dashed inside. Adamar heard a yelp and halted as the coyote was thrown out, followed by a displeased raccoon stablehand. The raccoon crossed his arms and glared at them.

"What're you doing coming into this barn?"

"We need to get our ancestor horses. We intend no harm. But we have to leave quickly." Adamar raised his ears in a non-defensive way.

"Why quickly?" The raccoon returned, his gaze tracking the three furs. "What's going on? Are you the ones that they're chasing?"

Ohanzee pushed himself off the ground. "Can we just get to our horses? We'll bother you no more afterwards."

The stablehand snorted, not noticing when Hmo quietly slipped away and around inside the stalls.

"I don't think I can let you in if you're being chased by the Galliv army. Not a good idea." The stablehand returned. He glanced at where Hmo had been standing, and opened his mouth to ask a question, but the crash of tools inside the barn stopped him. The stablehand ran inside, Adamar and Ohanzee rushing in after him.

"Hey!" The stablehand shouted, catching Hmo stepping over fallen pitchforks to slip a bridle onto Olie. Hmo ignored the raccoon as he continued tacking the three horses.

The stablehand lunged at Hmo, forgetting about the large ancestor animal standing near him, and began to wrestle with the bat.

Olie showed mild interest as the raccoon and bat rolled beneath his stomach. When the stablehand accidentally knocked into Olie's front knee, which was sensitive from an injury before he and Hmo came to Eadageth, the horse raised his hoof and slammed it down onto whoever was nearby.

The stablehand grunted as consciousness fled him, allowing Hmo to crawl out from beneath Olie and drag the stablehand away. Hmo looked up at Ohanzee and Adamar's surprised expressions. "Well, don't just stand there. Get moving."

As Hmo hid the unconscious raccoon, Adamar and Ohanzee quickly finished tacking the horses and gathered their arrows, slinging the quivers over their backs while they gripped theirs bows.

Adamar led Dakr out of the barn and mounted the horse. With Hmo and Ohanzee behind him, Adamar turned Dakr toward the opposite end of the Galliv, the edge closer to Darvin and unfortunately just as high off the ground as the opposing side.

While trying to keep his food in his stomach, the fox let out an irritated growl when he saw the army of Galliv at the exit, blocking it off and squinting through the setting sun. Galliv's archers notched their arrows and those with spears aimed the sharp metal points at the three furs.

Adamar relied on the sun to contort the army's view, and tightened the reins as he had Dakr leap forward. The horse bolted down the road, drawing Adamar closer to the army.

Adamar aimed his own bow and arrow at the warriors, loosing an arrow into one who shrieked and fell back, gathering the attention of those around him.

Dakr snorted and ran up an empty cart. He leapt over the unfocused army while his rider managed to grip the horse with his legs and keep his weapon simultaneously at the ready.

Dakr landed on the other side of the army, his hooves slamming into the dirt and skidding on dust before he gained purchase on the road. Adamar urged him to continue on galloping. Ohanzee and Hmo jumped their horses over the stumbling mass of warriors.

Adamar twisted back in the saddle and shot an arrow toward a warrior that was attempting to attack Hmo. The arrow bounced off the fur's helmet, making him startle and back away just as Olie reared. Hmo held on, and didn't let Olie stop when all four of the horse's hooves were on the ground.

Adamar and Ohanzee pulled their horses back into a quick canter, allowing Hmo to rush ahead and show them the way out of Galliv. The fox felt cheated as he saw it was just a winding, slowly inclining track stacked up against the side of the town. No deathtrap stone steps.

Once they were out Galliv, the three pushed their horses into a gallop until the mushroom town disappeared over a ridge and the Galliv army stayed within their town's boundaries.

Nineteen

You okay, fox?

Adamar looked over to the source of the voice, his ears pricking as the wind whistled across the treeless ground. The air ruffled the fire, making it leap and dance and send a few sparks into the air. Hmo shifted closer to the calming flames. Ohanzee tended to Galene.

You okay? The voice asked again, and Adamar noticed an ancestor fox watching him intently from behind one of the boulders that spotted the landscape. The field eventually gave way to the shadow-like forms of the Jdr Mountains sitting a few days' ride away.

"I'll be right back. Nature calls." Adamar told Hmo and walked over to the ancestor fox. As he approached, it poked its head further out from behind the rock, then pulled back and disappeared.

Adamar went around to the other side of the boulder, where he noticed a foxhole dug against stone. He could smell the ancestor's strong scent.

Adamar softly sounded out, *Ancestor? You call?*

Something scratched inside the foxhole before the answer came. *Yes.*

Why?

You okay, fox? The four-legged canine clambered out from its home and shook its fur, dust falling to the ground.

Adamar cocked his head. Ancestors didn't really ask about how one was doing. It wasn't out of cruelty, though. It was more for keeping the ancestor's words sacred and rare.

I am. Adamar responded. *Why?*

I heard. The fox sat down on its haunches, across from. *Heard meeting. Meeting got you far. You okay?*

Meeting? Adamar questioned.

The fox looked and smelled irritated. It waited a moment before responding. *Meeting with tall kind wolf.*

Adamar nodded, bringing the image of Azoth into his mind. Talking with the crazy wolf had to be the meeting the ancestor was talking about.

Yes. I remember meeting. Adamar sat on the ground. *How you hear? Ancestor communication?*

We not brainless, fox. The ancestor pawed at the ground impatiently. *We share when needed. On sharing, you be wary. Tricks come.*

Tricks? Adamar flattened his ears. *From Girbindon?* Tricks had already come.

Names are titles. With that, the fox got up and entered his foxhole, leaving Adamar with questions he knew the ancestor would not answer.

Adamar was still for a moment, churning over what the ancestor had said, and stood when he heard Galene whinny. His gaze glanced over to her. Ohanzee groomed her while Dakr pranced nearby, bored even after this afternoon's excitement. Ohanzee looked at Adamar and said that he'd take Dakr for a quick ride to work out his energy after he was done with Galene.

"Everything going well?" Hmo asked as Adamar sat back down across from him. Adamar looked at the bat over the fire, the flames skewing the bottom half of his vision.

He nodded and pulled his knees up to his chest, laying his muzzle on them. The wind ruffled his fur and danced into the tugged-up hood of his cloak, making him turn away from being directly upwind. He wished they weren't in the middle of the Zrad fields, where there were no thick, large forests to cover them. But at least there were a few trees, and the boulders gave them shelter.

"Someone's going to be trying to fool one of us or all into doing something." Adamar said. "I don't know when or where. The ancestor just said it would happen."

Silence responded to Adamar's words, leaving him to go over the frantic run from Galliv. The Galliv army was known to be overprotective of their town, but usually stayed on the mushroom whenever they were chasing an enemy off of their land. This time, however, their army's commander had decided it would be a good idea to climb down from Galliv and chase the three furs half a mile out, to where Galliv's boundary officially ended.

From there they'd slowed their tiring horses, but only to a fast trot. They had to reach Darvin before the time Girbindon had given them ran out.

Adamar stood and grabbed his bow to go hunting. He didn't want to think about Girbindon so much right now. He managed to kill a few ancestor rabbits, skinned them, and set them to cook over the fire. He smiled as he watched Ohanzee work Dakr some yards away. The coyote soon rode the horse back to his companions, removed his tack and gave him some feed Hmo had bought in Galliv.

"You two looked like sad rocks." Ohanzee chuckled, sitting beside Adamar.

Adamar looked at him. "How can a rock be sad?"

"I don't know." The coyote shrugged and grabbed a rabbit. "Anyone up for a spar after dinner?"

Adamar groaned. "Not another spar."

"Yes. We still have to do something. Instead of just running away from Galliv and running towards Darvin. We've been working out our strategies. But we'll have to do actual fighting. Sparring will make fighting Girbindon easier."

"Fine." Adamar finished his food and pushed himself to his feet. He moved a few feet away from the fire and drew a large fighting ring in the dirt.

"Ready?" Adamar asked, and when the coyote nodded, Adamar lunged at him.

The coyote ducked out of the way. He smiled when Adamar fell to the ground.

The two fought until Hmo nodded to Adamar as Ohanzee squirmed, struggling to get up from where the fox had knocked him to the ground. He managed to stand only to be pushed back down. Adamar pinned the coyote to the dirt.

"Alright, Adamar! Alright!" Ohanzee shouted. "You win. You've bested me."

The coyote stood, and glanced at Adamar. "How did you see where my weakness was?" Ohanzee rolled his shoulder, easing a discomfort. "It's hard to notice."

Adamar offered a smile. He'd seen a hesitation in Ohanzee's right arm and had used that to his advantage to win the fight. "I've gotten careful about seeing things when I have to. Making sure Miro's crib is near to flawlessly clean requires some careful work." The fox tilted his head. "How'd you hurt your arm again?"

"Remember when my stable collapsed a few years ago? You weren't there yet, Hmo. The roof just caved in and brought down the rest of the structure with it. Luckily no horses were inside, but I'd been just inside after mucking out the stalls. My arm was hit by a falling beam." Ohanzee rolled his shoulder again.

"I remember that." Adamar looked with worry at the coyote. "Are you okay?"

Ohanzee nodded. "Yeah. I'm fine. Just an old ache." He smirked at Adamar. "I'll get you tomorrow, though. I'm not going to spar again, right now. Sleep calls."

The coyote dampened the fire and then settled himself in front of it. Adamar sat back down.

Hmo spoke. "Have you noticed anything, Adamar?"

"What do you mean?"

"Have you noticed anything odd going on, any patterns, something that can help you try to figure out why Miro was taken. Have you noticed anything during the duration of this quest?"

Adamar was silent for a moment. Then, his words barely louder than a whisper, "I have. It's about Girbindon's furs. His influence. It's everywhere. And they want something, or want us dead. And my emotions, and briefly Ohanzee's, have been intense and sudden a lot."

Hmo gave a slow nod. He let the fox think over what he'd just said.

As Adamar hugged his knees to his chest and let his vision melt with the fire, Hmo reminded him that the hour was late, and they should get some rest.

Adamar lay down onto Dakr's unfolded saddle blanket.

Fog filled the fox's dreaming mind, clouding the edges of his thoughts and turning monsters into birds and birds into monsters. It drenched the world in white, covering everything with a fine layer of the translucent clouds. There were no scents in this dreamworld. Adamar rolled over in his sleep.

A voice called out in his dreams, at first making him wonder where it was being directed to and where it came from, but as the voice repeated itself, Adamar realized it was calling to him.

"Father. Father."

Adamar looked around, searching for the source of the voice and why it was calling him, why it was calling him that. Each turn he made in his sleeping world ended in a dead end, each wrong turn foggier than the last, enough to the point that Adamar eventually was turning blindly in his mind, panicking as he couldn't find any way out.

Adamar found words would not aid him; his throat wouldn't form sounds. His ears swiveled, but nothing was to be heard in the stillness of the fog.

Putting a wary step back, Adamar looked behind him, watching as the fog began to twist and mold itself together into different shapes.

"Father," a kit's voice said, "Come find me."

The fog became an image of a sleeping version of Miro, his thumb in his mouth and a peaceful look on his face. The voice repeated itself again, and Miro's image brightened, the detail thickening until it looked like Miro was truly right in front of him.

A different tone swirled into Adamar's ears, soothing for a moment until its words turned to ice, just as cold as what the voice was saying.

Adamar...Adamar...Do you not see what is good? Do you not see that your cub is alright? Look at him, Adamar. Look.

Adamar did, as the icy words flooded through his body, making his fur stand on end and him to shiver. He watched Miro roll over in his sleep, and Miro's tail briefly thumped against the ground; the kit was happy with something in his dreams.

Do you not see that he's fine? There's no need to worry about him. No need for you to risk your neck, Adamar, on finding him. Just leave him with me. I'll let him grow, be big, strong, everything you could want in a cub.

Go home to your mate. I know she's devastated with your leaving. She must be. Go home and relieve her with your return, with the news of your cub being kept safe and brought up well.

Adamar clenched his fists, his ears pressing back against his head while the rough, low voice of Girbindon echoed against the never-ending walls of the dream world. The voice bounced around, coming from nowhere at once, but then it stopped, seeming to emanate from just behind Adamar.

Unable to find the ability to speak, Adamar bared his teeth and turned, ready to attack the bear. When he saw nothing but fog standing in the bear's place, he scowled. He stiffened as the voice spoke again.

Adamar....give him to me.

An image came together from the fog, a fuzzy image at best, that depicted a teenage fox fur, a bow in one hand and a quiver of arrows in another. At first, Adamar thought the image to be of himself when he was younger, but as the fox in the fog turned, the mark on his chest wasn't the same as Adamar's.

As the fox raised its bow and strung an arrow, aiming at a target Adamar couldn't see, the elder fox felt Girbindon's presence again.

Watch how he lets the arrow fly like you do. I can train him to do that. Your pup will be strong. He'll be the best in a group of anyone, but only if you let me raise him. Or...

A gust of wind chased away the image and replaced it with a fox of the same age, same build, but thinner and sickly looking. The fox's muzzle was splattered with blood, sourcing from a deep gash that stretched across the fox's once white stomach.

If you do manage to come to me, find him, and take him home, this is what will become of your cub, Adamar.

Would you want to subject him to that? Look at the agony he must be in. That's not fair...is it?

The images disappeared, leaving Adamar alone. He was furious, but shivers shook his body every few seconds, making him look like a pathetic, trembling creature.

The fog began to descend on Adamar, growing darker, grayer, until eternal night had established itself over him. The fog seemed almost alive as it nudged up against Adamar, searching for new places to enter, searching to get into his lungs and drive him toward an option that he wasn't pleased of.

Make your decision, Adamar, Girbindon said, his voice swirling slowly about the fox. *Leave him with me and know he'll be strong, or take him home and dread the day when you see that wounded cub again.*

Adamar shook his head against the fading words. His kit wouldn't end up with Girbindon. He would find him. He had to.

Twenty

"Chilo, go, get a blanket and have some food warmed for him." Stupid told the jackal.

"But," Chilo protested, his hands resting nervously on the table, non-bandaged fingers tapping. "I just came in here to check and make sure Miro was ready for another session with the Great King Girbindon."

Stupid shot Chilo a quick glare. "Well, obviously, he's not! He's sick, you idiot. Do as I say and then report to King Girbindon."

"I'm supposed to only do what the Great King—"

"Now!" The hen shouted, pushing Chilo out into the hallway and sending him scampering for the supplies she requested.

With an irritated click of her tongue, the hen turned back to the kit shivering on the floor, curled into a ball as small as can be while his nose dripped snot into the dirt.

Miro sniffled and wiped at his nose as he'd been doing the entire day, feeling a fever rack his body and turn the world to be hotter than the flames that rose in dreams and colder than icy souls. Varying temperatures traveled throughout the kit while his stomach recoiled and roiled unhappily. His breaths had grown shorter as sickness attacked him, settling in his small lungs and making him cough violently, constantly.

The kit's delirious mind brought up random images that he could make no sense of. A tall creature danced with his father, purple ancestor horses ran across plains with the wind at their backs, and the sky turned a sickly shade of green.

So sickly, in reality, that Miro felt himself roll over and empty his stomach onto the dirt that blanketed his cell. He coughed, lying next to the previous contents of his belly. The sun slid in through the bars of the cell's window. He whimpered, shutting his eyes even tighter.

The hen moved over and opened Miro's cell, poking her head in as she surveyed the scene with a view unblocked by rusted metal bars. Her small eyes focused on the throw-up and she opened her mouth to yell at the kit, but Chilo came running back in, drawing her attention away.

"I have what you wanted. I can go tell the Great King Girbindon that there will be a delay." Chilo handed her the supplies she requested.

The hen scrutinized him. "Are you an idiot? Don't tell King Girbindon. He'll get mad. Just..." she shrugged, glancing back at Miro. "Stall him."

"But—" Chilo began. The hen glared at him and used a heavy wing to smack him across his muzzle. He got the message, and left, tail between his legs.

"Ah. Now." Stupid turned to the shivering kit. She set down the supplies and picked Miro up, holding him somewhat gently as she moved him away from his throw-up and onto the table outside his cell.

Miro squirmed weakly in her grip, and a quiet whimper escaped his throat as he was set down. He felt a cold compress mold to his forehead, and leaned into it, relishing the constant, cool temperature. He wanted his mother or father. They would make him feel better. He felt tears sit hot in his eyes.

"There." The hen said, rubbing his back with her free, feathered hand. "That feels good, doesn't it? Get well to greet Girbindon."

For minutes that seemed hours in Miro's mind, the hen tended to him, wrapping the kit in a blanket that was surprisingly comforting. She spooned some warm, soupy food into Miro's mouth, wiping it from his muzzle when most of it dripped down his fur. The hen picked up a rag to wipe his nose with, while keeping her back facing the window, so she could block the wind from reaching the kit.

While the hen was securing the blanket around Miro, who was half asleep, his head bobbing, Chilo came back in with a fresh claw mark along his muzzle.

"The Great King Girbindon orders you to bring Miro to him." Chilo managed, turning his ears out at the glare Stupid sent. "You can take no more time, he said. You must go bring Miro now."

Chilo yelped as the hen swung at him, ducking away from her blow before it connected with his face, and found solace in the corner. "If you could just give him to me, please, you can go about your other jobs." He cradled Miro to his chest when the hen handed him over, and ran out before she could try to hit him again.

As Chilo dashed to Girbindon, Miro leaned against the jackal, digging his fingers into Chilo's shirt. The hen had slipped some special liquid into the food she'd fed Miro, and unhappily, the kit felt himself start to waken from more than a half conscious state. He shook his head and attempted to go back to sleep, but that comfort wouldn't come. Miro started crying.

Tears wet the fox's face, soaking the blanket he was wrapped in. Chilo looked down in fear at the weeping pup.

"Miro," he growled, tightening his hold on the fox. "Stop doing that. Girbindon needs to see you as best you can be. Crying isn't the best. It shows that you're weak. Just stop, please."

Miro, per request, fell silent, and remained so for hours, even when Girbindon tried to get a rise out of him by showing an image of his father hurt. Miro watched with a curious face that quickly became one of horror. When the sickness attempted to return, he started crying again, much to Girbindon's dismay.

"I suppose Miro is being too ignorant today to decide to show us his skill." Girbindon sighed, glancing at the night that began to fall outside, darkening the land as the sun tripped behind the Jdr Mountains off in the distance.

"Take him back. Maybe tomorrow he'll be more cooperative." The bear turned, focusing on an awkwardly hanging tapestry, and began to right it from where he stood without lifting a finger. The words he spoke moved the tapestry.

As Chilo collected the fox pup, Miro sneezed. He shook his head just as a slow plume of fire began to smoke on Girbindon's short tail.

The bear didn't notice his fur being seared away.

"Uh, Great King," Chilo said, moving closer to Girbindon. "Your tail..."

"What about my tail, Chilo? I don't have all day for your endless, meaningless sentences." The bear scoffed, but as silence answered him, he turned his head and out of the corner of his eye glanced at the fire chewing at his flesh.

Girbindon yelped and tried to put out the flame.

"Did you do that?" Girbindon snarled as soon as he'd put out his tail, turning his back to the wall so Chilo and Miro weren't able to see the burnt flesh the bear had suffered.

Chilo shook his head. "No, Great King. It wasn't me. It was Miro." He cautiously moved closer with the fox kit.

"Miro?" Girbindon repeated, his eyes widening. "Miro did that? Miro did magic?"

The jackal glanced down at Miro, who stared back up at him.

"Give me him." Girbindon said, reaching out and taking Miro none too gently from Chilo's grasp. At a command from Girbindon, Chilo disappeared behind one of the tapestries, leaving the fox and bear alone.

Miro shivered in his blanket as Girbindon set him on his lap, the bear once again resting on his elaborately decorated throne. Despite having just been set on fire, Girbindon looked pleased, and grinned at Miro, his large teeth showing. His teeth continued to appear like weapons waiting to bite into flesh.

"Miro. You finally showed a sample of your magic ability. That's wonderful." Girbindon tousled the fur on top of Miro's head. The kit whined unhappily and shied away. He glanced over to the tapestry he'd emerged from, and made to go over there.

"No, no, Miro. You can't go just yet." Girbindon chided. "You have to show me what you can do." When the kit did nothing, a sheet of anger flashed over Girbindon's face. "Miro, show me. It's what you just did. When you created that fire."

Miro tilted his head at the bear. Why did Girbindon keep asking him to do something involving magic? How was he supposed to do...magic, anyways? And how could he expect Miro to understand what he meant by that? Miro wondered if his father would be able to figure out the bear's words. Come to think of it...where was his father? Miro hadn't seen him for what felt like ages.

Miro squirmed in the bear's grip, his thoughts on finding his father, even though he didn't have the first idea of where to look.

"Now, Miro. Show me how you created the fire." Girbindon brought Miro closer and held him up in the air. "Show me." The bear repeated, scrutinizing him.

Miro grunted and kicked out, his ribs being crushed by the bear's rough grip. He shook his head in an effort to get free, but was stopped when his nose began to itch. Irritated, Miro snorted, and a beam of green light appeared in the air and shot right into Girbindon's eye.

The bear cried out and put both furred hands to his eye, dropping Miro. The kit fell, landing on his back with the hard floor to cushion his fall. Tears began to trickle down Miro's face, though he didn't make a sound as bruises formed on his backside. The blanket had fallen off Miro, and he shivered as the sickness began to return, his fur no help to regulate his body temperature.

"Chilo!" Girbindon roared, keeping his eyes covered and stumbling around blindly. "Get me some bandages! Now!"

The jackal came running in. Stupid followed close behind with healing supplies.

"Get that fox out of my sight!" The bear shouted, swinging out with a fist and nearly catching Chilo on the nose. "He has caused me harm!" Girbindon raised his arm to strike out again, but the hen moved over to him and spoke quietly, her words soothing as she managed to calm the large bear and have him sit down on his throne.

Chilo picked up Miro, and as he was carrying him away from Girbindon, let a smile cross his muzzle. "Miro," he laughed quietly once they were in the hallway, "What did you do?"

Miro sneezed, yelping as a bit of flame appeared

on Chilo's hand, close to the kit's face. Chilo stopped and shook his hand, dispersing the flame and looking sadly at the burned bandage the small fire had left behind. Miro watched red seep from Chilo's now-open wound.

"Agh, Miro. That's what you did." Chilo sighed. He glanced back at where the hen was tending to a squirming Girbindon, and couldn't stifle another smile. "Nice going, Miro."

The fox kit giggled.

Twenty-One

"This time you will not harm me, right, Miro? Otherwise you will get punished." Girbindon growled, one of his eyes covered by a cloth wrapped around his head. The bear sat in his huge chair with Miro on the floor before him, the day after Miro had accidentally shot him in the eye.

Despite being injured, Girbindon was intent on making Miro do magic, which he wouldn't explain, and control it. As soon as Miro had been woken and was finished being prepared to see the bear, Girbindon had launched into an hour long rage on how Miro should be able to control his powers so he could grow and be good at the skill he had been given. How it didn't matter that he was supposedly too young for this; one was never too young for magic.

While Girbindon had been talking, Miro had just sat in front of him, playing with the carcass of an ancestor mouse he'd found lying in his cell earlier and ignoring whatever the bear was saying.

"Miro?" Girbindon narrowed his gaze. "Are you even listening to me? You better be listening to me. Because what I'm about to show you will help you in life." At the kit's response of silence, Girbindon sighed and grabbed Miro by his scruff, hoisting him into the air.

"You listen to me! You will not do any harm to me and you will do as I say!" The bear shook the squirming fox. "It's not hard! Just show me what you can do and you'll be obeying my requests."

Miro twisted in Girbindon's grip, struggling to get away from the frightening bear. His stomach rumbled unhappily, and Miro felt the sickness coming over him again.

"Miro!" Girbindon set the fox on the floor and watched as he tried to run off, but instead fell on his tail and began crying.

Annoyed, Girbindon opened his palm. A creature began to form in his hand, wriggling while its body solidified and blood coursed through it. Once the creature was completely alive, Girbindon stepped to Miro and bent down, holding his hand out to show the fox.

Miro sniffled, and turned, feeling the bear's presence behind him. He tilted his head, bloodshot eyes watching the reptile that crawled around Girbindon's furred fingers. Miro reached and picked up the lizard out of curiosity, holding it in the air and then dropping it to the ground. As the lizard hit the tile, a crack sounded and it writhed in pain. Miro, bored with the lizard but also worried that he'd harmed it, looked up at Girbindon, who was observing him quietly.

"There, Miro," The bear said, a grin stretching across his muzzle. "Wasn't that interesting? If you listen, that's what you'll be able to do. You'll be able to create different forms of life. Only small ones...but certainly that could impact some war you might fight in the future. Or you could make other, non-living things to help you fight." The lizard disappeared.

As the bear filled the air with unimportant words, Miro felt his body temperature rise, heated by the fur that he was covered in. His stomach disagreed with whatever was in it; food he couldn't remember. He threw up on Girbindon.

The kit sat down, sick splattering his muzzle, and watched through bleary eyes as Girbindon shut his mouth, staring down in surprise at what steamed on his feet.

A low growl rumbled in the bear's throat. His lips pulled back to show bare white teeth. Miro's eyes widened and he stood, running on shaky legs before falling.

Girbindon's massive hands scooped up Miro by his stomach, giving the kit a harsh squeeze before handing him off to Chilo, who had come running in at a signal Miro hadn't heard.

"Hey, sweetie. Wake up. It's time for you to eat."

A calm voice stirred Miro from one of his nightmares. He sat up, dirt from the floor mixing into his fur. Blood matted his side, the wound from getting whipped having reopened over the night.

A soft, slender muzzle appeared. Brown fur ran down the muzzle, then up to kind eyes and tall ears. Muddy irises circled the pupils that gently tracked the fox kit.

A simple dress hung off the deer's shoulders, trailing down to brush against the ground and nearly cover the deer's small hooves. The deer crouched down, reaching out with one hand, a piece of food resting in her palm.

Miro cocked his head at the bread, his fearful gaze glancing up to meet the deer's eyes. Miro turned and moved away.

The kit then looked back at the deer, and saw that she seemed to be one of Girbindon's workers, but no impatient scent drifted from her, nor the fear that always lingered on Chilo. She just smelled kind.

Nevertheless, Miro backed up until he was sitting in the corner. Her voice slipped through the air again, yet still Miro didn't obey her requests.

"Come on, sweetie. I'm not going to hurt you." The deer sat on the ground, legs folded next to one another, while her hooves that could easily crack a skull pointed away from Miro. She patted her thigh. "Miro, come here. You have to be hungry." Her gaze saddened as she caught sight of the blood in Miro's fur and on his bandages. "And you must be in pain."

Miro glanced at her with his ears back. But after a minute, he crawled over to where the deer was sitting, outside the cell, and reached for the food. He hesitated when his fingers came within an inch of edible substance, and looked up uncertainly at the deer.

The deer smiled and fondly rubbed the spot between his ears. "It's alright. I won't take away the food. Enjoy."

As Miro tentatively slid the food into his mouth, the deer picked him up and settled him on her leg, letting the kit rest against her stomach while he ate. She stroked his unhurt side, calming him until he stopped trembling and relaxed.

"See, Miro?" The deer's voice never rose above a calm level. "I'm not going to hurt you. Do you want me to heal your side? It shouldn't stay open like that."

Miro paused, glancing down at the red mass in his fur. He thought of pain, and shook his head.

He twisted and looked at the deer after a minute of silence. She smiled in return, her ears twitching as an angry roar echoed down the hallways. Miro's eyes began to leak tears.

"Shh, Miro, it's okay." The deer rubbed the fox's unwounded side.

As she soothed him, Miro noticed a woven bracelet encircling the deer's wrist. Its colors looked faded, as if it had endured years of use. But the deer didn't seem to be too old; she seemed to be the age of Miro's father, as far as the kit could tell.

Curiosity ran through Miro and he tried to take hold of the deer's bracelet, but she pulled her arm back and shook her head. "No, Miro. Don't touch that." The deer was quiet for a few moments, then started rocking Miro gently.

"Miro," the deer said, "You know how Girbindon's so mean? He's frightening?"

At the sound of the bear's name, Miro's ears pricked and he jolted upright, his wide eyes staring into the deer's.

The deer smelled his anxiety and tried to calm the fox, giving him more food. "Girbindon doesn't mean to be like that. He's frustrated with...everything. Getting you to listen, coordinating tactics, figuring out how to try and conquer more territory. He's a bit overwhelmed with everything."

She glanced down at Miro's lowering ears. "No, Miro," she chuckled, "I'm not taking his side. Don't think that. I'm just trying to bring you a different viewpoint. I don't know how long you're here, and only recently why he thinks you'll be a great help to expanding his empire."

The deer sighed. "There's much that you don't know, Miro. And much you don't understand. Yet, I know you're able to understand a little of what I'm saying. You're smart. You'll be able to figure out what things are, what they mean, all with your soon-to-be-hardworking mind. But, there's one thing I want you to figure out now, or at least try to."

Miro tilted his head. Was she leaving? He cuddled up against the deer, and whimpered pitifully in an attempt to get her to stay. He didn't want to go back to the bear, or the cold cell.

The deer looked behind herself, then glanced down at Miro and let a soft smile curve its way across her muzzle. "Alright, Miro. I'll tell you. I just have to hurry. Chilo might be coming in to check on you and make sure you're being treated fairly badly. Chilo is Girbindon's lackey. He does everything for

Girbindon that the King doesn't want to do himself. Which can be a lot, on some days."

Miro sneezed as dust tickled his nose, and he wiped his snout on his arm. A small flame appeared on the ground, which the deer put out with her hoof.

The deer shook her head and produced a rag from a pocket in her robes. She wiped at Miro's nose, chiding, "Use a rag, Miro. Otherwise you'll stay sick. Girbindon will stay mad."

Miro squirmed, trying to get away from the rough feel of the rag against his nose.

As Miro struggled, his hurt side brushed harshly against the deer's palms. He yelped in pain.

"Let's clean that wound. And, I know you're curious, Miro. I'll tell you soon what's going on. Everyone's born curious. Though, some get the curiosity beat out of them." As the deer hugged Miro to her chest, she sighed, her voice hollow, as if her thoughts were elsewhere. "Poor Chilo."

The deer brought Miro out of his cell and sat him on the table. She began to undress the wound. The bandages peeled away to reveal a mess of blood. But with the help of a cookie to distract him, the deer wrapped his wound.

After his initial meeting with the deer, Miro looked forward to seeing her again when she came in to bring his barely filling meals. His tail thumped against the ground with her presence, and the fox was always greeted by a kind smile that opposed the growls and demands of Girbindon. His kingliness's irritation never faltered, and whenever Miro managed to perform one of his "skills," the bear grinned, but only wickedly.

Miro's developing imagination became captivated with the tapestries that decorated the walls of Girbindon's throne room. His mind explored what could lie behind the wall hangings. He passed time by creating staircases that went to nowhere and tunnels connecting hallways that normally ended in dead ends.

Girbindon's interest in working on Miro's magical skills expanded to include the trickery that the fox could use one day. The bear explained how using trickery to deceive a fellow fur was an ample way to accomplish something, demonstrating it many times with Chilo, and Miro soon started to laugh as the jackal was often fooled into thinking something was the opposite of its true form.

Whenever Miro laughed at Chilo's torture, Girbindon's grin grew, and he seemed to almost nod to himself in triumph.

Twenty-Two

"We should work on shooting from horseback, in case when we get to Darvin we'll need the height advantage." Ohanzee suggested.

Adamar nodded. They were riding fast, to get to Miro as quickly as possible. Adamar hadn't mentioned his dream. He hadn't wanted to yet, and they'd been too busy, for after that dream a few nights ago, Hmo had realized they'd been going the wrong way. Bats could read the stars much better than foxes or coyotes could, and had noticed that they were too far to the left of one of the stars in the night sky. The bat estimated that they'd gotten off track when they'd run away from Galliv.

The three had left with great haste after that news, leaving in the early morning before the sun was yet up. But sunlight didn't matter too much; Adamar and Ohanzee both had their ancestors' ability to see in the dark.

After riding for hours at a quick speed, they'd let the horses slow down and take a break before picking up the pace again. The days counted down in Adamar's head, each one bringing more worry and despair than the one before it. Seven days to reach Miro.

Adamar looked at Hmo. "Is there a forest near here?" He asked, his nose straining to pick up the smells of trees.

Eadageth's archers worked to maintain their skills on horseback, going into the surrounding forest at least once every week to practice shooting at targets, and, if someone became hungry, an occasional ancestor deer would be pierced through with an arrow. But never would the furs aim at any creatures just for sport.

"Near the bottom of the Jdr Mountains." The bat said.

"Alright." Adamar looked at the mountains sitting off in the distance. Hopefully they would get on the mountains before nightfall. "Let's head over there and find something to eat tonight. We can mark trees for practicing."

The three drove their horses southeast, riding until a patch of trees rose up before them. The trees looked like insects against the large mountains behind them. Hmo guided Olie into the forest, disappearing to create a trail that would lead them through the woods as they practiced. Ohanzee and Adamar settled on the calls they would use to alert one another to the wounding of an ancestor for dinner.

A glance at the mountains brought fear into Adamar. He worried that they wouldn't be able to get over the mountains in time. And there was no other way around them.

When Hmo returned, he said that there were three trails passing through the forest. He took the middle one, while Ohanzee and Adamar grabbed the trails on the sides.

Once the three were ready, they nodded to each other and set off. Adamar held Dakr back from going faster for a short time, conserving the horse's energy so Dakr could reach the end of the trail without being ready to fall over from exhaustion.

As Adamar began the course, his mind wandered: if Miro would ever become an archer. If Adamar's kit would use his archery skills to seek out anyone that tried to recreate Girbindon's rule and shoot them through their heart.

If the images Girbindon had shown him would become true.

Adamar shook his head from the thoughts, knowing that Miro wouldn't have to choose a bow and arrow as his weapon of choice, and if he did, doing so would only be if Miro wanted to. No matter how much Adamar longed for him to.

The first mark came into view, and Adamar aimed, pulling his bowstring back to the end of his muzzle and letting the arrow fly. It lodged in the bark right next to the gouge of a mark. Adamar made sure his second arrow hit the next target closer to the center.

Halfway through the course, a branch appeared out of nowhere. The fox ducked. A smaller, tougher branch that grew beneath the thick limb seemed to reach out and snag Adamar on the arm, reopening the cut he'd gotten from Girbindon's workers when they had been captured.

Adamar hissed and felt blood trickle through his fur, staining the torn cloth of his sleeve. A target flew by. He ignored the pain throbbing in his arm and raised his bow again, notching an arrow as Dakr's hooves pounded against the ground.

A stinging twinge of pain jumped up Adamar's arm, and his shot faltered, the arrow falling into the dirt at the base of next target. Adamar narrowed his gaze, training his next arrow on the gouge in the wood as Dakr ran closer to it. Blood matted in his fur, but he managed to hit the center of the mark, and the one after it.

A howl echoed through the forest, pricking Adamar's ears. "Ohanzee," he breathed. Ohanzee had hit an ancestor. Hmo shouted, answering Ohanzee, and the bat rode to help bring down whatever ancestor it was that would soon be a meal.

Relying on his companions to take care of dinner, Adamar drove Dakr on, and slowed him into a trot after the last marked tree passed by. He rode out of the woods not long after, coming onto a small strip of land that stretched out along the base of one of the Jdr Mountains. Adamar gazed up at the mountains, their tips disappearing into gray clouds. A barely broken trail wound up the mountains, growing steeper and narrower as the mountains climbed.

Adamar turned back into the woods to retrieve his arrows. He eventually returned, his full quiver banging against his back. He dismounted and led Dakr to a tree on the edge of the forest, tying the horse's reins around the tree's trunk. He left his bow and quiver on a rock, out of the horse's kicking range. He rolled up his sleeve to look at the wound.

The gash was deeper than he had first thought, and had soaked the cloth originally wound around it as well as the sleeve of his shirt and the fabric of his robe. Blood oozed from the wound, thickening the air with the red crimson scent. The gash sent bolts of pain up Adamar's arm. It was maybe a few inches wide, but looked ghastly, and he suspected it was at least half an inch deep. It probed into muscle, causing him agony whenever he moved his arm. Sun hit his eyes as he turned and got a sinking feeling, seeing how close night was. They wouldn't be traveling at night on the mountains, per Hmo's request. One more day gone.

Adamar was cleaning the wound with the torn cloth of his sleeve, soaking up as much blood as he could, when Hmo appeared. Ohanzee followed a few moments later, a large deer slung over Galene's flank. The two furs dismounted and tied their horses to tree trunks. Hmo noticed Adamar first, and came over while Ohanzee pulled the deer down and began to skin it.

The bat met Adamar's gaze for a moment before he took the fox's arm and looked at the wound.

Hmo observed the blood running freely from the gash, then took the bloody cloth Adamar had in one hand and tied it around the wound, firmly applying pressure to stifle the bleeding.

"How'd this happen?" Hmo asked.

"A branch caught my arm and dug into the cut from when Girbindon's furs first attacked us." Adamar began to pull his sleeve back down, but Hmo pushed the sleeve back up and told Adamar to leave his arm uncovered for the moment.

"Be more careful, next time." Hmo chided, giving Adamar a disapproving glance before turning and helping Ohanzee with the deer.

Adamar lowered his ears, feeling like a pup that had just done something wrong. His arm throbbed with the pulse of his heart, but the blood flow soon stopped, and the wound then simply sent an ache up through Adamar's muscles. He put the poultice on the wound to cool the pain.

The fox began to help with preparing the deer for a fire, pulling off chunks of meat and slicing away the sinew.

"Adamar," Ohanzee said as the fox dug a knife through a thick piece of meat. Adamar glanced up.

"I can see the pain your arm's causing you. Just use one hand and let the other one rest. Straining that damaged muscle can't be good."

"I'm fine," the fox protested.

"No, you're not." Ohanzee pulled the meat away from Adamar. "Hmo and I can do this. It's just slicing deer meat. Nothing hard. You don't want to hurt yourself further before finding Miro." The coyote glanced at the trees. "How about you find some kindling for a fire?"

Adamar looked over at the forest, then at Ohanzee's stern expression. "Fine," he stood.

As Adamar collected wood for a fire, he speculated on how he'd be able to use his bow and arrow with such an injury. The muscle would take some time to heal, and time wasn't on his side as of late.

Adamar walked deeper into the forest, one arm clutching a pile of wood, and bent below the low hanging branch that had snagged him. He was about to walk on, when he paused. He turned, lowering his muzzle close to the end of the branch. Adamar ran his free hand over the pointed end, then put pressure against the sharp tip. Instead of digging into his flesh, the tip splintered and fell to the ground below.

"How could this have dug into my arm so sharply through thick fabric?" Adamar wondered aloud. He set down his pile of wood and pulled at the bandage about his upper arm, exposing the wound to the air.

Blood encircled the gash, making it appear worse than it looked, but Adamar licked his fingertips and cleaned the blood away from his fur the best he could. The gash stood out against his orange fur, the ends of it jagged.

Adamar was grateful that furs healed faster than their ancestors, noticing the beginnings of a scab on the wound.

The smell of night settling in began to permeate the air. Adamar pushed his thoughts about the oddly sharp branch to the back of his mind, gathered the wood, and went back to the clearing.

Once the deer meat was roasting and the bones had been buried the dead, Adamar, Ohanzee, and Hmo argued about who would get the best meat. Ohanzee suggested Adamar, since the fox made it out of the forest first, but Adamar countered with how Ohanzee and Hmo veered off their paths to bring down the deer.

The argument was eventually resolved by all three taking a share from the deer's flank, the heartiest part of the meat. They all gorged on the food until they could eat no more, and fell asleep with full stomachs that would last them some time trekking across the mountains.

Twenty-Three

Adamar pulled on Dakr's girth, tightening it for the trek up the mountain.

He then stepped away from Dakr, absentmindedly putting his hand over his pulsing wound.

Ohanzee noticed the fox's movements and went over to him, pushing up Adamar's sleeve as the fox tried to pull his arm away. The coyote caught the scent of the light scab covering the wound. "You shouldn't do anything with your arm today, Adamar." Ohanzee warned. "The cut smells like it's deep. How badly does it hurt?"

"I notice the pain."

Ohanzee checked the cloth around Adamar's arm, and then pulled Adamar's sleeve back down. As the coyote walked back to his horse, Hmo looked at the fox and coyote.

"Be careful. The mountains are not the easiest places to cross. And I'm unaware of how friendly any furs or clans who live on the mountain are. The faster we can get over them, the better."

Adamar nodded distractedly. What if something happened on the mountain, and he never saw Miro? Or if the clans were hostile and attacked them? What if Girbindon had sent some furs to kill the three in their sleep? He was getting paranoid. They'd all woken up early to get as far on the mountains as they could. The lack of sleep wasn't helping right now.

Adamar shook his head, banishing the ideas from his thoughts. He slipped his quiver of arrows across his back, wrapped his hand around his bow, and swung into Dakr's saddle.

Ohanzee rode over to Adamar while Hmo made a final check of supplies. The coyote brought Galene up alongside Dakr and cocked his head at Adamar, who was growing uneasy with the height of the mountains.

"Are you ready, Adamar? This is one of the few times you're going to be at the Jdr Mountains, let alone crossing them. Have fun. It's an adventure!" Ohanzee threw up his arm in celebratory exaggeration, and Galene reared, her front hooves clawing at the air as Ohanzee strained to hold on. When Galene set all four hooves on the ground again, Ohanzee gave Adamar a goofy smile. "See? An adventure."

Adamar rolled his eyes in amusement, but as Dakr fell into step behind Olie and they started up the path worn into the mountain, the fox's anxious gaze tracked the horizon that hid the tips of the Jdr Mountains.

As they rode, Adamar felt his anxiety growing. He knew he shouldn't be so terrified. Ohanzee was right. Finding Miro was an adventure. Not a pleasant one, but still. The path they were on actually grew wider, instead of narrower, as it rose into the sky, assuring Adamar only in the sense that he had more space to panic before he fell.

His mind turned to images of various ways of making a dramatic, accidental exit from the mountain, over the side of a cliff.

Hmo broke the silence. "Have you considered Girbindon's letter, Adamar?" his voice echoed off the rocks that followed the three along the winding trail.

"What do you mean?" Adamar sensed that the question wasn't just about what he was going to do in response.

"When dealing with an enemy, sometimes you have to analyze their words. Powerful enemies are masters of words, and often put hidden meanings into what they say, write, or think." Hmo explained, pulling his hood up over his large ears to shield them from the growing cold.

Adamar felt the cold try to touch his wound, but shifted his weight to close the tear in the fabric best he could. "Then no, I've not considered his options."

Hmo's response was commanding. "Do so. You too, Ohanzee."

Adamar and Ohanzee silently mulled over the words of Girbindon's message.

The letter had begun with Girbindon addressing Adamar, then saying the bear had Adamar's kit, and noting how Girbindon wondered if the three furs had enjoyed seeing his lackeys.

No, they hadn't; Adamar went back over the message's words. The bear knew Adamar wanted Miro back, and had called Adamar's passion for finding Miro desperation.

The challenge had confirmed Azoth's theories of the bear being cruel. The bear had begun with that he would be generous. Which, Adamar realized, implied that the bear typically wasn't so kind as to even give a fur a challenging task to complete.

"...you've to prove yourself..."

Proving oneself usually meant completing a trial of something that was being tested. So if Girbindon had said that he was testing Adamar, what for? He had tried to have Adamar killed. What purpose could he serve? Adamar swallowed anxiously on this thought.

Ten days...Girbindon had said ten days to find Miro. Six remained. Would they be able to cross the mountains in six and get to Darvin? And why did Girbindon steal Miro only to say that if Adamar came after the ten days were up, Girbindon would kill his kit? What was the point of that? Why did Girbindon mention he'd take the life from young Miro?

"Girbindon can still use Miro's body. He doesn't need him alive." Ohanzee's words were no louder than breath, but were strong enough to jolt Adamar back to the real world.

Twenty-Four

Adamar focused his gaze on Ohanzee, ears flicking back. "What do you mean?" he asked warily, hoping he had misheard.

"Miro doesn't have to be alive for whatever Girbindon wants him for. He may be more useful alive, but he can still get some use out of him dead." Ohanzee explained, bringing Galene around a bend to continue up the trail. As his horse turned, Ohanzee glanced sympathetically at Adamar.

"How'd you come to that?" Hmo questioned, tone calm.

"I did what you said. Analyzed the message." Ohanzee's ears pricked forward.

"Two minds can sometimes be better than one. Your past always influences your answer." The bat didn't let the two linger on his words for long, and continued. "So where did you get that information?"

"From one of the last few lines of what Girbindon said. He mentioned something about how if Adamar arrived in Darvin after the allotted few days, either Adamar or Miro would die. If Miro would die, then why would Girbindon have stolen him in the first place? I don't mean any offense, Adamar, but is there anything that you could offer in exchange for Miro?"

Adamar sighed. "Nothing that I know of. I could offer myself, but would just be another archer for his kingdom." A growl supported his words. "Another archer that would make it his goal to make sure Girbindon was dead as quickly as posisble."

"While your passion of despising Girbindon may be strong, Adamar," Hmo advised, "Do not let it blind your actions. You could do something that would devastate you or Miro forever."

Adamar was silent for a few moments, letting the anger subside. "So what is there that we can do about the message's meaning?"

"Mainly, nothing." Hmo replied, banishing hope from the mountain. Adamar's gaze fell with the news, and landed on the ground next to him. His eyes widened and he brought Dakr over, closer to the side of the mountain and away from the deadly cliff.

"Adamar, there's nothing to be afraid of. We're not that high up in the air. Try looking up instead of down. There'll be more to see as the trail climbs higher." Ohanzee said, watching Adamar. The tip of his tail wagged. "There should be a ton of snow, right, Hmo?"

"Yes."

Adamar laughed as his fear of heights faded, overcome by Ohanzee's enthusiasm for snow. Eadageth usually was covered in snow during part of the year, but no place got as much snow as the Jdr Mountains. On days when the archers would practice in the snow, various archers would have to go over and repeatedly pull Ohanzee out of the white fluffiness.

"You shouldn't play too much in the snow, though, Ohanzee," Hmo warned. "The Jdr Mountains are full of unexplored crevices and frozen lakes. One wrong step could cause you to become frozen in the mountain for all eternity."

Ohanzee's ears lowered. "I know." He raised his head. "Hmo, why won't you have a bit of fun? You should be happy sometimes."

"I am."

"Then show it. You never look or smell like you're enjoying anything." Ohanzee went on. "We're going up the Jdr Mountains, something that most furs never do. We're going to cross them. We're crossing the Land right now, all the way from Eadageth to Darvin! It's not exactly coast-to-coast, but it's fairly close. Have some fun. Come on." Ohanzee's expression turned sly. "I know I can beat you in a snowball fight," he said, taunting the bat. "You won't be able to overcome my awesome snow-throwing powers."

Silence answered Ohanzee for a few moments, but then Hmo quietly said, "You want to make a contest out of it?"

Adamar watched as the coyote celebrated in triumph, and felt a smile of his own creeping across his face. He decided that ruminating on what Girbindon had proposed would only hinder him over this mountain. In agreement, he added, "Ohanzee's right, Hmo. You know a lot about survival techniques and geography, but we haven't seen how well you know fun. Can you beat both of us in a snowball battle?"

Ohanzee cocked his head. "You do know a lot, Hmo. How do you know as much as you do?"

"How?" The bat repeated. "I learned."

"Well, I could've guessed that." Ohanzee said. "But from where? Did Chiropteram teach you?"

"In a way."

Ohanzee prodded the bat with more questions. But Hmo wouldn't respond, only speaking when they were closer to the top of the mountain, where the ground began to get hazardous.

Yeah, like there's something more hazardous this this deathtrap they had been walking on for hours; Adamar tightened Dakr's reins.

"We're about at the height where you can see the ground become rougher. There may be some rocks or crevices in the dirt, so you have to watch your horse is going—even more closely—so they don't accidentally step onto something that could hurt them. We're going to begin actually crossing the mountain instead of just going up it, so the path will get narrower." Hmo looked off at the foggy horizon. "If you see a place that looks like it would be a good spot to camp later on, make sure that there's an easy way to get there. We should be at least a third of the way over by the time it gets dark."

Adamar felt his fears returning, and hoped that the path they would be going on to cross the Jdr Mountains wasn't one that rose the highest off the ground.

The wind found the fox's wound, which he realized had been aching for the entire time they'd been riding. It felt unnaturally warm. The heat traveled up Adamar's arm, warming his shoulder until he shifted his elbow, allowing the tear in the fabric of his sleeve to be more open to the elements and hopefully cool down the gash.

While his wound cooled, Adamar drew in sweet breaths of the icy air, and was reminded of the snow that waited higher up the mountain. He focused on driving Dakr along the slowly, steadily climbing path.

An image of Avaha superimposed itself on a pile of stone Adamar passed by. His eyes widened, but he shook his head and the image vanished, the rocks becoming just rocks again.

Where did that come from? Adamar knew he was missing Avaha, but in the past few days, he'd been so intent on finding Miro and not going too far off the ground that she had been at the back of his mind. The image had been as if she'd sensed this, and somehow sent herself to remind him to keep her in his foremost thoughts.

But she wouldn't do that...Adamar argued silently. How could she? How could she know what he was thinking? She was his mate, but that didn't mean she knew exactly what was going on in his head.

The mountain flew past. Rocks and frosted ground became a blur that decorated Adamar's peripheral vision. He raised his gaze to look up at the mountain that stood, intimidating, before them. Adamar could see the path they were on wind up the mountain, make a turn, and then disappear before appearing some distance away against a multitude of other paths. Adamar furrowed his brow as Dakr's hooves pounded against the dirt. There seemed to be some sort of civilization where the paths emerged from.

When the trail became rocky once more, the three slowed their horses so they could maneuver more carefully about the slippery ground.

Eventually Adamar noticed that the sun was just starting to fall, slipping behind them and throwing beams of light at their backs.

"Adamar! Duck!" Ohanzee twisted in the saddle, startling the fox. He dipped his head beneath a gnarled, flaking branch from a Toreal tree, which only lived on the mountains. As Adamar passed beneath it, he could catch a scent of the poison that dripped off the Toreal's bark.

The poison stung Adamar's nose. It carried the smell of a rotten flower. He shook his head, shaking the poison from his nose.

"Not a good smell, is it?" Ohanzee asked, laughing as Adamar clawed at his nose. Adamar looked at the coyote. "You could've warned me sooner."

"Well, if you pay attention to things, maybe I wouldn't have had to." Ohanzee smiled, and turned to face forward again.

"Sometimes, Ohanzee, you seem like you're stuck between being a kit and being full grown." Adamar remarked. Ohanzee didn't turn around, but his tail thumped a couple times against Galene's saddle. The fox wondered how long it had taken Galene to get used to the fact that when Ohanzee did that, it meant nothing other than that her rider was happy.

Ohanzee's episodes of puphood reminded Adamar of Miro, and sadness filled him as Dakr trudged on.

What if Girbindon decided to kill Miro early? Or kill both him and Adamar? What would Avaha do if she found out? How would she find out? Of course she'd find out, if Adamar didn't return. And then she'd be able to say that she had been right.

Adamar loosened his grip on Dakr's reins, letting the horse have his head as he walked across the mountain.

Why did Girbindon want Miro? Why did he want Miro's body? And what could he do with him? Did he think he'd be able to...get something, harvest something from Miro? He seemed to think so, but what was it that he wanted? How did he even guess Miro would serve his purpose? Out of all the furs in the Land, how come Miro?

The path seemed to stretch endlessly on. The horses' hooves beat against the dirt. A few trees bordered the path, but none sat right on it, as if the trees were afraid of going too close to the furs that traveled across it every day.

As the sky grew darker, Adamar noticed ancestor animals begin to populate the tundra he went by, caribou raising their heads to glance at the travelers while mountain goats simply ignored them.

Snow began to drift along the trail. The Jdr Mountains weren't extremely tall, but they got snow and cold temperatures easily.

The three were silent until Ohanzee noticed a place where they could spend the night. Ohanzee turned Galene off the path and guided her to a circle on the ground. The circle was edged by snow. Frozen dirt could be seen in much of it, and Ohanzee guessed that a group of furs must've just left the site. He smelled the air and confirmed it.

Hmo glanced around the circle. "It'll do. It seems like whoever was staying here left for good, and probably moved to find another food source." He looked off toward the rising peak of the mountain. It was much closer than it had been earlier. And so were the multiple paths Adamar had noticed.

His wound throbbed as he jumped off his horse and began to prepare Dakr for a cold night on the mountain.

A howl split the night.

Adamar and Ohanzee spun, their feet making circles in the snow. Both held a piece of meat from the leftover deer, while Hmo sat on the ground, cocooned beneath the robes of all three furs and staring into a fire built on snowless ground.

Darkness had fallen by the time the three had begun to eat, sending them all into an alert state as they tried to take a rest from the day of riding. Olie, Dakr, and Galene were warming each other a few feet away, their saddle blankets draped over their backs in an effort to save them from freezing in the snowy air.

As soon as night had blanketed itself across the world, a gust of wind had sent more snow careening down, lightly coating the archers and their horses. While Hmo took their extra layers, Adamar and Ohanzee had scooped a fire out of the snow and managed to find non-snow covered kindling for it. Luckily, Ohanzee had thought of snow on the mountain, and had stashed a few dry twigs into Galene's saddlebags.

Adamar's pricked ears swiveled as his gaze searched the darkened land, looking for the source of the cry. His night vision was strong enough for him to see shapes and large details of the world. Ohanzee had the same ability, while Hmo was left in blackness except for the fire, his eyes at night as blind as his ancestors' daily vision.

"What was that?" Ohanzee asked, his voice barely above a whisper.

Adamar shook his head. "Probably something not too pleasant. Hopefully not Girbindon's warriors."

"It's not." Hmo said. "That was, most likely, just the clan of furs that were living here until a few days ago."

Ohanzee and Adamar exchanged alarmed looks. They both glanced at Hmo, who watched the flames from where he sat on the ground. "What should we do?" Adamar asked.

"Fight them. That's the best you can do. And watch their poisonous weapons."

Adamar scanned the horizon again, seeing nothing that could give a hint as to who had howled. His nose couldn't tell him anything either, as they were upwind of the howler.

"How big are mountain clans, Hmo?" Adamar asked, not taking his gaze off the land beyond their campsite. His tail swayed slowly, hackles rising as he searched for any movement. He was grateful that his fur was warm enough and it wasn't yet that cold, so Hmo could take his robe; the fox could move more freely without the weight of the heavy fabric.

"They can vary from having five furs to over a hundred furs. I'd estimate this was a clan on the smaller side. But, if they want to, clans will pack in closely together to conserve space and heat."

Adamar's ears flattened back. "Wonderful." He went over to where the bows and arrows were laying. He slid his quiver onto his back, taking his bow in hand as Ohanzee did the same.

"Do you know specifically what kind of weapons they would have?" Ohanzee asked, notching an arrow, but keeping it pointed at the ground.

"They're mountain clans. They make a lot of different weapons. Their weapons could be like yours, or they could be from the Toreal tree."

Another howl cut through the air, sending a shiver down Adamar's spine. The air seemed to suddenly become much colder, prompting Adamar's and Ohanzee's fur to raise. The fox wished they had Thayn to help them. They'd have better odds against whoever was out there in the darkness.

Out of the corner of his eye, Adamar thought he saw movement behind one of the trees that spotted the land. He looked over, and yelped as a sharpened stick came flying from seemingly out of nowhere and hit him in the side.

Adamar turned, drawing an arrow and pointing the tip toward where the stick had come from. In the stick's place stood a grinning mountain lion. A loincloth covered the mountain lion's lower section, but the mountain lion was otherwise without clothes. In the mountain lion's hand rested another stick, this one shorter and blunter.

"Who are you?" Ohanzee yelled, focusing an arrow on the lion.

"My name is Osima. And you are standing on the old site of my clan." The mountain lion responded, advancing a few steps.

Adamar bared his teeth. "Come no closer. Why are you coming back to this place if you have left it?"

The mountain lion let a growl end his words. "Why are you conquering it for the night?"

"We are just travelers, passing by. Let us be." Ohanzee moved closer to the snow bank, his feet scuffing into the light layer of white. He and Adamar smelled of protectiveness, of defending what they'd claimed as their territory for right now.

"So you are the ones we were told to attack. But we will let you go, if you leave." Osima answered. "If you do not, we will be forced to attack."

Adamar felt a bruise from the thrown stick forming on his ribs. The point had just missed breaking the skin. "You were told to attack us?" He tried to push down the thought that this circle had smelled so strong of other furs before; that they should have obeyed those smells and found somewhere else, even if it had been dark.

"Yes, by Girbindon, fox. He said if we killed you, then he'd leave us alone for a while. He and his fighters like to try going over the mountain a lot." His tail lashed as he continued to grin manically. "And you've wounded my clan's sacred ground with your fire. For this, we shall give you two choices. You may leave and never return, or we will attack."

As the mountain lion patiently waited, other furs began to gather around him, similarly clothed. Many held weapons, while some flexed their claws and shook their horns, preparing for battle.

Adamar glanced at Ohanzee. "We can't surrender. Miro is over there. And there's maybe seven of them in total. If we can get an arrow through them before they come too close, we won't have to be in any hand to hand combat, with any of their poisoned weapons."

Ohanzee folded back his ears, then nodded. "I don't see any other way." He looked to Hmo, as if he could try to coax more advice from him, but the bat and the three horses were nowhere to be seen. Tracks led into the snow, away from the mountain clan. Adamar guessed Hmo had left because with his eyesight, he couldn't help in the battle.

Ohanzee turned back to Adamar. "Hopefully he hasn't gone off too far." The coyote managed a slight smile. "This is just practice...right? Just practice for when we get to Girbindon?" Yet Ohanzee seemed uneasy at the thought of killing other furs like this.

Adamar shook his head. "I don't know." He leveled his gaze at the small clan, and loosed an arrow. One fur fell.

With a cry, the rest charged through the snow, wielding their weapons and showing their claws. Ohanzee landed an arrow into one of them, making the fur whimper and fall into the ground. Adamar was about to do the same when he was caught off guard.

Three of the remaining furs split off and made a circle around the campsite, teasing Adamar and Ohanzee to look their way while two still rushed straight at them.

Ohanzee turned, aiming an arrow toward the two while Adamar loosed an arrow of his own into a mountain goat. The goat collapsed into snow.

"You will regret coming here," Osima growled, coming within close range of Adamar. He laughed as Adamar aimed an arrow his way, and ducked when it flew into the air.

Osima sprung from a crouch, grabbing Adamar by the legs and tackling him to the ground. A second fur, a caribou that had been running alongside Osima, raised a stick over Adamar's head, waiting for the right moment to club Adamar's brains in.

Adamar and Osima struggled to get advantage over one another, using their claws to dig into flesh. Adamar's muzzle nearly caught Osima's neck, but the mountain lion squirmed out of his way and ripped a hole in Adamar's shirt, just missing his flesh.

The claws on Adamar's feet gouged a slash into the mountain lion's shin. Blood began to coat the ground. Adamar stole a glance up toward where he thought the sky hung, and saw the caribou get an arrow shot in his side.

Ohanzee flashed a smile at Adamar in triumph, only to be clawed by another mountain lion that had seemingly risen from the dead snow. The female mountain lion hissed and ducked from under Ohanzee's swinging fist, swiping a gash into his wrist. As Ohanzee twisted out of the way, the lion flicked a blunt stick along his arm.

Adamar noticed a sort of liquid shimmer on the stick. His eyes widened.

Ohanzee growled at the mountain lion and lunged at her. He missed when she turned away. The mountain lion smiled, and an accent swirled her words together. "I hope you like Toreal poison." She then turned and dashed away over the snow with the remaining fur, leaving only Osima against Adamar and Ohanzee.

Anger flared in Adamar's veins as he saw how close the coyote had come to being poisoned. He slammed a fist into the lion's nose, using his other arm to catch Osima as the mountain lion tried to twist out of his reach.

The mountain lion's tail lashed as he squirmed, struggling to move away from Adamar's clawing fists. When Osima seemed to be fading from consciousness, Adamar stood, uncurling his fist and letting his bloodstained hand rest by his side.

As Adamar turned to Ohanzee, Osima shot up from the ground and buried a claw into the wound continuously throbbing on Adamar's arm. The fox snarled in pain. Osima laughed and followed his clan members into the night. "We'll be back to kill you!"

Adamar put a hand over the blood dripping down his arm. He quickly looked for any other attacking furs, and when he found none, went over to Ohanzee.

The coyote sat in the snow, carefully rubbing the poison off with balls of hard snow. He looked at Adamar. "It's not in my blood. I'm okay."

Twenty-Five

"Where'd you go?" Adamar asked Hmo as he helped wrap Ohanzee's cut.

Hmo had appeared a few minutes ago. "You don't need to know a place well to find a spot to hide."

"You can see we both got hurt."

"Yet," Hmo countered, "The amount of blood on this snow can't have come from just two furs. And I had to step over the body of a mountain goat I assume one of you killed."

"I killed it." Ohanzee remarked. "And nearly got poisoned myself."

"If you start to not feel well, Ohanzee, eat some snow." Hmo advised. The coyote nodded, and the three mounted their horses. After Hmo made a quick check that they hadn't left anything nor were being trailed by an unhappy mountain clan, they set off.

"There has to be another way across this."

Adamar stared, wide eyed, at another death trap in front of him. While dawn had broken, the three had ridden until they came to a bridge that smelled and looked like it was made of ice, suspended over a fissure in the mountain that, Adamar guessed, went down for a good mile.

Fog curled up from the split in the mountain, shielding the bridge that ran across it. Adamar noticed the eerie sight with his tail between his legs.

Dakr, smelling the fox's nervousness, whinnied anxiously and backed up from the bridge.

"Unless you can fly, I don't know of another way." Hmo said, gazing at the bridge before them. "This mountain fissure extends for miles to its sides. To try and walk around it would take more time than the trip is worth." He looked at Adamar. "I'll go first. When you go, tie a cloth around Galene's and Dakr's eyes, so they don't see the drop on either sides of them. It'll make crossing the bridge easier."

Adamar scowled, hiding his fear. "Maybe I should do that to myself..." He ignored Hmo's glare.

Adamar dismounted and took off his shirt, tying it around Dakr's eyes. His arm throbbed while he held Dakr's reins. Ohanzee did the same to Galene.

He watched Hmo guide Olie over to the ice bridge, and help the horse put a hoof on the slick surface. The bat's claws clicked while he walked. He constantly spoke to Olie, rubbing the horse's nose while guiding him over the bridge.

Adamar watched with growing dread as Hmo helped his horse onto the other side of the mountain, then looked back and nodded for Adamar to bring Dakr over.

The fox's tail stay tucked between his legs. The bridge seemed to stretch into nothingness, growing thinner until it was just a collection of ice shards. The drop below the bridge fathomed out into an endless fall.

"Adamar!" Hmo called, trying to shake the fox from his fear.

Adamar looked at the bat.

"Think of Miro! What would happen to him if you don't reach him, don't cross this small crack in the mountain?" Hmo said. "Adamar, it's not a long bridge."

Trembling, the fox managed to cross the icy death trap, Dakr behind him. Adamar struggled to not look at what swirled far beneath him. Adamar collapsed into snow, letting the white fluffiness cool his overwhelmed mind as Ohanzee and Galene crossed the bridge with no problems.

Twenty-Six

As they climbed higher into the Jdr Mountains, more snow fell, thickening until the three furs had difficulty seeing more than a few feet in front of them. Every little while they had to dismount and brush the snow and ice from their horses' nostrils.

Emotions were riding low, dampened by the weather and how blizzards made the world seem so bleak, meaningless, as if the three would never be free from the relentless snow, would never be able to find Darvin and put an arrow through Girbindon's neck.

Adamar thought of how he'd felt Avaha's presence a couple times now, while Girbindon was present seemingly everywhere they turned. Except, he was hidden from a first impression.

But their minds stayed mainly on trudging through the snow, all other thoughts banished by the instinct of survival. They continued to move in the direction they believed was toward the Darvin kingdom. Hmo helped to guide Ohanzee and Adamar, but all three of them kept on becoming confused in the snow.

The snow had slowed when Dakr abruptly stopped, and shook his head in protest. The fox tried to get the horse to keep walking. Hmo and Ohanzee trotted up and did the same, but the roan horse wouldn't move a muscle.

Adamar gave his bow to Hmo for a moment. He dismounted and pulled the reins over Dakr's head, tugging on the horse's reins. "Come on, Dakr,"

Adamar grunted, hearing his words get lost to the wind.

The horse's nostrils flared and his ears flattened back against his head. He looked at the fox, smelling of defiance.

Adamar tried again to have Dakr move forward, but the horse dug his hooves into the ground and leaned back, fighting against his rider.

Frustrated, Adamar swung back into Dakr's saddle. The fox held Dakr's reins in both hands.

Adamar clucked his tongue against the roof of his mouth. "Dakr." His voice was stern as he made another attempt to show the horse that he was in charge. "Walk forward. Walk."

Adamar felt Dakr raise a hoof, and relaxed for only a second. The horse then snorted, turned away from the blizzard, and took off.

Adamar heavily settled his weight into the back of the saddle and pulled on the reins, struggling to calm the horse. Dakr tossed his head and bucked. Adamar tightened his hold on the reins. The horse put on another burst of speed. Adamar heard the pounding of hooves behind him and hoped it was Ohanzee and Hmo following, instead of some mounted mountain clan.

"Dakr!" Adamar shouted, wrenching the reins back. The horse spun in the snow, facing the storm, sending up a shower of the snow and coating Adamar, who lost his grip on the reins. Before the fox could wipe the snow from his eyes, Dakr sped off again.

"What...why would he?" Adamar stammered, holding his knees against his chest as he stared into a fire.

Dakr had galloped for nearly a mile, with his displeased rider clinging on for dear life. Ohanzee and Hmo had driven their horses after Dakr.

Eventually Hmo had managed to catch up with Adamar and surpass him. The bat had guided Olie in front of Dakr, and turned Olie so his side was facing the incoming roan horse. Dakr had continued galloping into the blizzard, but as soon as Olie's scent had whipped towards the roan horse and Olie came into view, Dakr whinnied and dug his hooves into the ground. Snow flew up, but Dakr stopped, sides heaving.

Ohanzee came up behind Adamar, and the three turned back in the direction they thought they were going, but the blizzard had covered all tracks in the snow. They'd then agreed on traveling towards where it seemed that southeast rested until they found a place where they could wait out the storm.

"He got us lost." Ohanzee grumbled from where he now sat next to Adamar. The coyote growled in annoyance when the fuming wind blew the fire out for the fourth time. Adamar went to try and spark a flame again, but Hmo told him to just leave it alone.

The bat had called for the three to stop some time ago. Ohanzee, Adamar, and Hmo had dismounted, tying their horses' reins around the trunk of a tree and spreading their saddle blankets over their backs.

"Why would Dakr do that?" Adamar asked, directing the question toward himself. He pulled at the sleeve of his robe, trying to cover the wound. The torn fabric didn't help. "I may not be Leona, but I know Dakr doesn't bolt like that."

"Unless he had a significant reason." Ohanzee said, his words sounding like whispers in the storm.

Adamar glanced over at Ohanzee, narrowing his eyes against the blowing snow. "What do you mean?"

Ohanzee sighed. "Every animal has multiple senses. Horses do too. We can't speak with Dakr because he's a horse and we're not, but if we could, maybe he'd have something to say."

"Which would be?"

"He refused to go forward because there was a danger we couldn't detect, that he noticed. Galene and Olie didn't seem to do the same, but they weren't standing right beside Dakr. So we can't be sure if they noticed whatever Dakr did." Ohanzee shrugged. "Just a thought."

Adamar pressed his back against a pile of snow he'd scooped together earlier, and closed his eyes. "Maybe. Whenever this storm lets up, we'll find out. We'll head back towards that spot." The cold wind blew, and he wished that Avaha was here with him. On the coldest nights in winter, they'd always cuddle close, keeping warm as a storm ranged. And now that Miro had been born, their kit would always be between them, wrapped in toasty blankets.

"Do you think the scent of us will still be there? What if we just pass the spot that Dakr hates?" Ohanzee asked, drawing Adamar out of his memories.

"I don't think we will."

Hmo scraped away snow while Adamar and Ohanzee stood back, holding on to the horses. Dakr pranced uneasily.

The storm had cleared overnight, and the three had mounted their horses, riding towards where Dakr had bolted. They hadn't needed to do much guessing and backtracking; it was as if something was pulling them toward the notorious spot.

"It's a trap." Hmo said, pulling something out of the snow. He held up a plant with round leaves that were pointed at the end, and had berries climbing up and down the plant's stem. The leaves were oddly green for being buried beneath snow for hours. "Girbindon intended to have this explode right beneath Dakr's hooves."

"How could he do that?" Adamar asked, ears lowered. "How could he know when Dakr was just going to step there?"

Hmo shook his head. "Girbindon can answer that." He stood and placed the plant in his palm. "I can't remember its name, but this is part of a fairly explosive plant, which is probably why Girbindon used it."

"What should we do with it?" Adamar asked. "If we just leave it here, could it go off?"

Hmo's ears flicked back. "I don't believe so. This was set to explode just when Dakr came across it. Now that it's been taken from where it would be a weapon, this is just a harmless plant. I'll drop it somewhere as we continue to cross the Jdr Mountains. The prolonged cold should kill it."

Uneasy, and fearing for Miro's safety once again, Adamar swung into Dakr's saddle. The horse shifted at Adamar's weight, but didn't spook.

Adamar settled his grip on his bow and the reins. The wound in his arm throbbed, and the fox thought he felt a warm liquid trickling down through his fur. It give off a sickly, moist scent.

Twenty-Seven

The deer crouched behind a tapestry, hidden in the shadows of a corner. She leaned against the wall and listened. Her ears pricked forward, alert.

She'd been wandering the halls, looking for work to occupy herself with, when she had heard a foreign voice wander in from Girbindon's throne room. Her curiosity had been peaked, and she'd hidden behind a tapestry.

"Sit, sit." The King Girbindon said. The deer heard a chair scraping across a floor and a creak as someone sat down in it.

"Thank you, My King." A squeaky voice said. "I have come with news."

"Yes. Wonderful. Good news, I presume?" Girbindon responded.

The deer shifted her weight and carefully brushed aside a corner of the tapestry, holding the fabric back with her thin fingers as she glanced at the scene beyond.

Girbindon relaxed in his large chair. A cloaked fur sat across from him, perched on the edge of a simple, smaller seat. A hint of a muzzle poked out from the fur's cloak, and ended in a small pink nose that looked like it belonged on a mouse. The deer could smell possum.

The flames flickered on Girbindon's face. "Remove your hood, Badr." The bear commanded.

The possum reached up and pulled his hood back. "My King," he acknowledged.

"Did your travels go well?" Girbindon inquired.

Badr nodded. "They did. Your using the spells to bring me back home was a unique experience."

"Unique?" Girbindon's face gathered a displeased expression. "How so?"

The possum's nose scrunched. "I've never traveled by your way, before, My Great King. The experience left me a bit ill, I'm sorry to admit."

Girbindon raised his head, as if to further demonstrate that he was above the possum. "As you should be. You may have to travel my way again, Badr. Make sure your body becomes acclimated to the process. Chilo did not, and used the magic I had given him to leave an incriminating mark in Miro's room. He was rightly punished."

The possum nodded and folded his hands in his lap. "Of course, My King."

Girbindon grinned. "Now, do tell me of what you discovered. Did anyone suspect you of working for me?"

"None, My King."

"Good. List your accomplishments."

"I was accepted into Eadageth's archers with no difficulties, as you've been aware. I became acquaintances with none. However, I was able to observe the fox. He does not appear to be conscious of what skill he has the potential to possess. And he does possess what you are after."

The deer saw Girbindon lean forward in his chair, and she too scooted closer, hesitantly edging her muzzle out through the tapestry to see the scene better. Hopefully the bear and possum were too busy to pay attention to her scent.

"Does that mean the fox had the mark?" Girbindon asked, his tone coated with eagerness.

The possum nodded. "Yes. Adamar did."

"And where was it?"

Badr was silent for a moment as he thought of the answer. "It was on Adamar's chest. A spot of brown right next to his heart."

A grin spread across Girbindon's muzzle. "Wonderful! Wonderful." He said. "You're sure that he has no idea what it's for? When did you find this out?"

Badr seemed to beam with pride. "I asked him myself, My Great King. And Adamar just thought it was a mark he'd been born with. Which means he does not remember his fur turning a different color. I inquired about it during a lunch break. All male archers practice shirtless, so they don't become overheated. They do not clothe themselves properly when they sit down for the midday meal."

"I see." Girbindon said. "So Adamar gave no hint that he knew what the mark was for?"

Badr shook his head. "None, My King."

"I was correct, then, in sending out some furs to grab or kill him. He will be useful, like his cub, dead or alive."

"And what're you doing here?"

The deer turned around, eyes wide, and saw the hen that had been taking care of Miro stood over her, hands on her hips. The hen clucked and whispered, "What happened? Are you listening in on our Great King Girbindon?"

The deer shook her head. "I just tripped. My hoof caught on a rough edge of the wall, from where Girbindon had had another of his rampages and tore at the stone with his claws. My hoof should be fine. I'm just checking to be sure."

The hen eyed the deer suspiciously for a moment. "Well, be quick about it. Even if you've got no work to do, there's always work to be done."

As the hen strutted away, the deer let out a breath of relief and turned back towards the tapestry. She poked her muzzle through the tapestry once more.

"Did you see her coming?" Girbindon asked the possum. "She should be here soon."

"Unfortunately, I did not, My King. She must be priming herself for an entrance. You know how she loves to greet you with the utmost kindness and greatest appearance." Badr reported. "May I ask you a question?"

Girbindon shifted his weight. "You may."

"How has Adamar's youngling been doing? Has he been responding?"

A look of frustration slipped onto Girbindon's muzzle. "In a way, Badr. But no more talk of that."

The possum stood. "Then, My Great King, I will attend to the preparations for Adamar's arrival. Is there anything I can get you while I'm around?"

Girbindon shook his head. "No, Badr. Your information and sleuthing is well appreciated."

The possum smiled, his rat's tail flicking across the ground. "I'm glad, My King." Badr turned and went to a tapestry depicting a large bear laughing at hundreds of petrified, minuscule furs. Badr lifted the wall hanging and slipped behind it.

As soon as Badr disappeared, the deer straightened, questions dancing about in her mind, but one stood out, prominent. The possum had entered with a certain scent following him, one that the deer had caught traces of when she'd been tending to Miro.

And Adamar? So Girbindon was trying to kill Miro's father? But he also wanted something from him. What did he want?

Twenty-Eight

"Adamar...I miss you..." A voice rang, tumbling through the mist that bordered Adamar's fitful dreams.

Adamar shook his head. He opened his eyes to see the swirling fog everywhere he looked. His ears pricked and he propped himself up on his elbows. He tried to stand, but his body wouldn't cooperate, and a faint ache coursed through his body when Adamar attempted to move his legs.

"Adamar...my lovely Adamar. When will you come home?"

Adamar's eyes widened. Avaha's voice was in his dreams. His tail began thumping against a ground he couldn't see. He tried to call out to his mate, but his voice was gone, as if she'd stolen his words away.

Avaha's muzzle appeared out of the mist, and her head soon followed, hovering directly above Adamar. Her soft snout and loving face smiled down at Adamar as her arms appeared and reached out to him. She gently took his muzzle in her hands while her body came into view. He noticed the fine purple dress that formed to her body and elegantly displayed her bushy tail as it swished behind her back. A veil draped about her ears and fell down behind her shoulders, giving her appearance even more wonder.

"My sweet Adamar. I've so missed you." Avaha knelt by Adamar's side and put her lips to his. Her

gaze met Adamar's, but seemed distant, as if her thoughts were somewhere else.

Avaha smiled and folded her legs beneath her, placing her hands over her lap as she sat back. *"I wonder where you are, Adamar. I worry so much."* She glanced off, and her voice was laden with sadness. *"I sometimes wish you hadn't gone to search for Miro. But, as you've been gone, I've realized my mistake in trying to get you to stay. You'll come home with our wonderful kit, or you'll die trying. Hopefully the latter will happen."*

Avaha sighed and shifted so she was sitting next to Adamar, absentmindedly stroking the spot between his ears. *"Come home soon, Adamar."* she said. *"Bring Miro back, please. Our home is so empty without you two."*

Adamar's ears flicked forward, watching her as she stared off into the fog for endless moments. Then Avaha turned and gave Adamar a soft smile. She leaned forward to kiss him again, but just as her muzzle was an inch from his, a drop of blood fell from her nose.

"Oh, my." Avaha put her hands to her snout. *"Bloody noses are always troublesome."*

Adamar watched her quizzically and with increasing worry. Avaha lifted a piece of her veil and put it to her nose, but the blood flow only increased, flowing steadily until her hands had been soaked red.

A growl of frustration rumbled in Avaha's throat. *"No matter."* she snarled, dropping her hands and lunging at Adamar, who couldn't defend himself too well.

"I miss you." Avaha opened her mouth to reveal bloody fangs, while her soaked hands pressed down on Adamar's shoulders, pinning him to the ground. Avaha grinned. *"Yes! Curl your tail, Adamar. Curl your tail. Be afraid. Be afraid of me."* She laughed and put her muzzle close to Adamar's. *"Remember that I miss*

you."

"I think I should go home, Adamar." Ohanzee's hands packed snow into a ball.

Adamar's ears pricked, and he looked up, wide-eyed. "What makes you think that?" he inquired again, thinking back to the first time Ohanzee had said this.

The coyote shrugged. He appeared exhausted from the day of riding, but his gaze, when he met Adamar's, was older and even wearier. "I'm worried about my family." Ohanzee looked up at where the horses were standing, resting and eating in a scooped out snowdrift with their heads bent close to one another.

"I know." Adamar said. The fox hated how the words resonated in his ears, sounding cold and unsympathetic, unlike what he'd intended. "Why do you think you should go?"

"What if what happened in your dream is real? What if someone...I don't mean to point out Avaha...but if a fur tried to attack my family while I was away?" Ohanzee's ears flicked back. "They could defend themselves, but I still would like to be there."

Adamar turned the coyote's words over in his mind. He'd woken Ohanzee and Hmo in the middle of the night, when his dream had ended and sent him screaming into the real world. Ohanzee had instinctively interpreted the dream, inferring that the nightmare was trying to tell Adamar that danger would soon come.

"Would you be able to get home without Girbindon's furs following you?" the fox asked.

"Hopefully. I'm not you. So I don't have as much importance to them. But, still." Ohanzee rolled back onto his heels and crossed his legs beneath himself, tossing the ball of snow back and forth between his hands. "I wonder how they're doing. My mate...she's very strong and extremely knowledgeable, but I still worry. I wonder how my pups are faring without me being there."

Adamar was silent for a moment. His wound throbbed. "Though it may be my kit that we're going after, I'm not the leader in this quest. None of us are. We're just furs going after him and looking to stop Girbindon from doing whatever it is he plans on completing. So I can't say whether or not you should stay."

A sad smile made its way across Ohanzee's muzzle. "Then, I'll be leaving. I'm sorry."

The wind howled in protest, its power increasing from the breeze it had been moments before.

Snow flew up as the wind raced over the mountains as if racing with itself. The wind roared, its cry growing louder and louder until Ohanzee and Adamar were barely able to understand the words in the wind.

"You may go home." The wind brought the voice of Girbindon to the furs' ears. *"You may leave your friend, coyote, and you may go home. But if you do, I can say you will never like what you'll see. You'll regret the decision for the rest of the days.*

"If you go home, I will have my furs rip your mate to shreds, and leave her eyes attached to your door, so when you arrive at home, you can see that she'll always be watching you.

"Then your cubs will die, bleeding from the inside out. They'll be able to see you before they die, but only in their last moments, and then will collapse onto you as you hate yourself forever for making that decision."

Adamar glanced worriedly at Ohanzee, who was trembling in fear as he sat in the snow.

"I hope you make your decision wisely, coyote."

A laugh echoed through the wind, and then

vanished as the wind stopped rushing, becoming just a breeze again.

Adamar looked at the coyote. "Ohanzee, I'm so sorry." His ears turned out when the frightened coyote didn't respond and the smell of fear froze the air. "I never meant for Girbindon to threaten your family. I—"

"Stop talking." Ohanzee growled. "You don't need to apologize. That was Girbindon's decision." Ohanzee closed his eyes, still trembling and smelling strongly of cold, cold fear. "Girbindon had motives behind that. Not just to keep me following you, but maybe to make me mad at you. And make it easier for him to conquer."

Adamar recoiled. "Mad at you? How?"

"Because when one is angered about something," Hmo said, coming over and sitting before the two. "One tends to look for something to blame. And they tend to blame the first thing that comes to mind. In this case, that would be you, Adamar. Because if your pup hadn't been stolen, then this whole quest would probably have never happened."

"I do not blame you, Adamar." Ohanzee said. His hands again began shaping another ball of snow, fingers shaking as he worked. "I blame Girbindon for this whole mess. Though I'm seeing little to get mad at you for." he sighed, and a knowing smirk crossed his muzzle. "However, Girbindon just made a very bad mistake. I'll remember his threatening my family when we find your pup." He looked at Adamar and laughed. The trembling slowly eased from his body. "And you should remember to save a piece of the bear for me. I want to make sure the pain I cause him hurts greatly."

Adamar allowed a worried smile. "You're sure, though, that you're okay?"

The coyote shrugged. "I'm somewhat terrified of the bear...but everyone has to be afraid of something." he turned and held up the snowball resting in his hand. Adamar noticed that the coyote's tail was between his legs.

"Hey, Hmo!" Ohanzee laughed as the snowball slammed into Hmo's back.

The bat turned around in time to see Ohanzee dive into a snowdrift, and chased after him.

Adamar watched as the two fired snow at each other, and would've joined them, but an unknown exhaustion tugged at his body, forcing him to just sit in the snow.

A few rounds of snowball fighting passed by, and a slightly displeased Hmo eventually declared Ohanzee the winner. As soon as Hmo trudged out of the snow, Ohanzee tackled him, only to end up pinned beneath the soaked bat. The coyote smelled strongly of happiness, with the fear sitting idly on standby.

"You did well in the snowball fight," Hmo remarked. "However, practice using different throws. There's a way to imbue a poison into snow, and if you're ever up against an enemy in a place like this, it's a good skill to know. If your enemy notices you have only one way of throwing, they will focus on destroying that way so you'd be left unarmed."

Ohanzee rolled his eyes, but nodded, as if Hmo was an old teacher talking about the history of the Land.

Heat danced up and down Adamar's arm. The wound hadn't really healed. An unpleasant smell had begun to drift up from the open gash, even stronger than before. Adamar began holding his arm at an awkward angle so he wouldn't have to smell the rancid scent.

As the morning broke over the mountains, he felt his body temperature rising to an almost unbearable point. He rolled around in the snow in an attempt to get cool, but the snow did little to help him.

Wooziness appeared almost as soon as Adamar got on Dakr and told the horse to start moving, so Hmo grabbed the fox's bow from him. Adamar held tightly onto the reins, along with a piece of Dakr's mane in his free hand. He felt like any moment he was going to slip off Dakr and see his breakfast once again. He didn't think too much of Miro, other than the fleeting thought that time was running out and they had to hurry. Was it three days left? No, two. Right?

His stomach churned as they rode, disagreeing with the rhythm of Dakr's hooves. Adamar hoped the ill feelings were just a result of having eaten too much of something, but the logical part of his mind told him otherwise.

Adamar heard Hmo's voice, but the words sounded as if they were underwater, and only made sense to Adamar a few moments after they'd been said.

"We're walking into a particularly treacherous part of the Jdr Mountains," Hmo announced. "So be extremely careful. The good thing, though, is that once we pass this hazardous area, we'll be nearly over the Jdr Mountains, at which point we can go to the village of Hile. We crossed onto the other side yesterday."

"Great." Ohanzee remarked. His wrist was still wrapped in cloth from the mountain clan attack and was now laxly holding Galene's reins. Adamar had half an idea that even if Ohanzee was bleeding, lying upside down on Galene's back, she'd still walk in the direction he wanted.

"Are the furs in Hile friendly? I don't think any of us want to go through a Galliv experience again." Ohanzee inquired.

Hmo shook his head. "They're as friendly as Fride should've been."

Ohanzee shook his head. "You know, that really reassures me."

The bat shrugged. "Glad to be of service."

A smirk crossed Ohanzee's muzzle. "At least I beat you in a snowball fight."

Hmo said nothing.

Adamar watched through a weary gaze as ice began to slick the path, eventually covering it in a thin sheet of dense and hardened snow. The horses' hooves dug into the ice.

Trees began to populate the edges of the path, as if fencing the three in from whatever lay beyond the trail. Adamar noticed figures dart in and out of the trees to his right, but none move on his left. The fox wondered if the figures were real as the heat in his body that never cooled.

Adamar was jerked alert, when Dakr slid on a sloping patch of ice.

Dakr neighed anxiously and attempted to back up, only to be pulled downward by gravity. The horse's nervous steps brought him and his rider close to the edge of the path, giving the two a glimpse of what lay beyond the trees.

Darkness dropped into a crack in the mountain, and snaked along the uneven edges that ran the length of the crevice. The crack seemed to continue on endlessly, disappearing into the edges of Adamar's blurry vision. Part of the mountain dipped toward the opening, as if beckoning in all who passed by.

Adamar's feet slipped out of Dakr's stirrups, but his delirious mind didn't alert his body to the event.

As Dakr slid toward the crack, he whinnied out of fear and jumped forward, desperate to get away from the death that was staring the two in their faces.

Adamar's arm moved with the horse's thrashing, and a knife of pain shot up toward his shoulder. Adamar dropped the reins in surprise, letting go of Dakr's mane just as the horse scrabbled his rear hooves away from the edge of the crack.

Adamar tumbled out of the saddle and landed on the crevice's sloping brink. He felt his lower legs hang out over the crack, but didn't move as aches climbed throughout his body.

He laid on the edge for a moment, then rolled carefully over and put his hands down on the smooth ice that rested on top of stone. The fox dug in his claws, and tried to pull his feet up under him, but the ice cracked and gave way. Fear put adrenaline into his blood. He couldn't see his comrades.

Hmo and Ohanzee were already past the downward slope and riding forward, but when they didn't hear Adamar directly behind them and they smelled the strong tang of adrenaline and Dakr's fear, the two turned.

The fox dropped into the crevice. Shards of stone jutted out of the sides of the crack, and tore at Adamar's flesh as he dropped down toward the center of the mountain.

A shard of stone plunged into his ankle just before a slab smacked up against Adamar's back, driving the wind out of him.

Bruises began forming all over the fox's body. Blood funneled itself out through the wound in Adamar's leg. The fox lay on the ground, searching for a breath of air to call his own.

Little oxygen entered his lungs, and Adamar found himself growing heavier. The calls of Ohanzee and Hmo filtered down to his ears, but he couldn't distinguish one from the other.

The gash that burrowed into his bicep ached, sending waves of heat over his battered body. Pain radiated from everywhere, but he felt the blood trickle out of his ripped foot more prominently than anything else.

Exhaustion stole Adamar away.

Twenty-Nine

"My King," someone gasped, her voice entering Miro's dreams. "You know you don't have to confront Miro here. We would all be pleased to bring him to you, clean and prepared for the honor of meeting with you."

"I want to deal with him." Girbindon's voice paused. "Alone."

As three-toed feet scuttled off, Miro rolled over and opened his eyes, ears flicking back at Girbindon's presence. He immediately smelled for the deer, but upon not finding her anywhere, he moved back against the wall.

Girbindon grinned and shook his head, his gaze tracking the kit. The patch on his eye had disappeared since he'd last seen Miro. "Nice try, Miro. But I won't have any of your antics. Today I'm going to be showing you something very interesting. I'm sure you'll enjoy it." A laugh followed Girbindon's words.

The bear unlocked the cage door and reached in, grabbing Miro by the scruff of his neck as the fox kit tried to get away. Miro twisted in Girbindon's grasp, grunting in frustration when his efforts failed.

"Shush, Miro." Girbindon spoke into the kit's orange ears. "I'm taking you to a place that's very secret. A place that no one else except I, and soon you, know about. You only get to know about it because your father will never get you, and you will become strong like me." The bear held Miro close. He stepped out of the room. Instead of turning towards his throne room, Girbindon went in the opposite direction and continued past more prison cells, each danker and dirtier than the last.

Miro's nose caught the scents of the empty cells, and he looked up at Girbindon, curious as to the purpose of so many rooms.

Girbindon smirked, expression proud as he focused on the hallway that waited up ahead. "Those are for the traitors that'll betray me when my kingdom expands. So far the only furs in the Darvin kingdom are those you see in this building, but that won't be for much longer."

Miro clung to Girbindon while the bear walked down confusing hallways and corners.

After some immeasurable time passed, Girbindon came to a set of stairs sunk into the ground. Girbindon waved a free hand, and torches placed along the staircase walls lit up with flickering flames.

"Miro, welcome to my greatest hidden secret." Girbindon said after he'd traveled down the stairs, and came to a stop at a wooden door that stretched nearly to the rocky ceiling.

Metal swirled from the doors' hinges and combined to make a spider web stretch itself across the wood, ending at a metal handle that locked the door and what rested beyond it from curious furs.

Girbindon placed his hand on the wood, stretching his furred fingers wide as a soft glow began to light up around the bear's hand. Green mist twisted, hissing around Girbindon's fingers.

Silently, the door swung inward into a lightless room. Miro tilted his head at an image that barely moved.

As soon as Miro realized what he was looking at, he whined and buried his face into Girbindon's chest, desperate to get away from the faintly lit green eyes that watched him in the dark.

Thirty

Girbindon waved his hand once more as he stepped into the room, smiling. A torch lit up the unknown space. The bear shut the door behind him, the loud sound it made jolting Miro. The kit looked up and took in the scene before him.

As if it had been cut out from the ground, dirt and rock lined the walls of the irregularly shaped room. Torches served as the only source of light, and were placed in holes carved out from the soil, where they hung out from, and flickered over, the tiled floor. The room was bare of anything except for a bookcase and table that stood in a corner, and a cage that dominated the room.

Girbindon walked over to the shelves of books and ran his hand across the leather spines, breathing in the scent of old parchment and dried ink. "These, Miro, are the books that contain knowledge about the darker side of the skills I've been trying to get you to do." The bear's grip on Miro tightened. "And hopefully, once you see who is here, you will be motivated to better perform what I request."

Miro whined and turned his head, tired of being held by the bear. He wanted to leave. The room smelled weird and unfamiliar. His gaze settled on a figure that lay in the cage. The cage looked as if it had been made from the ground up; no entryway could be seen, and other than having a metal floor, the cage was a set of iron bars that extended a few feet into the air until they met a metal covering that wasn't high enough to allow for an adult fur to fully stand. A bowl of fresh food lay in a darker corner of the cage.

Girbindon moved closer to stand a few feet from the cage. "Miro," he said, keeping his gaze on the figure. "Meet Ecetal, a dragon."

Miro glanced at the fur, his head tilted. Reptilian-like furs were rare.

Unmoving, a dragon lay on its side on the metal cage floor, its eyes cautiously tracking the two furs. Light green scales encircled the dragon's body, changing only at its chest and the front of its torso, where bright red scales rested. A band of dark, forest green scales made a circle around the upper part of the dragon's tail. Dark gray spikes walked down the length of the dragon's spine; starting at the back of its head and ending at the tip of its tail.

The dragon's thin body showed that the dragon hadn't been fed in a while; its collarbone threatened to push through its thick skin. Claws extended from the dragon's feet, and smaller, yet just as sharp talons ended the dragon's slender fingers.

The dragon's head was covered in the same scales that decorated its body, but the scales were smaller, like the scales on the dragon's fingers and toes. A tubular red tongue, forked at the end, flicked out of the dragon mouth's as it tasted the air. Its nostrils flared while it took in a weary breath.

"Ecetal is a dragon." Girbindon remarked. "You don't see dragons very often here. They're not as common as a fox or weasel is, Miro. A while ago, dragons were known for having great power. And that is this thing I like to think of as the magic heart. In the books I have here, it's formally named the Magician's Lev. It is this part of a fur's body that matures with them, and allows them to perform magic.

"Which is what I wanted you to do, Miro. It's what you tapped into when you set my tail on fire. When you did that, that meant that you're going to be someone who is strong in the twists of magic. The Magician's Lev doesn't show on one's body until a fur reaches teenage years, when the magic usually but not always begins to show. It is typically found on someone's chest. You can tell by an oddly colored spot of fur or feathers. But for a dragon the Magician's Lev lies in a dragon's tail, which is one of the most powerful parts of a dragon's body."

Girbindon laughed. "But enough of this boring nonsense!"

Girbindon took a step toward the dragon, and Ecetal's eyes flashed anger. The bear ignored Ecetal's displeasure. "In a dragon the Magician's Lev is much larger and much more powerful, because of all the different types of furs that went into forming him. The physical size of your Magician's Lev determines the strength and how much of the magic you can do. But the darker, better side of magic describes a way of harnessing the power of a Magician's Lev from another fur." Girbindon walked to the side of the cage and pointed at a tube with a black liquid flowing through it. It snaked out of Ecetal's ankle and vanished into the ceiling.

"Ecetal's been a great friend, and he's given me much of the power that once allowed him to perform magic so well." Proud of himself and his accomplishments, Girbindon bared his teeth in a ruthless grin.

Miro's ears pricked forward. He'd heard of his father having friends, and had gathered that friends helped each other. He hadn't seen friends giving almost all of their energy to help another friend, and do so seemingly against their will.

"I was your friend, once." The dragon hissed, its words nearly silent as it struggled to do more than just lie on the floor. "I was your only friend, Girbindon. But you imprisoned me. And stole my magic. And in doing so, my energy." Ecetal drew in a breath, and was silent for a moment as he gathered his strength. "You're a monster, Girbindon."

The bear scoffed. "It's King Girbindon."

Fury flickered over Ecetal's gaze again, and he met Miro's curious eyes. "If you're going to be as strong as Girbindon says you will be, you're going to be fighting against a lot." The dragon watched as the kit squirmed, uncomfortable, underneath his gaze. "But much of what Girbindon says cannot be trusted. Look what happened when I put faith in him."

Ecetal looked back over at Girbindon. "You know I can't last forever, like this. One day, I'll die. And then you'll have nobody to steal power from."

Girbindon growled. "If you're going to use up your energy to talk, replenish it at the same time. There's a bowl full of fresh food in the corner. Eat."

Ecetal's eyes narrowed, but he said nothing.

Sighing in disappointment, Girbindon looked down at the kit. "Ecetal is where you'll get much of your strength from, Miro. He is how you were able to perform some magic a few days ago, by making it easier for you to do so at such a young age. His magic is pumped into a few of the rooms here, including my throne room." The bear placed Miro on the ground. "You should know where things you use come from. So go to him." Girbindon nudged Miro in the direction of the dragon.

The fox kit faced Ecetal, his orange ears flicking back against his head warily. The dragon didn't move while Miro approached, putting one shaky step in front of the other until he was right up against the cage bars. The reptilian scent sat prominently in Miro's nose as his legs gave out and he fell forward. His muzzle missed hitting the bars, but his arms went through them, and a hand brushed against Ecetal's snout.

Miro looked at his palm, twisting his black-furred hand back and forth in wonder. The scales that had just brushed beneath his fingers had a foreign touch, and Miro reached out again. He ran his hand over Ecetal's muzzle, and did so a few more times. A soft humming echoed from the dragon's chest, and his eyes closed for a moment as he relished the touch of someone not prone to violence, a touch that Miro faintly guessed Ecetal had not felt for a long time.

As if in answer to Miro's young thoughts, Girbindon said, "Ecetal's been helping me for a few years now. When he first came in, he wasn't as cooperative as you might see. He was nearly strong enough to overpower my guards." Girbindon chuckled. "But that ended soon, right, Ecetal?"

The dragon glared at Girbindon. His gaze then shifted to Miro. "Never listen to anything Girbindon says." Ecetal repeated, voice full of harsh warning. "He'll trick you with his knowledge of words. A master of words is the wisest and most wicked fur around."

Miro cocked his head at Ecetal. He couldn't understand why the dragon was so tired that he could barely sit up. The fox whimpered.

Compassion draped a thin cloth across Ecetal's face. Slowly, Ecetal began to move. The dragon trembled as he put bone-thin arms on the metal cage ground. He pushed against the metal, struggling to push his weight up into the air and bring his body up. Ecetal closed his eyes, concentrating, and the black liquid flowing from his blood stopped moving for a moment.

Girbindon gave a shout of protest as Ecetal redirected his magic and pushed his body up into a sitting position. Ecetal swayed, his long legs lying awkwardly next to him, but the dragon pulled his tail around. The thick limb dragged across the floor with painstaking slowness until it rested against Ecetal to support him.

Miro's eyes widened. He snatched a piece of food from the plate that rested nearby, and handed it to Ecetal.

The dragon smiled weakly and accepted the fruit. "Thank you, Miro." Ecetal's claws ran absentmindedly around the food. "In the past few days, you've probably been getting a lot of advice on how you're going to be when you're older." Ecetal drew in a shaky breath. "But I don't think anyone's told you to be careful."

Ecetal cried out and collapsed to the ground, his eyes closing off his view of the world as his head thumped against the hard metal. The dragon laid still, the piece of fruit leaking juice from where his claws had pierced it.

Miro stared at the unconscious dragon, then looked over at Girbindon, who was twisting the intravenous line that ran into Ecetal's ankle. The bear's displeased expression morphed into a wicked grin as he scooped Miro from the ground.

"It was such a shame that I had to redirect the power of the Magician's Lev embedded in Ecetal." The bear mused. "But Ecetal's energy is important. And when he wastes it on meaningless things, I'm prompted to show him that doing so isn't the wisest of choices." Girbindon looked at Ecetal, whose chest rose slowly as he rested on his side. "While he's getting back to performing his job, allow me to begin your training."

Girbindon walked to the bookshelves and set Miro on the edge of the table. The bear reached up, running his hand across the spines of worn books, eventually settling on one he deemed suitable.

"I haven't used this in a while." Girbindon admitted, opening the leather manuscript and blowing dust off the cover. The bear flipped the book's pages until he came to a page he read aloud: "'Magic is an old skill that every fur is capable of possessing. But only a few furs are born with an element in their body that allows them to produce magic. This is called the Magician's Lev. Predominantly, the Magician's Lev is located near the sorcerer's heart. The Magician's Lev has a limit to its use. The greater in size the Magician's Lev is, the stronger the sorcerer is in magical capabilities. Thus, the smaller in size, the weaker the sorcerer is. If a sorcerer expends himself to the limit of his Magician's Lev, he risks destroying his skill forever.'"

Girbindon moved to the next page. "'With the training they receive as they grow, sorcerers are usually taught in their puphoods the basic skills of magic. However, some sorcerers go to different learning establishments, where they can study the art of magic more in depth.'"

The book cracked as Girbindon snapped it shut. He grinned at Miro. "Most of what've I told you about is what is mentioned in the beginning stages of this book. But not all of it is accurate, sadly. During the Far-reaching War, many strong sorcerers were killed for their skill, since furs with no talent believed those who had the power of magic had an unfair advantage. So the Magician's Lev began to die out, until it became like how it is now—rare. It's especially rare to see it both in a father and his pup." The bear's grin seemed to grow. "Just like you, Miro."

Thirty-One

Miro crawled along the edge of his cell, his nose pulling him toward a scent that was leaking from a corner of the stone. The kit couldn't identify the scent, but he thought it smelled similar to what had been in the room where Ecetal was kept.

His mind had already begun to forget what Ecetal had said, but Miro remembered the effort it took for Ecetal to just sit up. Miro didn't understand why, or how that tube had been inserted into the dragon's leg. Miro wondered if the magic liquid that Girbindon had been talking about flowed through a fur's bloodstream, and that was why the tube was in Ecetal's ankle, instead of in his tail, so it wouldn't get tangled.

But these thoughts quickly danced away from the kit as he edged closer to the corner of his cell, and the scent grew stronger. It seemed to be almost beckoning to him. And just as a voice called out, Miro noticed a strange pile of dirt in the corner, a pile that he didn't remember making when he'd gotten bored yesterday and had started to dig up the floor of his cell.

"Afternoon, Miro." The deer placed a tray on the table, unlocked the cell door, and ducked into the cell, where she stood behind the kit with a curious expression. "What are you doing, you silly fox?"

Miro squeaked in surprise as gentle hands grasped him around his torso and lifted him into the air. The deer smiled at Miro, bringing him close to her muzzle. "You can explore later. I have some food for you."

Miro sat in the deer's lap while he ate, managing to keep the old bread in his stomach. The deer kindly rubbed his back, speaking soothing words.

The deer turned her head when Girbindon roared orders that rang down the halls. Miro noticed that the deer's woven bracelet had fallen onto the ground near her leg. He picked it up and sniffed it curiously, and caught a faint scent like the one that had been in Ecetal's cell.

Miro opened his small muzzle and bit down on the bracelet.

Heat rushed through Miro's mouth, sparks flying at his palette and burning his tongue. Smoke filled the fox's mouth. Miro whined and coughed violently, clawing at his mouth.

The deer looked at Miro at the fox's cries of pain, and her ears flicked back. She took her bracelet, slipping it onto her wrist. She wrapped her free hand around the handle of a pitcher. The deer opened Miro's mouth and eased water onto his painful tongue.

"That's why you shouldn't play with my bracelet, Miro." The deer gently chided, lessening the agony the kit felt.

Tears soaked Miro's fur. His mouth felt like someone had set fire to it, and each drop of water that fell on his tongue he swallowed with eagerness. The water cooled the burn, but the kit still felt pain...pain that the deer had caused because she had the offending item in the first place.

As soon as his mouth felt somewhat better, Miro crawled away from the deer, his tail curled between his legs and his ears pressed flat against his head. He whimpered pitifully when the deer looked at him with an expression reflecting his own sadness.

"Miro, why're you running away?" The deer placed the water pitcher back on the table. "I didn't hurt you. If you come back, I can explain why your mouth hurt like it did."

Miro shook his head and curled into a ball, shutting his view of the world from sight. The thought that if he couldn't see her, she couldn't see him, drove into his mind, only to be destroyed when hands picked him up and cradled him.

"It's okay, Miro." The deer said, rocking gently as he squirmed. "You won't be hurt again if you don't bite my bracelet. It's a very special bracelet." The deer shifted to holding Miro in one arm and put her free hand into a pocket on her dress, bringing out a cookie. "Do you want a treat while I explain?" she offered.

The kit stared at the cookie, contemplating whether to eat it or not. His stomach won over, and he snatched the treat from the deer's hand, stuffing it into his muzzle and onto his burnt tongue.

"Better now?" The deer asked, smiling. She scratched the spot between Miro's ears. His tail began wagging.

Folding her legs beneath her, the deer sat down again, placing Miro before her. She wiped his grimy muzzle with a rag.

"Miro, there's this thing that you might've heard of. It's called magic. And it's pretty amazing. This bracelet has magic in it." The deer smiled. "It lets me perform little magic tricks. I can't perform powerful magic, like knocking a hole in a wall. But I can do other things." The deer spoke a few quiet words, and handed Miro another, bigger cookie from thin air. The fox eagerly bit into the treat.

"When magic is placed on inanimate objects, like my bracelet, it also gives a guard to these objects. So when you bit down on the bracelet, it reacted in self-defense. That's why your mouth hurt." The deer smiled and picked Miro up.

Miro hesitantly ran his fingers along the woven bracelet. He pulled it off her wrist, holding it up to the light and turning it, his curiosity rekindling.

"See? It's not scary." The deer said. "And, you don't have to be with Girbindon today. That's what he was just yelling about. He has to deal with something else, something that he said is more important than you."

The deer sighed and shook her head. "Though I don't understand how that could be. You're fairly important, Miro; even just a fawn, you're kinder than all the furs I've met here."

Thirty-Two

Ecetal lay in his cage, unmoving, his eyes closed. His head throbbed from the fall, though his tough scales had protected him from sustaining any more than a large bruise. A soft pain echoed from his ankle, where the tube entered into an artery and pulled the magic from his Magician's Lev. The pain had been at first agony, but over the few years he'd been trapped by Girbindon, Ecetal had gotten used to the pain, and now barely paid attention to it.

Other than his leg and his head, nothing ached in the dragon's body. He rarely felt pain. He was always so drained from unwillingly serving Girbindon that everything was bathed in an everlasting numbness. It was bittersweet.

Most of the time, Ecetal would lay half conscious, conserving whatever energy he could find for a later time, when Girbindon was gone, and when the dragon would eat. Food was always available, brought down by the king himself, but Ecetal refused to eat his food in Girbindon's presence. If he scrabbled for the food as soon as it appeared, he'd look weaker than he felt, and more like the loyal slave Girbindon was trying to get.

When Ecetal ate, peace would fall over him. Eating gave him more than just a little burst of energy; it became a break in the continuous and often monotonous day.

No one except for Girbindon had seen Ecetal in the years he'd been trapped, until the fox hatchling had come with the bear. Ecetal had sensed when he'd heard Girbindon's footsteps that it wasn't an ordinary visit. Girbindon had already appeared today. For him to come down a second time, and not during mealtime, was a strange occurrence.

When he wasn't bringing food, Girbindon only visited Ecetal so he could find someone to talk to about his plans—someone he knew wouldn't be able to tell others of what he was thinking about.

Ecetal had opened his eyes to see who was with Girbindon when the door had swung inward, and at first the dragon had thought he was in another of his dreams, dreams that depicted an unknown figure rescuing him from this torture.

Miro had never seen a dragon before, something that Ecetal had expected. Most furs went their entire lives without seeing a dragon. The ancestors of the dragon furs were gone, so the remaining few two-legged dragons were all on their own, and often lived solitary lives.

Ecetal hadn't been sure what had empowered him to use his stored energy and sit up for the fox hatchling, but he was glad he did. He'd shown great respect for a hatchling that would probably never remember meeting him, yet Ecetal had the sense that the fox just might hold on to the memory. The fox had seemed different from the other pups he had met when he was training in magic years ago as a young one himself. The fox wasn't as loud as the normal pups; he'd been so quiet and reserved, that Ecetal wondered how old the fox's soul was.

For a dragon to show that they admired another fur was legendary, Ecetal knew. Dragons, even when they had been soaring through the skies, were rare and strange creatures with souls much older than their physical bodies. The rumor that dragons were wise was accurate, but Ecetal didn't always believe himself to be so wise.

He was thrilled that he'd gotten a visitor. He mulled over the fox's name. Miro. The dragon wondered what it could mean. Probably nothing, but it was a task nonetheless, something Ecetal could do to keep his brain stimulated. Sometimes the dragon replayed and analyzed memories. Other times he would use magic and create small things as Girbindon slept.

As soon as night would fall, Girbindon would prepare himself for a night's rest, a time that Ecetal savored even more than mealtimes.

Like most furs who were able to use magic, Girbindon didn't practice the skill in his sleep, which allowed for Ecetal to perform little magic shows of his own.

The line that entered into his artery pulled energy and power regardless of whether it was day or night, but Ecetal had worked over the past few years to perfect a trick he found, where he could stop the flow of his Magician's Lev into the tube, and instead use the magic for himself, but only for a short time. It wasn't enough for him to be able to break the cage, which Girbindon had protected with a lot of magic, but it was sufficient for entertainment.

Girbindon never noticed that the magic supply had briefly turned off as he tossed in his sleep.

Ecetal would recite spells he'd learned from training and cast them upon the rocky walls, or light up the room in sunlight—something he hadn't seen in a while. Doing so always entertained the dragon, as well as keeping his vision better than it would be if he looked only into darkness while he was stuck here.

Ecetal would sleep throughout the day to save scraps of energy for the night, even though it was against his natural instincts to be a nocturnal creature.

Sometimes he would plan what he'd do when he was free from Girbindon's grasp. He figured he'd die of exhaustion before that happened, but his imagination always showed him otherwise.

The dragon repeated the phrase his teachers had taught him—how it was good to know one's enemy. Having grown up with Girbindon helped, and allowed Ecetal to disappear into the memories of the days already past, the days before Girbindon had turned into a power-hungry monster.

In his training, the younger furs had taunted Ecetal about not having wings. They'd repeatedly asked why he was incapable of flight, and he repeatedly gave the same answer: Ecetal's ancestors had come from the forests. They hadn't found a need for wings, only found them a nuisance, and eventually wings disappeared from their bodies.

Ecetal sighed, running over Girbindon's flaws in his mind for the hundredth time.

Being a bear, Girbindon had a trace of the horrible eyesight that plagued his ancestors, but he tried to mask this every day by some magic spell he'd probably found in the piles of books he owned on magic.

Like many conquerors, Girbindon was afraid of failure. He hated being second best at anything, and had regarded Ecetal with jealousy whenever the dragon did better than him during training. It had been a friendly jealousy, but Ecetal had been so busy exploring the boundaries of his skill that he hadn't notice Girbindon's flaw transforming into his life's goal.

Ecetal focused his energy on redirecting the flow of power, and felt a jab of pain as the intravenous tube stopped working; no liquid was traveling through it. The relief from his Magician's Lev not being drained dry overwhelmed the pain. The dragon opened his eyes and spoke softly, sticking his snout through the bars of the cage and projecting a memory on the ceiling.

A younger, teenage version of Ecetal stood before his and Girbindon's teacher, an old and strict wolf. A teenage Girbindon, much thinner than he was at his current age, was next to Ecetal. His arms crossed as the dragon twisted his hands and pulled a dancing particle from thin air.

Their teacher smiled and his tail beat against the tree stump he rested on, praising Ecetal for his work, for doing something that in his long years, the wolf had never seen before. Ecetal nodded and bowed appreciatively, then turned toward his friend, who was watching him with a competitive expression.

In a joking manner, Ecetal told Girbindon that the bear would do better next time, but Ecetal's friend only rolled his eyes and playfully pushed the dragon to the side.

The two began walking across the campus grounds, chattering about nonsense. They'd been selected by the school to train in the arts of sorcery when they were a few years younger, and had lived at the school ever since, practicing and refining their rare skill.

As they had grown older, the two had been assigned jobs teaching the younger furs basic skills. Most often Ecetal would be the one to instruct, while Girbindon simply assisted him. From Ecetal's arrival at the school, it had been clear that he was capable of great power, especially because he was a dragon, while Girbindon only had the power of an average sorcerer.

Nevertheless, though, because of the rarity of having a Magician's Lev, Girbindon had been sent to the school without question.

Girbindon was rarely truly happy when he was training, and was only happy when the attention was on him, and he'd done something the right way.

Ecetal watched this memory and sighed. Girbindon had defended Ecetal as an actual friend would do when the other students would tease him about being flightless.

But Ecetal realized he probably would've settled for having any other fur as a friend. Training at a school to become highly skilled in magic led one to be often lonely, and finding companionship in anyone was common.

The teenage Ecetal was guided over to a clearing on the edge of the campus, where Girbindon directed him to take a seat and watch his performance. The dragon did so, his thick tail curled around his side as Girbindon focused his concentration and set a tree aflame. Ecetal smiled and congratulated him. The bear grinned and extinguished the fire.

The image disappeared. Ecetal forced himself to sit up. He pulled the bowl of food toward him and began to eat quietly in the dark. As the dragon ate, he smirked, thinking of how Girbindon had absolutely no night vision, which Ecetal had often used against him when pulling a friendly prank during their training.

Maybe, if they knew that, the dragon mused, Girbindon's enemies could do the same, throwing darkness at Girbindon and forcing the bear to fight blindly.

Though, it seemed that Girbindon already was fighting blindly. His methods of conquering were without guidance from anyone else, and he was attempting to use old methods to his advantage. The bear often spoke of how he believed he would be able to gain control of all the Land, one day.

Ecetal drank from a jug full of cold water, his raised snout keeping his gaze on the ceiling. He glanced at a shadowed corner that stood just above the door, in a spot that Girbindon never noticed. Recently, Ecetal had felt the urge to create a tunnel from one of the first cells in Girbindon's palace down to where he was imprisoned.

The dragon had devoted most of his nights to scooping out this tunnel, purely by magic. At first, he hadn't understood why he was doing so.

Now he realized why.

Thirty-Three

As night fell, the strange scent grew stronger, and Miro's curiosity did the same.

Once the deer left, Miro crawled over to where he had been searching before. He discovered a rough hole sitting nearby the foreign dirt pile, and stuck his nose into it.

The scent seemed to be emanating from the hole, which, to Miro's delight, appeared to be an endless, unexplored tunnel. The kit wriggled his body into the tunnel, the scent seeming to almost beckon for him to crawl down the tunnel.

And so he did.

Miro relied on his nose and night vision as he pulled himself through the dirt. His fur quickly became covered in dusty soil. He sneezed a few times. He was surprised when a spontaneous fire didn't follow his sneezing, and turned around in the tunnel, searching for the fire before he became bored and continued on his way.

The tunnel grew wider as he crawled through it, until it ended in a hole large enough for him to easily squeeze through. He went flying through the end of the tunnel, and yelped when something soft cushioned his descent. Air. He lowered to the ground.

Cowering, Miro hugged his tail.

"You're okay, Miro." Ecetal said. Miro jumped and turned around.

Ecetal was sitting up in his cage, leaning against the metal bars for support as the intravenous line laid still, not pulling any magic out of the dragon.

Ecetal smiled softly at Miro. "I'm not going to hurt you. Come here." he watched as the kit contemplated this decision, then slowly made his way over to the dragon and sat in front of his cage.

The dragon reached behind himself and pulled an apple from a food bowl, which he handed to Miro. The fox sniffed the fruit for a moment, then sank his teeth into it.

Ecetal was quiet as Miro chewed, apparently focusing his concentration on some task that had him close his eyes and murmur soft words.

Once the apple had been eaten, core included, Miro poked the dragon through the bars of his cage and whimpered for more food.

"I'm going to do something that you will not understand. And something you probably won't for years. But one day you'll find it useful." The dragon said, opening his tired eyes. "I don't know if by the time that day comes around I'll be dead or not. Nevertheless."

Ecetal reached out and gently rested his forefingers and thumbs on the sides of Miro's head. The kit twisted and shied away, still unused to the leathery touch of Ecetal's scales.

"Miro, it's okay." The dragon said. "This won't hurt. Just stay still."

After protesting for a moment more, Miro quit fidgeting.

Ecetal closed his eyes and began speaking softly. A ball of light started to form between the dragon and fox. The light danced, turning as it rounded into a smooth sphere. Pastels and sharp colors floated around its surface. Miro stared in wonder, and giggled when the sphere began to move toward him, stopping only when it was resting in front of the space between his eyes. The kit's gaze crossed in an effort to continue looking at the light.

"Stay still, Miro." Ecetal repeated, his voice sounding like it came from far away.

The ball of light disappeared into Miro's forehead, and his eyes rolled up into his head.

When Miro woke, he found himself lying against Ecetal's tail, which had snaked through the bars and curled protectively around him. Miro laid against the dragon's tail for a few moments, enjoying the warm heat from his scales.

"Miro, it's time for you to go." Ecetal said, exhaustion heavy in his voice. "I believe the day will be coming soon. It would be a good move to go back to your cell."

The fox whined, but complied, crawling over to the wall below the hole he'd come from. He looked at Ecetal for help to getting back into the tunnel.

The dragon spoke a few words. The dark liquid began to flow through the intravenous line again as an unseen force lifted Miro up, and propelled him into the tunnel.

Miro turned, and saw that the tunnel had caved in, rocks blocking his way into Ecetal's room. Miro then sniffed the air, and his nose caught the scent of food.

Hungry, the kit followed the smell, already forgetting what Ecetal had just done.

Thirty-Four

"I've brought up some books for you two."

The deer paused in her walk, holding a bucket of Girbindon's dirty clothes in one arm. Her ears flicked toward an open door that she hadn't seen before.

The deer pressed herself into the shadows and listened. She knew she shouldn't be eavesdropping on King Girbindon and his business, but her curiosity was peaked. If she was caught, she'd be able to say she had gotten lost, considering she was the newest fur to join Girbindon's staff.

The voices that came from the open door were familiar, and the deer could connect two of them to the possum Badr, and to Girbindon himself, but the third she hadn't heard before. It sounded sweet, while conniving, as if whoever owned the voice had many tricks up their sleeve. The deer smelled the air. The third voice belonged to a fox.

A rustle of papers preceded Girbindon's words. "So this is what should be built to do the task." The bear grunted. "It doesn't look like it will take too much time, but you'll have to be careful about getting everything just right. If the measurements aren't perfect, that could kill him and what we want, therefore rendering the whole job useless."

"We will take care of that," Badr said. "When do you want it finished?"

"Last I heard, my workers had placed something in his path to stall him long enough to let me keep Miro. But if not, within a couple days." Girbindon's voice carried a smirk.

There was a pause.

"Other than building this, are there any other things we need to do before his arrival? Or will you take care of all of that, My Great King?" the fox asked.

"You should be sure that you can fight off whoever comes with him. I expect that that should already be done by the time he gets to this room, but one can never be too sure. However, I will take care of all else."

"Your generosity is kind." The possum responded. "Who will be performing the deed?"

"You mean doing the actual extraction?" Girbindon shuffled around and flipped a page in something. "This states that it is best for a relation to complete the task. That will make the entire process easier, apparently. And you know how I love when things are easy."

"We do." The fox confirmed.

Girbindon sighed. "The problem though is that Miro is still stubborn. I've been unable to get him to do much."

"Maybe, My King, maybe he's too young to fully understand your wise words." Badr suggested.

Badr cried out as he was struck by Girbindon's fist.

"You idiot! Don't you think I've already thought of that? I've known furs dumber than him and twenty times his age." The bear scoffed. "Miro's just playing stupid. He understands all I'm saying. He refuses to acknowledge it."

"I'm sorry, My King. My mistake. I've heard that Miro was raised well, and taught to understand multiple riddles." The possum apologized.

"That's good." Girbindon acknowledged with a touch of anger. "Now if he will just show it."

The fox moved closer to Girbindon. "I suspect you should give him time. I do not mean to offend, My Great King, but I did raise Miro for many months, for this very purpose."

Girbindon considered this for a moment. "I suppose."

"To be clear on this," the fox confirmed, "Will he be led up here by your warriors, or will we have to escort him ourselves?"

"I've not decided yet. I believe I shall see how it goes, how easy it is to capture him."

"Alright. This process should not take long?"

"Correct. It shouldn't be too long. Your goal is to do the job, then, if you've any compassion for him, sew up the wound that will be left. But I suspect you won't. You're quite cruel when need be."

The fox laughed, her laughter sounding sickly sweet. "I have had much time to become so. Your training, My King, has also aided in my skills of being merciless."

Girbindon stepped closer to the door, and the deer pressed herself back against the wall. She pulled her cloak up over her ears.

"We will continue this meeting later." Girbindon said. His tone suddenly acquired a snake-like quality. "Now, I shall say it was a good idea I left this door open."

The bear appeared in the doorway, stepping out of the room with a grin on his brown muzzle. He smirked at the deer, and before she could move, gripped her throat and lifted her up into the air.

As the laundry basket clattered to the ground and the deer scrambled for air, Badr appeared behind Girbindon, watching with an expression of amusement.

"And why is it good that you left this room's door open, My King?" he asked.

"Because it allows me to catch the spy, the spy who has been running around this place supposedly undetected." Girbindon tightened his grip on the deer's throat.

The deer kicked out, her hooves clipping Girbindon in the chest as she struggled to take in air. The bear recoiled and dropped her to the ground.

"She thought no one knew about her. This spy was wrong. Take her to my throne room. I'll question her there."

Thirty-Five

New scents assaulted Adamar; herbs, metal, canine, and others he wasn't conscious enough to determine.

Dulled pain flooded up through his body, and he shifted, feeling a soft cotton sheet beneath his fur. He opened his eyes.

He lay in a small, wooden room, with metal beams spanning the ceiling. A table full of herbs and varying sizes of mortars and pestles was pushed against the corner of the rectangular space. His cloak sat next to it, folded and smelling freshly cleaned, though torn. A window stood in the wall to Adamar's left, where the sun filtered through and fell across his abdomen.

As Adamar took in his surroundings, his ears flattened back in alarm. He didn't know where he was, and he immediately threw off the blanket, ignoring the various scabs that decorated his torso, and put his legs on the cold floor.

Pain shot up through Adamar's paw pads, centering on his right ankle, which was wrapped in an unmoving and thick white bandage. Blood coated the edges of the cloth and reached Adamar's dry nose. The fox's tongue licked at his nose, wetting it so he could smell better.

Still panicked, Adamar tried standing, keeping weight off his injured foot and grabbing the corner of two intersecting walls that jutted forward, only to realize that he was stark naked.

The fox pulled the blanket off the cot and messily tried to assemble it about himself. A fur with a black and orange coat came in. He recognized her scent as one of the stronger ones in this room, but also one he'd smelled recently.

She pushed against his shoulder and easily helped him lie back down.

Adamar propped himself up on his elbows, ears flattened and his lip curled back to reveal his teeth in a defensive snarl. If he was correct, she was a jackal.

But a male jackal had taken Miro. Adamar hadn't smelled a female jackal near Miro's crib.

"Oh, stop it." The nurse chided. "No one's going to harm you, here, Adamar."

The fox let a growl precede his words. "How do you know my name? And where am I?"

"You are in Hile, where there is no need to be as defensive as you are." The fur responded, putting her hands on her hips and meeting Adamar's gaze, challenging him.

Adamar returned the look for a few moments, then huffed and looked away. "So how do you know my name?" he asked again, his voice quieter.

"Your friends told me what it was when you were brought here." The nurse shook her head. "I hear you had quite a fall. The Jdr Mountains are extremely treacherous. Especially on this side."

Adamar fell silent, and began inspecting his wounds.

Cleaned bandages encircled the wound on Adamar's arm, while small scabs danced up and down his torso, covering scrapes. His legs were just as hurt, the only difference that his ankle and the top of his foot were heavily wrapped.

When Adamar curiously lifted an edge of the bandages on his arm, the nurse slapped his hand away.

"Don't do that. You won't heal as fast, and you want to get better quickly, right? Your friends mentioned that you three were on a quest."

Adamar glanced at the nurse. "How much did they tell you?"

The jackal shrugged. "Enough. The name's Rowena, if you were wondering."

Adamar fell back onto the pillow. "How long have I been here?"

"A bit over a day. You were pretty bad when you were brought in. Covered in blood and running a high fever. But some herbs and a bit of Rowena's special smear, your fever broke and you looked better."

"'Rowena's special smear'?" Adamar questioned, wary.

"Yes. It's this special concoction made from the fine herbs you can find in pretty much any woods. No, don't ask, I'm not going to tell you what's in it."

Adamar nodded slowly, and cocked his head at Rowena's strange fur. Her coat was mostly a sandy color, while a black and grey patch of fur covered the back of her head, disappeared into her clothes, and was on the back of her tail. She appeared fox-like, except for her much taller ears.

"May I ask..." The fox said, wanting to confirm what his nose thought. "What species are you?"

Rowena rolled her eyes. "You forest furs are so uneducated. I'm jackal . My ancestors migrated here during the Far-reaching War."

Adamar nodded, wondering if she had a connection with Darvin. But he figured, as he lay here injured, he should leave that idea alone for a little while. "Where are my friends? Can I go to them?"

"If you can fly, sure. You're going to have a hard time putting weight on that ankle. Some of your muscles got ripped there." Rowena pushed Adamar down again. "I'll go find your friends. They've been waiting for you to wake up. Stay."

As the jackal left, Adamar sighed and closed his eyes. He couldn't even begin to fathom how many more days, if any, he had left before Girbindon's challenge was over. Fright burned through him.

No. No. Miro would not die. He couldn't.

Time passed, and Adamar sank into sleep.

"Adamar! You're awake!" Ohanzee shouted. "Or, well, you were."

Adamar groaned and opened his eyes to find Ohanzee and Hmo standing at his bedside, both dressed in new clothes. Adamar sat up.

"How are you doing?" Ohanzee asked, sitting on the edge of the bed.

"Alright. My foot doesn't feel so great." Adamar shrugged. "How did I even get here?"

"When we saw you fall into that ditch, Hmo went to the nearest village he could find, this one. I stayed near the ditch, with Dakr and you. I wasn't sure how Olie galloped so fast, but by the time it had started to get dark, Hmo had run down the mountain, gotten warriors from Hile to follow him, and was back up to where you had fallen. Apparently we were extremely close to the edge of the mountain. You just couldn't tell because of the mountain's geography. And the interesting thing is that they came from below you."

Adamar glanced at Ohanzee. "What do you mean?"

"There are tunnels under the Jdr Mountains." Ohanzee explained. "Hile's warriors said that the tunnels are for use by anyone who lived near or on the Jdr Mountains, and cross below almost half of the mountain range. There are these steps carved from rock that allow you to go almost the entire way up the ditch you fell in.

"You fell onto one of the first steps. Hile's soldiers were able to climb up and bring you back down." Ohanzee looked at Hmo. "You were in the tunnels with them. I couldn't see what happened after."

"Not much," the bat said, focusing his gaze on Adamar. "They carried you down through the tunnels—a much faster and shorter route than trekking the rest of the way down the mountains. Then they brought you here and Rowena took you under her wing."

"I've never heard of tunnels beneath the mountains." Adamar admitted.

Ohanzee shook his head. "Very few have."

"What's gone on since yesterday?" Adamar shifted his weight and began picking at a scab.

"We've been getting ready to fight Girbindon. But other than that, exploring." Ohanzee smiled. "They have some great training places here. They look like so much fun. And everyone's so welcome, despite what surrounds Hile."

"What're you talking about?" Adamar asked, dropping his hand.

"There's this giant wall that encircles the city." Hmo said. "You can see it when you're better."

Adamar began to stand. "Or I could go look now. I'm fine. It's just a little pain." He grimaced as his foot touched the ground, but tried to keep pain from his face and smell.

"Adamar, I wouldn't do that." Ohanzee suggested, watching the fox uneasily.

Rowena walked into the room, and scowled when she saw Adamar out of bed. Without wasting a second, she moved over and pushed him back down.

As he protested, she pulled a jar out from a pocket in her apron, and held it in front of his nose.

As Adamar felt his body growing heavier, the world becoming more like complete air, he heard the jackal mention how she'd given him something that should keep him calm and healing for the next few hours.

"My, you really must miss your pup."

Adamar blinked open bleary eyes. The sun's bright light hit him in the face. He turned and sat up, glancing at Rowena, who stood in the corner of the room, her back to him while she ground herbs.

Adamar's nose scrunched as the pungent scent of crushed leaves filled the air. "What did you say?" he slurred, still waking.

Rowena didn't turn to him. "You were saying your pup's name a lot in your sleep. You must've had a nightmare."

Adamar rested his head against the wood wall behind him. "I can't remember."

"I understand your pain." Rowena went on. "I had a pup of my own once. But I didn't have him for long."

Adamar tilted his head, thoughts of Miro threatening to take over his mind. "What happened to your kit?"

Rowena sighed and set down her mortar and pestle, pausing a moment. "The fur you're chasing, Girbindon, he has my pup. He's an older teenager by now."

Adamar's ears flicked back. "How did Girbindon get hold of him?"

"I know what you're thinking, Adamar." Rowena faced him and leaned her back against the table. "Girbindon did not steal my Chilo like he took your pup. I voluntarily gave him over. It was hard but—"

Adamar snarled, the pain he felt setting him on edge too quickly. "You gave your pup to Girbindon without being forced? You gave him to Girbindon? You helped that monster?"

Rowena's ears flattened back and she allowed a growl of her own to taint her words. "I had no choice, Adamar. Chilo and I would've died had I not accepted help from Girbindon. I do not like how the situation resolved either, but it had to be done. There were complications with giving birth to Chilo...and Girbindon offered, with one request. I thought it was better to let my pup live, instead of die before he smelled his first scent."

As Rowena tried to approach Adamar with a cream on her hands she claimed would help heal his wounds, the fox bared his teeth, a deep growl emanating from his throat.

"Stay away from me." Cornered, Adamar waited for Rowena to come closer. He'd snap at her if needed, as she would give him no option.

The jackal watched him. "Adamar, please. I don't mean you any harm."

"You sure?" Adamar accused. "Because your pup stole my kit from me! He's the one who started this whole quest of madness! If you hadn't given him over to Girbindon, Miro wouldn't have even been stolen!"

"Adamar, I had no idea that would ever happen. Please, you have to calm down." Rowena attempted moving closer again.

A flame flew up through Adamar's body, stemming from an area near his heart. At first the flame burned relentlessly, giving the fox agony, but he merely grimaced, not taking his gaze off Rowena as his mind turned her into an enemy.

The flame began to settle into soothing heat that still raged in Adamar, but with a passion rather than a cruel fervor. The fox glanced at Rowena, who was cautiously standing at the foot of his bed.

Adamar prepared to attack the nurse, but two hands from different furs caught his arms and pulled him back.

"What's wrong with you?" Ohanzee yelled, tugging on Adamar's wrists in conjunction with Hmo, and dragged the fox off his cot, away from biting Rowena.

Adamar barely felt the pain as his body slammed to the floor and spikes drove up through his injured ankle. He struggled against Hmo and Ohanzee, but his attempts were fruitless, and only revealed that a sliding blanket was about to show Adamar's naked body.

Hmo grabbed the edges of the blanket and managed to pull the ends of it around and behind Adamar, as he gripped Adamar's wrist in one hand.

Together, the bat and coyote dragged Adamar out of the room he'd been recovering in, through a hall with furs waiting patiently for their various wounds and scrapes to be seen, and past a strange little white ball of fur that had a muzzle.

The scent of fresh air struck Adamar as he was hauled outside, around a bend, and into a courtyard.

Ohanzee and Hmo threw Adamar near a solid stone bench, where he snarled at them and made to stand up, his claws searching to dig into flesh.

Out of desperation, Ohanzee let his fist land on Adamar's furred chest.

The fox yelped and collapsed to the ground, whimpering as pain shot through his body once more, overwhelming the fire and making Adamar's vision dance in and out of focus.

Once his vision returned, Adamar raised his head and looked guiltily at Hmo and Ohanzee, who were standing over him and glaring.

Ohanzee opened his mouth to speak, but Hmo cut him off.

"What. Were. You. Doing?" The bat snarled, his fangs flashing. "Why did you do that? If we were in any other village, these furs would have attacked you. And Rowena was just trying to help you."

Adamar couldn't meet Hmo's gaze. "I don't know...something just came over me. It was as if my thoughts weren't my own. I couldn't control myself." He had no idea what had happened. Just...great rage had come over him. Now, all that was in his mind was the idea that Girbindon had something to do with that.

Hmo's narrowed gaze tracked him for a few moments. "Work on behaving better." Then the bat turned away and strode off, disappearing into the center of Hile.

Adamar glanced at Ohanzee, whose face had softened somewhat.

The coyote sat down on the bench, his tail occupying the space next to him. "I don't know what that was, but I know you really made Hmo mad. No one makes Hmo mad easily."

Adamar's ears turned out. "I know." He struggled to stand, clutching the blanket about his lower section as his leg protested each movement he made. The fox could feel pulses of pain from where Ohanzee had punched him.

The fox fell back to the bench and looked at Ohanzee with a weak smile. "You throw a good punch." he said. "I'm sorry."

"I get that you are." Ohanzee rolled his eyes, forgiving the fox already. "You look lovely in that blanket dress, by the way."

Adamar glared at him.

"Let's move past whatever that was." The coyote suggested. "Look around." he stood. "I'll go grab you some clothes."

Ohanzee went back into the infirmary, Adamar pulled himself up onto the cement bench and allowed his thoughts to drift away. He looked around.

He had been dragged out in a small, courtyard populated by a few other furs, all in various states of relaxation. Bushes danced around the space, blocking the view of what lay beyond the foliage, making the space seem calmer. A garden ran up against a building, where Rowena practiced medicine.

Ohanzee returned carrying Adamar's cloak, and tossed it at him.

As the setting sun warmed his face, Adamar started to wonder how many days had gone by in total. He accounted for the trip over the mountains, Galliv, and lastly, his injury that gave him no doubt time had slipped away. Nine days gone by, including today.

The fox sighed and focused his thoughts on Miro. He wondered how his pup was doing, and whether or not someone was adequately taking care of Miro. He hoped that if someone was, they were doing a good job of it. They better be.

With images of Miro coursing through his mind, the thought of Rowena's kit, Chilo, appeared. How had Chilo endured Girbindon's wrath for years? Did he know where his mother was? Who she was?

"Hey, Adamar," Ohanzee said, coming up to him and startling him out of his stupor. "Rowena told me that you have to drink this. It'll help the pain."

Adamar eyed suspiciously a bottle that Ohanzee held out. "It's not poison, is it?"

Ohanzee chuckled. "No, Rowena doesn't want to kill you for this morning. She actually says she understands." The coyote shrugged. "She said it's a thing all parents with lost pups know."

Adamar drained the liquid, and soon felt a numbness settle over the more prominent aches in his body.

"The furs of Hile also say that they've all encountered Girbindon's small army at least once before." Ohanzee said.

"So then they know of Girbindon? That's different, compared to Eadageth." Adamar shifted on a wooden bench, in front of Rowena's shop, which he'd ventured out to after a few hours inside, resting, planning, and eating.

Ohanzee nodded. "Girbindon and the Darvin kingdom aren't too far from here. Which explains the wall they built around Hile. Girbindon attacks this place once a month. They don't know why."

"Maybe because of Hile's proximity to Darvin?" Adamar suggested. "Easy land to conquer because of that, if that's what Girbindon wants to do."

"Could be."

A voice shouted.

"Why are you talking about Girbindon?"

Ohanzee whirled around to see a two-legged horse walking closer to them, wearing a leather apron that could only suggest the horse was a blacksmith. The smell of metal and the red-hot iron tool the horse held in his hand confirmed the assumption.

"What's your business with that fiend?" The horse asked, and stopped before Ohanzee and Adamar.

"Why do you want to know?" Adamar responded, uneasily eyeing the crowd that began to form around them.

The horse stamped his hoof into the ground. "You're not thinking of going after that bear, are you? Because we've had some of our own furs try to kill Girbindon. We've never seen them again." The horse snorted and glared at Adamar and Ohanzee. "You two look like the next sorry creatures to be torn apart by Girbindon."

Ohanzee's ears faced backwards. "And what if we are? How does it matter to you? We're just furs passing through."

The horse gestured to the bandages on Adamar. "By the looks of it, you aren't."

Ohanzee looked at the furs standing and chattering around them. "Furs of Hile," he said, raising his voice to be heard better. "We don't mean you any harm. If you would please just stop speaking about us."

Adamar grit his teeth. "That's only going to work against us, Ohanzee."

The coyote flinched. "Sorry."

Adamar's ears pricked as whispers began to float toward him and Ohanzee.

"They're crazy for even thinking of that idea."

"They'll die out there."

"But they don't care. They're insane."

Adamar noticed that the horse had melted into the crowd, and felt cornered once again as the furs of Hile gathered together to see the commotion.

"We're not crazy!" Adamar shouted, his gaze searching the crowd for a kind face.

Someone asked, "Isn't he the one that disturbed Nurse Rowena? I heard he went insane."

The whispers and taunts grew until Ohanzee and Adamar got up to leave. The furs blocked their way, but then Hmo appeared and guided them through the crowd.

Hmo was silent until he'd brought the two into the front room of Rowena's shop.

The bat crossed his arms. "You can see why it's a good idea to not share your intents in public. I don't think there are any furs from Girbindon here, but if this was a town that wasn't a fortress, then that event could have finished totally different." Hmo left.

Thirty-Six

A ball of fluff slammed into Adamar's uninjured leg, making him jump.

After Hmo had left, Adamar and Ohanzee discussed how much they missed their pups and their exact strategy for attacking Girbindon. Rowena tended to her patients, occasionally asking Ohanzee and Adamar if they needed anything. She gave Ohanzee a drink for his arm, which had begun to hurt again. Adamar watched her gaze each time she came over, but the jackal always had a calm, neutral expression, to Adamar's relief and worry.

Adamar looked down and saw a small wolf puppy grinning up at him. The wolf was panting from a run in mud, mud that was smeared all over his pure white fur. The youngling's blood-red eyes startled Adamar.

"You know," the youngling said, dragging a wooden sword at his side, "I don't think you're stupid. I think you're brave for getting ready to fight that big, mean bear!" The wolf pup scrunched up his nose as he caught scent of Adamar's healing leg wound. He cautiously poked the bandage with the edge of his wooden sword. Adamar managed to stifle a flinch. The wound wasn't hurting nearly as much as earlier, thanks to Rowena's amazing healing skills.

The fox smiled down at the pup. "Hey," Adamar said, and tussled the fur between the wolf's ears. "What're you doing?"

The wolf looked up at Adamar, his head tilted as he considered the question. "I'm telling you that you're brave."

Adamar chuckled. "Thank you."

The wolf's tail wagged with glee. "You're very tall. How'd you get to be so tall?"

"Oh, Sky, stop bothering strangers." Rowena chided, coming over and picking up the wolf, who squealed and began to squirm in her grip.

"Put me down! I want to talk to the fox!" The wolf began smacking Rowena with his sword.

Rowena growled and put a hand around the wolf's muzzle. Sky whined, but stopped squirming. The jackal dropped her hand.

"Sorry about that." Rowena apologized, keeping a firm grip on the wolf. "He's a little rambunctious sometimes." Rowena took in the smells of the room, and glanced at Sky. "That, and dirty! Sky! I told you to not play in the mud."

Adamar and Ohanzee laughed, delighting in the wolf pup's antics.

"I'll just put him outside...and lock the door." Rowena gave the wolf a glare before she turned to go.

"He wasn't bothering us," Adamar said, trying to ignore his eagerness for the wolf pup to stay. The wolf reminded him of Miro, only older. "We can watch over him while you tend to other furs." The fox wouldn't admit how welcome the distraction would be, from Miro and Girbindon and his leg and Avaha and his nightmares.

Rowena glanced at the coyote and fox, and then at Sky, who nodded in agreement. "Please, Miss Rowena?" the wolf asked.

With a sigh, Rowena set Sky down on the ground. The wolf pup ran to Ohanzee and Adamar, tail waving furiously.

"He's actually named Skyor, but he likes to be called Sky." Rowena said, and sent a stern glance to the pup. "Be good."

Sky smiled as she walked away. "I'm called Sky because I'll go as high as the sky!" he exclaimed, and tried to climb onto Adamar's lap.

Adamar grimaced when Sky stepped on his foot, and gently pushed the wolf over to the coyote. "Go bother Ohanzee."

Once Sky had efficiently stabbed Ohanzee with his sword and deemed him not a threat, the wolf pup plopped down in front of the two archers. He looked up at them inquisitively. "Where did you come from?" Sky asked, ears pricked forward.

"Eadageth. It's almost the entire way on the other side of the Land." Ohanzee answered.

Sky began asking various questions about life in Eadageth, and became particularly passionate when Adamar mentioned how both of them usually carried around a bow and arrow.

"Arrows?" The wolf pup said, standing. He stabbed his wooden weapon into an imaginary foe. "Swords are better than arrows! Swords are stronger!"

Adamar leaned forward, his elbows on his knees. "Can a sword fly as far as an arrow?"

The wolf's determined face dissolved into concentration. "No, but a sword could if someone used magic."

Adamar chuckled. He wasn't going to deny that magic existed, but he wasn't going to confirm it either. He had no knowledge about it, so he couldn't say whether it existed or not.

Ohanzee, on the other hand, seemed to be enthralled by the prospect of sorcery.

"Magic?" The coyote repeated. "What kind of magic? Is it the kind that made your fur so white?"

The wolf pup giggled. "It could be. But Rowena said I was born this way. So isn't that magic too?"

Ohanzee tilted his head, watching the wolf pup as he pranced around, sparring with invisible enemies. "Where are your parents, Skyor?" the coyote asked, his voice quiet.

Sky glanced at Ohanzee. "Rowena told me that they were jealous of my fur. So they gave me away when I was littler." The wolf pup walked over to Ohanzee. "That was over three years ago, she said."

Ohanzee's ears flicked back. "And how old are you now, Sky?"

Sky held up the number of fingers that corresponded to his age. "Four," he said proudly, and then looked at the two. "How old are you?"

"I'm twenty-five, Ohanzee's twenty-seven." Adamar tussled the fur between the wolf's ears. "But those are just ages."

Sky stabbed the wooden floor with his sword. "Can we go play outside? I want to run in the dirt again. Miss Rowena says I shouldn't, but it's still a lot of fun. Can we go? Please?"

Adamar laughed, but shook his head. "Sorry, Sky, we can't. Neither of us would be able to run too well. You'd beat us."

Sky growled and crossed his arms. "That's what all the big furs say."

Ohanzee and Adamar exchanged a glance. The coyote leaned forward and gently tapped Sky on the shoulder, bringing the wolf's attention to him.

"Hey, Sky, we understand that many adults have probably told you that you'll beat them, so they don't have to spar with you. Adamar's foot is hurt and my arm aches from an old injury. We honestly would if we could, but we can't." The coyote offered a sad smile.

Sky looked at Adamar's foot, and cautiously put his hand against the bandage wrapping the fox's foot. Sky withdrew his palm, but glanced once more at it with a curious gaze.

Sky sighed and said, "Then can you tell me a story?"

"Sure." Adamar said.

"I've heard furs talk of something they call the Far-reaching War, especially when that big scary bear attacks us every month, like the scary bear will start another war. What are they talking about? What's the Far-reaching War?"

Adamar explained. "It was a war that spanned over the entirety of the Land. It nearly destroyed every single fur ever alive. Some species of furs did go extinct over the course of the fighting."

"Why did it happen?" Sky pulled himself into Ohanzee's lap.

"Furs got greedy when disaster ravaged one of the islands close to here." Adamar said. "A long time ago, longer than many can remember, a giant wave came over an island and completely destroyed it, killing many furs as well as destroying the chief exports of that island. The furs on this island, Kleak, became sick from the debris that was piling up everywhere. As their bodies grew ill, so did their minds.

"The furs began to steal from one another and kill each other as ways of gaining the supplies that they needed to survive. Some furs that hadn't been affected as badly by the illness tried to organize a system so food could be passed around equally. This started out well but failed terribly."

Adamar noticed that the other furs waiting for Rowena's care were watching him. The fox saw no hostile expressions and smelled nothing other than curiosity, so he continued.

"There were varying numbers of the species of furs who lived on Kleak. Furs began to divide the food among them, a good idea, except that different species got different treatment.

"Many aquatic furs lived on Kleak. These furs, such as the dolphins that live there now, had varying eating habits. Species such as sharks and even the non-aquatics that were there, any fur that had an ancestor who could go without food for a little while would be put on the bottom of the food waiting list.

"This caused civil war. Furs began to fight over the food. It was chaos. The queen's army tried to break up the fighting, but they couldn't stop it.

"Soon this war spread here, when furs from Kleak had gone to a neighboring island and then, from there, migrated here. Luckily, they didn't bring the illnesses, but they brought their weapons."

Adamar paused. The pain didn't ebb too much from his foot now. "The war spread across the Land. It was everywhere. You couldn't turn without seeing an enemy waiting to kill you. Furs tried to figure out ways to stop this—furs who had high positions in the queen's palace and were thus protected from this madness—so they turned to using, I believe, furs who had great skill and used their strengths from something they were born with. I'm rusty on this part, so I think the old histories that say they were born with this skill meant something like their minds; they were born with powerful minds." Or maybe with the magic Sky had mentioned, Adamar thought with amusement.

"A method was put into place, and it was using these furs to either eliminate the fighters or to stop them from fighting. Somehow, this worked, but only for a little while. After a while of this method, fighters began to get smart, and so they stole these skilled furs and used them against their enemies.

"Different species had different skills, which

meant that there were a few species that excelled in having powerful minds. As these species were captured for the fighters' use, they were worked to death, and so these species, as well as their ancestors, started to go extinct. Griffins, dragons, okapis, were nearly all but dead by the time the Far-reaching War ended."

"How did it end?" Sky asked. He leaned forward in his eagerness to know what happened next.

"It ended with a fur with amazing skill sending something across the Land. I don't know what it was, as I say it now it sounds like it could only have been magic, but it stopped the war completely. That was good. The Land and those still alive began to recuperate, and realize just how much damage had happened during the war.

"Many species had gone extinct. You will never see an ancestor dragon in the sky, nor an okapi roaming the forests. Furs were completely obliterated from the land. It is legendary to see a fur whose ancestors had been persecuted during the Far-reaching War, especially if you gain the chance to talk to them.

"Once the war had settled, furs began to choose where they would live again, and it ended up with furs staying in specific regions. You'll see wolves and coyotes like yourself and Ohanzee on the mainland, and if you go to the islands, you'll see aquatic furs, or furs that are able to withstand much warmer climates.

"That wasn't anyone's intent, but that's how it remains today."

Adamar fell silent as the last words of the retold history reverberated throughout the room.

Sky spoke, breaking the silence. "Adamar, what's a shark?"

Adamar looked down at the curious wolf and gave a small, relieved smile.

Thirty-Seven

"You didn't have to watch over Skyor." Rowena said, pulling up a bench and sitting down across from Ohanzee and Adamar.

"It wasn't much of a difficulty. He was fairly calm for a young pup." Ohanzee said. Night had fallen and many furs had left. Skyor had been sent to his room, carrying a book of drawings of different species of furs and their ancestors.

The jackal smiled tiredly. "Nevertheless, it was appreciated. With this weather growing colder, more furs have been slipping and coming down with illness. I've been fairly busy." she shot a glance at Adamar, who shrunk back, sheepish.

"I heard about what happened earlier." Rowena went on. "I'm sorry to admit this, but you must expect at least a small amount of that teasing for the rest of your stay in Hile. Girbindon hasn't attacked in over a month, so the entire city's uneasy."

Adamar's ears pricked. "Do you know why that is? Why he attacks?"

Rowena sighed. "I, actually, do. But it is something you two must agree to never mention to anyone outside this room. It might upset the usual peace that's in Hile. You can know because you're not from here, and you're not staying for long.

"When I was about to give birth to Chilo, I had complications. As you know, Adamar." Rowena's eyes were downcast. "Girbindon helped, but he helped by using magic. After the process, he mentioned how there were two kinds of magic: bad and good. Or, more as he liked to call them: dark and blankness."

"Blankness?" Ohanzee asked. "Wouldn't that be light?"

Rowena met his inquisitive gaze. "Girbindon mentioned blankness. For now, I'm just going to call it that." she continued her story. "The reason that I can't find a better source is that, I believe, there are books on magic, the use of, the history, everything, locked away in Hile's library. The king of Hile keeps them away from public sight, down in a section of the library he calls 'the archives,' so no one suspects anything."

The jackal paused. "A likely reason that Girbindon attacks Hile so often is because he wants these magic books destroyed. I think that Girbindon knows how to use both dark and blankness magic, but prefers the darker side of magic. Since he prefers this, and he wants to conquer more of the Land, he wants these books destroyed so the blankness side of magic can never be revived and used against him."

"Girbindon used dark magic on you?" Ohanzee inquired.

"I certainly hope he didn't. He never said which he used. But I'm worried that it could have affected Chilo."

Adamar tilted his head, mulling over something Rowena had said. "Rowena," he asked. "What do you mean that Girbindon wants to conquer more land?"

"Every time Girbindon would attack, he'd have his warriors yell battle cries that always mentioned how the bear would conquer everything. So I'm assuming that Girbindon is eager to do so."

Ohanzee and Adamar looked at each other. "Girbindon's reasons for taking Miro might be bigger than we thought." the coyote said.

Adamar nodded miserably.

Rowena glanced at the two of them. "Well, I'm sorry for that saddening piece of news. But Ohanzee, if you wouldn't mind, could you go upstairs? I'd like to speak to Adamar in private for a little while. It's nothing that you should worry about. Besides, you'll need to rest for fighting Girbindon."

Ohanzee sighed, bid them a good night, and disappeared.

"Come sit," Rowena said, pulling two chairs away from a fireplace.

Adamar pushed himself to standing, and with effort, limped over to one of the padded seats, into which he collapsed, grimacing as his foot protested.

Rowena went into a back room, and came out a few moments later with two steaming mugs of tea. Adamar accepted one with a grateful smile, and cupped his hands around the warm mug. He sipped carefully at it.

The canine crossed her legs and looked at Adamar. "How has your foot been throughout the day?"

Adamar shrugged. "It still hurts a little, but it feels a lot better."

"I would expect that. You know you really shouldn't be putting weight on it. Staying in bed and letting it heal will be a faster process in the long run." Rowena advised. "I know that we can heal much faster than our ancestors, but that doesn't mean you can be careless."

Adamar's gaze was on his tea. "It's just that I don't have the time to rest. With searching for Girbindon and Miro, time has slipped away."

"You don't find time, you make time." Rowena replied and took a sip of her own tea. "Speaking of Girbindon, are you doing alright, now that you've gotten past this morning's episode?"

Adamar stared into his mug. "Yeah. Sorry. I didn't know why—"

"I get it." Rowena said, cutting him off. "I understand why you did that."

"What?" Adamar looked up, surprised.

"You heard me." The jackal responded. "I get it. You miss Miro. You're in pain. And I'm connected to who took your pup."

Adamar was silent for a moment. "I suppose."

Rowena smiled. "Hey, it's okay. Everyone has outbursts. Even the calmest furs cannot contain their anger all the time. They just may not express their outbursts in a way you can notice."

"I appreciate your not throwing me out." Adamar said. He sighed, feeling the pulsing pain start to climb up his leg again. Pain or no pain, he had to leave soon for Miro. "I believe I should go, so you can get some sleep as well."

"Go?" Rowena smiled. "You'd go about ten feet to your room over there. Anyways, I've some thoughts about fighting Girbindon."

Adamar cocked his head. "You do?"

"Yes. And it actually comes from Sky. I don't particularly prefer the tactic, but you might think otherwise."

Adamar nodded slowly. "Sky said something about how his parents had given him away. Is that true?"

"Unfortunately, it is. Sky's parents didn't want an albino pup, so they left him here when he was very young. I've been caring for him ever since."

Adamar flicked his ears back in anger. "What kind of parents would do that? I know that he would have problems hunting, but in the winter, he'd be a wonderful asset. And besides that, there's nothing wrong with him."

Rowena shrugged. "Some furs just care about their public appearance too much. Luckily, though, Sky doesn't, which makes it easy for me to watch over him. His tactic is that when he spars with someone, he runs straight at them. He doesn't try dodging or sneaking up on them, like you'd expect.

"You probably won't use that tactic, but nevertheless, I'm going to suggest that you at least think about it when you're getting close to Darvin."

Adamar turned the idea over in his mind. "Why? When Sky employs that, does it work?"

"If the fur has never faced Sky before, it does. Which could help you, if you fight Girbindon only one time. But I fear that that will not be so." Rowena placed her empty mug at the foot of her chair.

"Girbindon may be cruel, but he is clever. He usually does not do things without having a plan for them, first. I do not know why he took your pup, though I can suspect it has something to do with magic. This could mean that more will be in store for you, if you want Girbindon dead. He'll use magic at his disposal. He has a lot of power with magic, and is not afraid to use it when he wants to."

Adamar sighed. "This will not be one battle."

"No, it won't. And, for future reference, magic was the skill all the persecuted furs had in the Far-reaching War."

Rowena stood and left Adamar alone. The fire crackled as Adamar gripped the mug tightly in his hands. He kept drinking the tea, even as it grew cold, something he didn't notice.

Darkness blanketed the fox while he stared into the dying flames.

Getting Miro back was going to be a greater problem than he thought. Killing Girbindon would be another challenge altogether.

Thirty-Eight

"Adamar, wake up." Ohanzee said near the fox's ears.

Adamar fell out of the chair where he'd spent the night, nearly smacking his head on the stone fireplace. He groaned and turned over onto his back, noticing Ohanzee standing over him, watching him curiously.

A ball of fluff appeared behind the coyote. Sky pounced onto Adamar, and sat on the fox's chest as he pointed the end of his wooden sword at Adamar's vulnerable throat.

"Die, fox! I will defeat you when we spar today." Sky growled, a playful look crossing his snout. "So can we? Can we play?"

Adamar stared at the ceiling, feeling the weight of the wolf sit heavily on his ribcage. "Sky, get off."

"Never!" The wolf jabbed his sword into Adamar's throat.

Even though it was only made out of wood, Adamar snarled as the sword nearly hit his jugular. When he forced himself to relax, he noticed that the wolf had jumped off and was hiding behind Ohanzee's legs, white tail tucked between his own legs.

Adamar rolled over onto his stomach, and pushed himself to a standing point. He shook out his leg. His foot had continued to heal overnight, but it was stiff from sleeping in a chair.

His ears flicked back and he walked to the hiding wolf. He crouched to the wolf's eye level. "I'm sorry for scaring you, Sky." Adamar said. These outbursts were getting out of hand. "You accidentally struck a sensitive area. You know how your nose is sensitive?"

The wolf nodded, watching Adamar with naked fright.

"So your throat is also sensitive, too. There's no protection of your throat, other than your flesh and fur. And since I'm not a reptile, I don't have scales over my throat, which makes it all the more vulnerable. That's why I reacted like I did."

A dark shadow moved across the room.

Adamar rose and saw Hmo standing behind Ohanzee, watching calmly with his arms crossed over his chest. Adamar expected the bat was there to reprimand him further for yesterday's outburst.

"Your arrows were destroyed when you fell down that ditch." Hmo said, looking at Adamar. "You need more. I've found that there's a fletcher in Hile, whom we're going to visit. He's supposed to be extremely good at fashioning weapons."

Adamar nodded, and glanced at Sky. "Can he come?" the fox asked Hmo. He wanted to show the wolf pup that he wasn't scary. And besides, he liked the wolf's company.

Hmo considered the idea. "No. There are weapons there. You'll have to stay with Rowena, wolf."

The wolf pup growled. "I want to come. No one ever lets me go anywhere."

Something flickered across Hmo's face, and the bat looked down at the pouting Sky. "Alright." Hmo said, scooping up the wolf and holding him in his arms. "I'll take you out to the fields of Hile. We can spar there." Hmo glanced at Adamar. "Follow the scent of wood. That'll lead you to Briscoe's place."

As Hmo walked away carrying the happy wolf, Adamar and Ohanzee stared after him, not able to believe what they had just seen.

Ohanzee looked at Adamar after a moment. "You watched that too, right?"

The fox nodded slowly. "Yeah...let's get to that fletcher's place before things get stranger."

Adamar limped down a dirt path that ran along the edge of one of Hile's surrounding walls. The stone fortress blocked out most of the woody scent from nearby forests, but Adamar caught the thickening smell of oak, pine, and other trees as he grew closer to the fletcher's shop.

Up ahead stood a simple, small house that looked like it was mostly unoccupied: windows were cracked and the roof was falling in. A paddock rested against the house, and had a lone horse grazing in it, occasionally flicking at the flies with its tail. Next to the house sat a larger barn, with wood just inside the doorway.

Adamar knocked on the doorframe. "Is Briscoe here?" he shouted.

A wildcat stepped into view, wearing a leather apron. The cat sneezed, and shook sawdust off his sandy fur. "Yes, that's me." He looked at the fox and coyote. "What do you want?"

Adamar kept his weight on his good foot, and stood straighter. "We heard that you make good arrows, and we're looking to buy a quiver full of them."

The wildcat narrowed his eyes. He noticed Adamar's injury. "What happened to you? Are you an enemy that decided it was high time to sneak into Hile and raid all that we have?"

Ohanzee shook his head. "We intend to do nothing of the sort. We're just here for arrows."

The cat huffed, but turned and beckoned for them to follow.

Adamar walked into the wildcat's workspace, and immediately noticed just how vast the place was.

A large fire dominated one of the longer sides of the barn, where wood was stacked, ready to be burnt, and a small fire was dancing inside the rocky alcove. Various types of wood were stacked along the wall opposite the fire, their colors and sizes shifting and changing as much as the clouds that rolled across the sky. Tools were piled into messy heaps and spilled onto a cloth-covered mass.

"So you need arrows?" Briscoe asked as he stoked the fire.

"As soon as you can, please." Adamar said from a few feet behind the wildcat. Ohanzee's canine nose had taken him to the canvas mass, and he was lifting up the edge of it to look beneath when a knife flew at him.

The coyote yelped and jumped out of the way. He glanced with wide eyes at Briscoe, who offered a glare.

"Do not investigate what is not said to be investigated." The wildcat hissed. He looked to Adamar. "What kind of arrow are you looking for? Thin, fast, heavier for more damage?

"Just arrows, really, Briscoe. We need them as quickly as possible." Adamar said. He had to leave soon, and couldn't be held up by making a specialized arrow.

"Just arrows?" The wildcat repeated, and threw his hands into the air. "Just arrows, and you call yourself archers?" He glared at the two. "Where are you from?"

"Eadageth." Ohanzee met Briscoe's gaze.

"Eadageth..." Briscoe muttered and turned to his piles of wood. "How about we try something different? What are you looking to do with your arrow? Are they just practice arrows, or do you need them for something else?"

Adamar spoke his words quietly. "We're going to fight Girbindon with them. Girbindon, the fur that's been attacking Hile. We need good piercing and killing arrows."

"I know who he is, fox. And I'll tell you, you're going to have a good chance of failing. But I'll make the arrows anyway. I don't like refusing service to well-meaning furs."

Adamar gave Briscoe the required dimensions, and turned to go.

"You're not leaving just yet, orange fox and small coyote." Briscoe disciplined, a knife in his hand and a thick piece of wood in the other. He began whittling an arrow shaft down to size, and gestured at two stools with his blade. "You two are going to watch, so you can learn for when you go back home, maybe teach those Eadageth furs a little about arrows."

Adamar and Ohanzee restrained their displeased reactions to the insults and occupied the two stools.

Silence thickened the air for a few minutes as Briscoe worked, wood shavings falling to his feet, and the branch becoming thinner, more arrow-like.

Briscoe looked up at the two, his whiskers twitching. His knife didn't stop moving.

"You two can talk while you're in my presence." Briscoe said. "It's not like I'm to punish you for doing so. Not like I have much authority though, I'm just the wildcat who makes weapons."

So Ohanzee asked, "Briscoe, how long should making these arrows take?"

Briscoe shrugged. "I'm to make this first one, and then I'll have a model for the rest of them. Not long. Probably by the time the sun goes down, you'll have your arrows."

"I hope Girbindon can wait that long." Ohanzee said. "I think the time has passed for you to find Miro."

Adamar's ears went back in fear. It had? How out of it had he been, on the mountain? He didn't want to think about the time anymore, even though the thought was constantly bothering him, making his mind race. "Maybe Girbindon's decided to be generous."

"What do you have to do with that bear, since you're killing him?"

"He has my kit. I'm going to get Miro back." the fox answered.

Briscoe chuckled and went back to his whittling. "Say goodbye to your kitten. You're going to have a hard time of finding him. I'm not saying you can't, I'm just saying you won't find the same kit that was taken from you however long ago it was. He'll have changed by then, even if he had been a newborn. No one goes to Girbindon and comes out unscathed."

"Do you think we should stop trying to find Miro?" Not that he would stop even if the wildcat said a resounding yes.

Briscoe rubbed wax over the arrow shaft to protect it from wet weather. Or blood. He opened a black pot hung over the fire. "I prefer to make arrows the way I've found has been the most successful, whether anyone agrees with me or not." the wildcat explained. Briscoe pulled the top off the pot, and steam blasted into his fur. He began slowly warming the arrow over coals, turning it while he spoke.

"Do I?" Briscoe echoed. "Why do you care about my opinions? You just met me. How could I matter to you? How can you know that, if I have some opinions, they're any good?"

"Still, though. Do you think we should stop?" Ohanzee asked out of curiosity.

Briscoe rolled the arrow over the heat. "You're too far along in your quest to stop. You'd come all this way and just go back home? What kind of courage is that?" The wildcat shook his head. "Keep going. You're almost there. No point in going back now."

Briscoe pulled the arrow away from the fire and laid it on a cooling rack. He pulled his knife out and carved a notch in the back of the shaft.

The wildcat gestured to a bucket sitting next to the fire. "Go and take that out to feed Enki. He's the horse in the pasture."

Ohanzee stood and did so.

"Do you feel ready to take on Girbindon? You seem doubtful." Briscoe asked, not looking up from his work.

Adamar shrugged. "As ready as I can be."

"You'll want to be. He isn't a bear to mess with. I should know."

Adamar's ears pricked, and he looked over at where the wildcat was beginning to shape a metal arrowhead. "What do you mean?"

"I didn't choose to make weapons without having known what it's like to use these weapons." Briscoe said. "This intruding wall in Hile wasn't here ten years ago. But I was. I was twenty-four, and I joined Hile's band of warriors. We had a great time. We never went into battle. Except for right before the wall was created. Girbindon attacked, and it was one of the worst attacks he's dealt in the entirety of his hatred on Hile."

"So you fought Girbindon?" Adamar's curiosity was growing.

"I did." Briscoe replied, and picked up a metal tool to shape the arrowhead. "He was a tough one. I was one of the few to survive. He used this...skill that none of us, except me, knew of back then. If I say, you'll never know. So don't ask."

Yet Adamar leaned closer. Rowena's warning drifted in his thoughts. "Was it magic?"

Briscoe dropped his arrowhead in surprise, and yowled as the sparks hit his flesh. He turned to Adamar, eyes wide and fur bristling. "How do you know of it?"

When Adamar didn't answer, Briscoe scowled. He started to smell of contempt. But as he looked back at the fox, the wildcat's gaze softened and the smell faded. "There is something you should know, that Girbindon might try to use on you. If he knows you're coming, he could bring out horses."

"Horses?" The fox repeated, wondering if Briscoe had lost his mind. "You mean like the one Ohanzee's feeding?"

Ohanzee walked back in, and set the empty bucket down. He glanced at the two with a curious expression. "What're you talking about? Something about me and horses?"

Briscoe picked up his work, putting a design into the metal. "Girbindon has found a way to give magic to ancestors that originally did not have the power of magic. He's only been able to do it with horses, so far, which is probably because of their large chests. I think he also only wants ancestors that are regularly used for war." he set the arrowhead to cool and began rooting around in various spots in the barn. As he searched, he continued to explain. "If one of his horses has a white star on its forehead, there is a good chance that it is imbued with magic. The horse cannot control this magic, unless it is trained to do so, or if it is entirely white, like my horse is.

"Girbindon does not train his horses. So they are wild beasts that only listen to their riders and will kill anything they are designated to destroy."

Briscoe sat back on his stool, holding a few darkly colored ancestor feathers in his hand. He attached the feathers to the end of the arrow, and then took off a ribbon that he had been hiding beneath the fur on his tail. Briscoe put the ribbon around the arrow's fletchings, and murmured words beneath his breath.

"What are—" Ohanzee's question died away as a deep purple surrounded the feathers on the back of the arrow, stemming from the ribbon. The purple swirled, and disappeared as quickly as it had come.

Briscoe smiled, put his ribbon back on his tail, and ran his fingers along the edge of the arrow. "Magic."

He handed the arrow to Adamar, who turned it over as he inspected it.

The arrow didn't weigh much. Its arrowhead was made of a similar weight of metal, and sunken into it was the image of a flower, its petals dancing around the head. The feathers at the end of the shaft were dark ancestor duck feathers.

The fox handed the arrow back.

Briscoe began whittling the shaft for the next arrow. "Your arrows will be strong, but not too heavy, and I'll put a bit of magic in a few so the arrow will fly without a chance of being disturbed by the wind. It should hit its target."

Ohanzee looked at Briscoe. "How did you learn all this? And get this magic?"

The wildcat's tail rocked with proud glee. "Reading lets you be what you want to be. Hile's library used to be a great place."

"Used to be?" asked Adamar.

"Before the king of Hile put some books into archives and kept them away from the public eye. The magic books are in the archives now. They detail much history about both sides of magic, and talk about how some are born with the skill of a sorcerer, and some are not. One of the books was a guide on how to be somewhat of a sorcerer, even if you aren't born with this skill. It described what tools to use to get some magic."

Briscoe picked up another piece of wood. "I used that book. You saw that this ribbon I wear has magic in it."

Adamar and Ohanzee listened in awe. "How would you know that someone has the power of a sorcerer?" the fox asked.

Briscoe shrugged. "That page was ripped out of the book. Just gone. I don't know what happened to it."

"Is there any way to access the archives now?" Ohanzee said.

"Sadly, no." Briscoe shook his head, turning the shaft. "Only the king is allowed to go down there. And he'll never go."

"Could you bring up the issue with the king, and maybe ask if he'll release the magic books?"

Briscoe laughed. "It's obvious you're from Eadageth. If you unlock the archives, the furs in Hile will be curious and know about the unveiling. So they will look through the books, and if they find magic, there could be problems. I only found the books when I got lost, before the king locked them away. Books now in the archives have always been in the shadows. Furs never knew about them...because they're all ignorant idiots."

Adamar and Ohanzee were quiet for a moment.

"Could we see your horse, Briscoe?" Adamar asked. "Just to see what we're up against."

The wildcat set down his work and slipped the knife into a pocket in his leather apron.   "You can." Briscoe said. "And it'll be fun."

Briscoe's horse looked up as the three furs approached.

The horse's coat was as white as Sky's. Briscoe had Adamar and Ohanzee wait at the edge as he slipped through the fence, a halter and lead in hand.

As soon as Briscoe stepped into the pasture, his horse dashed off, intent on making Briscoe chase him. The wildcat scowled and ran after his horse, chasing him around the paddock.

Adamar and Ohanzee laughed at the spectacle.

When Briscoe eventually caught his horse, he slipped a halter over its head, swung up onto its back, and rode bareback over to the waiting furs.

The horse snorted and dipped its head toward Adamar and Ohanzee.

"This is Enki." Briscoe affectionately patted his horse's neck. "He's completely imbued with magic."

"What does that mean, exactly?" Ohanzee stroked Enki's nose.

"It means that more magic went into him than if he was only partially affected by it. It's in his blood a much greater deal. His whole body being white indicates that. It also means that he gets more power than other horses. He gallops faster, has a greater stamina, is stronger, and also can do this little trick. Back away."

Adamar and Ohanzee stepped out of range, away from the fence, and Briscoe had Enki rear.

Enki's hooves cried through the air, sparks flying off them, some hitting Briscoe's house and scorching the wood. When the horse planted all four of his hooves on the ground, a thunderclap echoed overhead, and the horse swished his tail happily. Adamar shivered at the sound of thunder.

Briscoe dismounted and offered the two furs a ride, insisting when they both refused. Ohanzee got on Enki and gripped the horse's mane and lead in his hands, his legs tense against the horse's sides. The coyote looked at Briscoe for instructions.

"When riding a horse affected by magic, you will be able to notice a change in them. Though ancestor horses are already quite intelligent, Enki is even more so. And he will take advantage of you the minute you stop concentrating on what you want him to do.

"This also means that if you're thinking something, it better not be fear." Briscoe rested his elbows on the fence. "Tell him to walk. He will only listen to the fur riding him, and no one else. Unless he deems you an enemy."

Ohanzee applied pressure to the horse's sides, and Enki started off at a quick walk, following the fence that ran around the pasture. When Briscoe asked the coyote to increase the horse's speed, Enki jumped right from a walk to a canter. Ohanzee's ears folded down sheepishly, and had the horse slow to a trot.

Adamar glanced at Briscoe. "What just happened?" he asked, storing the information for when he confronted Girbindon.

Briscoe kept his gaze on his horse as he answered Adamar's question. "It seems that your friend likes to ride fast. Ohanzee wanted to do more than just a trot. So Enki responded accordingly. Somewhere in the recesses of your friend's mind, there was the suppressed urge to canter, which Enki sensed."

Adamar chuckled. "Ohanzee seems stuck in between a pup and an adult sometimes."

Briscoe twitched his whiskers, hissing unhappily. "He should get over that. Riding a horse with magic in it without being observant is not a good idea."

Adamar glanced at the wildcat, and defended his friend. "Ohanzee is observant. We all have our moments."

Briscoe dismissed him with a wave of the hand and climbed up onto the fence, where he perched, sitting casually on the wood. His tail swung in a lazy fashion behind him.

Briscoe called out across the pasture, and Ohanzee followed the wildcat's command, pushing Enki into a gallop. The horse tossed his head, and seemed to be restraining himself from something he desired.

Adamar watched as the horse kicked up swaths of dirt as he ran, Ohanzee on his back and making sure that falling off would not be an option.

The fox glanced at Briscoe, who was watching the scene with a knowing smirk. "Is that as fast as Enki can go?" Adamar asked.

Briscoe waited until Enki was running along the opposite end of the pasture, and then yelled, "Celertato!"

Enki whinnied triumphantly and leapt forward. His hooves appeared to barely touch the ground as he ran around the pasture with Ohanzee sitting on his back. When the horse had increased his speed, Ohanzee had yelped in fear, but a moment after that he'd caught onto the rhythm of the horse's gait, and was laughing with joy.

Adamar watched, amazed. "What did you just do, Briscoe?"

Briscoe laughed. "I had Enki go into another gait. That was a word from an old language, the ancestors' language. It means speed. So a horse's walk has four beats, a trot two, a canter three, and a gallop four. This speed has one beat. It's almost like he's flying."

"That's impossible."

"Look right in front of you, fox. I think that Enki states otherwise. Horses that aren't completely imbued with magic can't run this gait."

As if in response, Enki neighed.

Eventually Adamar and Briscoe left Ohanzee outside, as the coyote was thrilled to ride Enki, and the horse was having an equally great time. Adamar and Briscoe went back inside the cat's workspace, where Adamar helped whittle shafts while Briscoe outfitted them with fletchings and specially designed arrowheads.

Once twenty-four arrows fit snugly into Adamar's quiver, Briscoe had the fox practice with a target posted on the far end of the barn.

The sun had begun to gone down, but Adamar lifted his bow, notched an arrow, and pulled the bowstring back to the beginning of his muzzle.

He let go, and the arrow cut through the air. It corkscrewed as it flew, but it maintained its flight path, angling just slightly up above the target, and then getting pulled down by gravity until it drove into the middle of the bulls-eye.

Adamar stared at his bow, and began inspecting it to see what had caused a strange feeling from the bow when he'd loosed the arrow.

Briscoe crossed his arms, coming closer from where he stood, behind the fox. "That's the magic making it strange for you. What did it feel like?"

Adamar shook his head. "I don't know how to describe it. Just...different." But relief washed over him. He had arrows now. He had more of a fighting chance in getting Miro back.

"That's normal." The wildcat replied. "Magic is a strange thing. It has strange effects. All except for a few of those arrows are imbued with magic, so if you don't like using an arrow with magic, you aren't stuck with them. But when you do use one, it makes the projectile more deadly."

Adamar cocked his head. "Why is that?"

"Because when the arrow spins, it doesn't just stop spinning if it hits a target. It keeps spinning, even if not at the same speed. If something is spinning inside you, it will cause damage and rip apart more of your body."

Thirty-Nine

Night came and went, and turned into day.

Adamar woke to see Rowena bending over him, undressing the wound on his foot. The fox pushed himself up to a sitting position, curious to see what the wound looked like.

Rowena didn't make any acknowledgement of him while she pulled the last of the soiled bandages away and dumped them in a bucket of dirty cloth.

A smell of mixed herbs hit Adamar's nose as he leaned forward and observed the wound.

A gash at least an inch wide ran from his ankle to the top of his foot. The wound looked like something had gouged his flesh. The ends of it were pink, and a light scab had formed over it as it tried to heal. The center of the wound was a darker red, and was where Rowena began to apply a poultice.

The canine dipped her fingers into a jar of some cream, and gently worked it into the wound. Adamar gritted his teeth as pain flared, but stayed still, watching while Rowena worked.

Once she had efficiently covered the wound in a light coating of Rowena's special smear, she closed her jar and began to bind the wound, making sure that it was snug around Adamar's foot, but was also loose enough so the wound could breathe and heal faster.

"Drink up." Rowena handed a bottle to Adamar, who compliantly drank it, and gave the empty bottle back to Rowena.

He felt the pain in his foot lessen, and smiled

in relief. He waited for Rowena to leave so he could put on actual clothes.

Rowena gathered up her supplies and indicated the corner opposite the end of Adamar's cot. "There's some new clothes for you there. Yours were so torn and bloody that they had to be recycled."

Adamar nodded thankfully, and stood once Rowena had left. The fox stumbled over to the pile of cloth and shrugged on a new long-sleeve t-shirt and pants. He clasped a strip of fabric from one side of his pants to the other, over the base of his tail to keep his pants up, and shook out his fur, feeling the cloth settle nicely on his body.

Sky ran in just as Adamar was about to leave, wielding his sword and giggling. Rowena came after him, her arms outstretched as she tried to scoop up the mischief-causing wolf.

Adamar chuckled while Sky squealed and ran around. Sky grabbed the fox's leg and hid behind him.

"Sorry about that." Rowena said, while Adamar reached down and removed the wolf from his leg.

He held the wolf pup on his hip. "It's fine." his ears flicked back for a moment of anxiety; he had to leave. But he knew Rowena wouldn't let him go right now. So he offered, "I can take care of him this morning, if you need." Adamar moved his nose away from the point of Sky's sword.

Rowena nodded, and then glanced disapprovingly at Adamar standing on his foot. "You can, but only if you remain sitting down."

Adamar sighed and did as asked, resting on the edge of his bed with the wolf in his lap. Rowena nodded and disappeared. His thoughts drifted. He had to get to Miro. He couldn't keep sitting here and resting.

Adamar spent a couple hours with the wolf pup, and was surprised when he learned that Hmo had taught Sky how to read simple words. But he still read some of the stories in Sky's book to him, laughing when the wolf would jump to the floor and reenact some of the scenes he heard. Every so often, he would stand and walk around the small room to strengthen his foot and ankle. After the midday meal, Briscoe appeared, and had Adamar practice outside with the enchanted arrows, to Skyor's delight as he listed how his sword would be superior to these arrows.

Hmo and Ohanzee followed Briscoe's arrival. Ohanzee sat on the edge of Adamar's bed, holding Sky, while Hmo stood before them.

"I believe it is time we are off." The bat said. "Girbindon does not seem like a fur that will be patient. Your foot is better than it was, Adamar. And we are out of time."

Adamar nodded. "I've been wanting to leave since I woke up here. I want to get to Miro." As informative as Hile had been, he would be relieved to leave this town and get closer to Miro.

Sky cried out and struggled against Ohanzee's arms. "No!" The wolf pup's red eyes grew even redder with tears that soaked through his fur. "You can't go!"

Adamar looked at the wolf with a sad smile. "We don't have much of a chance, Skyor. It was fun being with you for a little while, but time has flown out of our reach."

The wolf whimpered and broke free of Ohanzee's grip, running straight at Adamar. "No! Please don't go!"

"Sky, we have to. You have your picture book. You can remember us through that."

"It won't be the same." Sky protested, meeting Adamar's gaze. "I don't want you to go."

Adamar glanced at Hmo for help. The bat shook his head and looked at Skyor.

"I will not say that we are sorry for having to go, Skyor." Hmo said. "For that would be inaccurate. However, I am saying you will do well without hanging around the adults all the time. The other pups may not take to you at first, but that doesn't mean it will be the same thing forever."

The wolf sniffed, but quieted, and oversaw the three furs' preparations to leave. Rowena had Adamar walk back and forth across her waiting room a few times, correcting him on how he walked, as to help him not reopen the wound. As he worked hard to strengthen the hurt muscles, Adamar could smell her displeasure at letting him leave so soon in his healing.

Hmo led him and Ohanzee over to the stables, on the other side of Hile. There he stuffed extra bandages Rowena insisted he take into Dakr's saddlebags.

The three saddled their horses, and swung up into the seats. Adamar felt his foot protest as he rested it in the stirrups, so he dropped his right stirrup, allowing his foot to sit mostly painlessly.

They rode their horses out into the city, robes settled over their shoulders and quivers slung across their backs. They trotted to one of the few openings in Hile that led to the outside. Two massive wooden doors stood in replacement of stone, traveling almost all the way up the wall, until they collided with a rocky bridge that crossed the top of the wall. Iron brackets ran across the doors. Hmo signaled a fur atop the wall to open the door.

Adamar felt a smile growing on his muzzle as he thought of how much closer to Miro he was. The reminder that Girbindon's allotted time had passed by tried to drown him, but he pushed it away.

Then the blacksmith from the other day ran in front of the doors and ordered them to stop.

Forty

"You cannot leave Hile. You will die out there." The two-legged horse snorted.

Hmo encouraged Olie closer and gazed down at the blacksmith. "That is not your business. Whether we survive our expedition or not should not matter to you."

The horse glared at Hmo. "And die right after you leave Hile? You'd tarnish this place's reputation." The equine fur glanced to his sides, where other furs were gathering and forming around him.

"You've no record of us. How could you? You barely know who we are." Hmo countered.

"There's more of us than you. That doesn't matter." The horse crossed his arms, smirking. At least twenty furs from Hile were standing behind him, some holding weapons, while others stretched their claws.

Hmo looked up to the furs that patrolled the top of the wall, ignoring those before him. "Open the gate!" he said.

No response.

As Hmo prepared to charge through the mass of furs, the blacksmith yelled a war cry and had his band rush forward. They attacked. Galene and Dakr reared in fright.

Adamar yelped as someone struck his injured foot. Someone yelled out the weak spot they'd found, and more furs ran towards Adamar, who was stuck in the mass of them. The fox pulled an arrow from his quiver and aimed it at anyone who was nearby in an attempt to scare them off.

Out of the corner of Adamar's eye he saw a canine-like figure run into a smaller door embedded in the towers of the gates. Rowena climbed the spiraling stairs in the tower until she reached where the guards of Hile were.

The chaos on the ground increased, only to be stopped by an echoing creak. The doors groaned as they began to swing outward. It became obvious to Adamar that many furs came in from the mountains, but did not exit out the other side, where Darvin was.

The large doors revealed a thin length of grassy field before the field gave way to a dense copse of trees.

The Hile furs turned, surprised, and the three mounted riders took the opportunity. They pressed their rides, urging them to dodge those that were frozen in shock and gallop through the gates.

Angry cries erupted, but few crossed through the doorway after them.

Ohanzee whooped in joy and ran toward the forest, his ears flopping back with the wind's strength. He gripped his bow and tightened the strap on his quiver of arrows, so it wouldn't bounce uncomfortably against his back.

Adamar smiled at the coyote's joy, but dread now rested in his mind, throbbing in the same time with the pain from his wound. What if they were going to die? What if Miro instead was the dead one?

Never.

Adamar shook his head to throw the thought out.

The three didn't have their horses break stride until they had crossed the border of the forest and were shrouded in shadows, out of sight of Hile. The village shrank behind them, and branches cracked beneath their horses' hooves.

As they headed toward Darvin, Adamar's mind drifted back to Miro. He hoped his kit still hadn't been harmed, and that he'd find him just as Miro had been before he'd been taken.

His mind told him that his anticipations were wrong.

Forty-One

Time passed by, yet the deer didn't show.

Miro sat up in his cell, his legs sprawled in front of him, tail curled loosely around his side. His stomach clawed at itself with hunger.

Miro strained to hear the sound of someone coming down the hall, toward him. He didn't smell anyone, either.

Silence drew on, and Miro felt the pain of his hunger ache at his ribcage. He started frantically wondering where the furs could be. He wanted the deer to come, but neither her nor the hen nor Chilo were in sight. Not even mean, scary Girbindon.

Maybe...Miro's mind danced into odd possibilities. Maybe his father had come and killed them all, so he could get to his kit.

But if he'd killed the deer, Miro wouldn't be pleased with that.

He whimpered as desperation grew in him. He curled into a ball, hugging his tail and sliding his thumb into his mouth.

"I've some news, Miro."

At the sound of someone's voice, the fox raised his head, only to growl when he saw that Girbindon was standing before him, dressed as classily as ever.

The bear placed his hands on his hips. "You will not growl at me, cub." Girbindon ducked inside the cell and pulled Miro out. The kit whined in response, but didn't protest further, knowing that doing so wouldn't end well.

Girbindon carried Miro to his throne room, where the bear seated himself in the elaborately decorated chair and placed Miro on his lap.

"Ecetal has a Magician's Lev, and so do I." Girbindon began.

Miro just watched the bear.

"Your father also has a Magician's Lev, Miro." The bear smirked and met Miro's gaze. "The side of magic I prefer has ways of controlling his, like with Ecetal. However, because your father isn't here right now, I can't take the fuel in his Magician's Lev. But I was able to use your blood, which is similar to his, to control him." The bear chuckled. "And it was joyful."

The bear went on. "I made your father very angry, and had him attack whoever was nearby. I imagine it must've been hilarious. When your father comes here, even though the time has already passed for him to retrieve you, I'll be sure to put a little more torture to him through the Magician's Lev, which he still doesn't know he has."

Miro twisted his head to look at the corridors hidden by tapestries, straining to see or smell the deer coming. He wasn't having fun and the deer was a lot kinder than Girbindon. When Girbindon attempted to force him to look at himself again, Miro grunted and squirmed in the bear's grip.

Despite Girbindon's commands, Miro didn't let up, only stopping when the bear grabbed him by the scruff and shook him.

"Shut up, you idiot." Girbindon held the writhing fox in the air, ignoring Miro's futile attempts to claw the bear's fingers away from his throat. "Your deer isn't here today."

Miro kicked out at the bear. Girbindon snarled and shook the fox again.

"When your father comes here, do you want him to be hurt even more than he will be?"

Girbindon dropped the fox to his lap. "Are you so stupid that you'd endanger your father's welfare?"

The bear paused in his tirade for a moment. "You probably don't care anyways." Girbindon stood and picked Miro up. The fox whimpered but didn't struggle this time, as he tried to ignore the pain in his empty stomach.

Girbindon brought Miro back to his cell. He locked the door with a disapproving expression, and left without giving Miro any food as if he intended to return some time later. But as the day dragged on and Miro's stomach shrank further, the kit began to doubt that anyone would ever see him again. His hunger-filled mind told him that life was over, that he'd die soon.

Then the hen came in with food and joy settled over him. He tore into a piece of bread with his tail thumping behind him.

Forty-Two

The scraping of a plate sliding across the floor stirred Ecetal, and he focused on the sound.

Girbindon was near, filling his bowl with food and leaving it in the corner, as he always did. The bear was muttering to himself. Ecetal tried to pay attention to the words, but his limited energy didn't aid him, and he sank into the comforts of being half-conscious.

"When the fox's father comes, you should be glad." Girbindon said.

Ecetal glanced at him through a barely open eye. The cage bars obscured the image of the bear, and in the dragon's occasionally delirious state, he was able to imagine the bars as swords that were hacking Girbindon to pieces.

Girbindon noticed the dragon's partial consciousness. "Morning, Ecetal. How's the day been?"

Ecetal ignored the prompt. "Why?" his voice was barely audible. Girbindon had been soaking up as much power as the dragon's Magician's Lev could give, without completely drawing the life from him. But the dragon nonetheless felt worse than usual.

"Why should you be glad when Miro's father comes?" Girbindon confirmed. "Because when the extraction happens, I won't have to use your power as much as before. You'll be able to rest, and it'll give you a chance to rationally think about options I am giving you."

Ecetal met the bear's gaze, his curiosity overriding the note his mind was sending: that he shouldn't trust a word of Girbindon's.

Girbindon smiled at his triumph of having captured the dragon's interest. "Once the extraction is complete, and successful, I will give you the chance of standing by my side and ruling with me. Your power and mine combined would make for a wonderful empire."

Ecetal's nostrils flared as he drew in a shuddering breath. "Your power is my power, not yours."

"I did forget about that." The bear responded. "So only a minor change can be made. You'll just have to continue giving me some of your power. You won't be as strong as you truly are, but you'll get out of that cage I know you adore."

Ecetal narrowed his eyes. "What about freedom?"

Girbindon laughed. "How funny. I'd let you not have to stay in that every day, but I'd still keep a tight grip on you, Ecetal. You wouldn't leave my side, like you didn't when we were younger."

That had been voluntary. Ecetal attempted to speak the words, but they slid off his tongue, and in his exhaustion, he had little reason to bother worrying about them. He closed his eyes.

"The arrival of Miro's father will be wondrous. I'll grow more powerful than ever before. Darvin will finally rule the land. We won't have to do as we did, what my father did, just struggling to keep this kingdom alive. I'll have power. Amazing power." Girbindon pulled a book from the shelves and paged through it. "But the annoying thing is, I have to get even more power just so the task can be completed. Once that's done, though, Ecetal, you'll be able to rest easy."

Ecetal searched his mind for questions to ask. He wasn't intent on Girbindon staying any longer, but the dragon concentrated on depleting any stock of energy he had. When Miro's father came, Girbindon would be immensely tapping into his and therefore the dragon's magic supply, and Ecetal wanted to be asleep for the potentially painful experience.

"How much power does the fox have?"

Girbindon glanced at him. "He has power. He's just a fox, though."

"Then why," Ecetal paused. "Why did you choose him?"

"You know the story of the Far-reaching War." Girbindon said. "Because the Magician's Lev died out in everyone. It's extremely rare to see it nowadays. I had to pick one that had a young cub, young enough to manipulate before the cub would remember his parents, so I can keep the cub and make it a future ruler of Darvin. Avaha helped with that when she became Adamar's mate."

With the war, everyone's ability to perform magic had gone extinct. Only a few were born with the strength. Ecetal sighed. Except for dragons. All surviving dragons had Magician's Levs, and always would.

Ecetal recalled that the royal courts of every kingdom had at least two sorcerers hidden secretly away. In Itador, there were more than a dozen furs that dealt in magic and using it in defense.

"Does the queen know of you?" Ecetal asked, looking at the bear with no offensive expression for once.

"She will." Girbindon responded. The bear set his book down and studied Ecetal. "Now I'm going to try something on you. So hold still. It worked on Miro's father, but that was at long range and he doesn't have a Magician's Lev as powerful as a dragon. Maybe if at close range a smaller amount of power would work..." Girbindon grinned and spoke words under his breath.

Ecetal watched the bear closely, unclear of what his former friend was trying to do.

Ecetal's tail warmed with fire, and energy shot through his body.

The dragon cried out at the foreign release of power, and rolled over, writhing in pain as sensation cleared his ever-present fatigue.

He disregarded the intravenous line twisting around his feet while ideas fled into his mind, sending a flame down his limbs once more.

An urge to attack come up from somewhere in him, but he fought the impulse. He gripped his hands into fists as it grew stronger, his eyes shutting tight with the effort. Ecetal hissed and found himself unconsciously rising to his knees.

The dragon gave into the urge and launched at the end of the cage, toward Girbindon, his claws outstretched to slice the bear into pieces. His tail throbbed with the energy flowing from the band near the base of his tail.

With a yelp of pain, Ecetal smashed into the side of the crate. Dark red bled down his nose. He slumped to the ground and curled into a ball, terror flooding his body and his aching mind. When Girbindon spoke again, the dragon recoiled, as if solely words were necessary to hurt him.

"It works." The bear grinned. "Wonderful." Girbindon stared down at Ecetal. "There are so many uses to a Magician's Lev. It's amazing. The thing that creates some power gives you so much power if used correctly." The bear crouched down to Ecetal's eye level, and put his hand through the bars.

The dragon hissed, showing his teeth in a desperate moment of protection. "Do not touch me." He warned. As he said the words, he could feel the energy start to ebb away from him.

Girbindon sighed, but pulled his hand away. "As you wish. I was only going to heal your nose. It must hurt."

Ecetal glared at his enemy. "You've caused me more pain than a hurt nose. This is nothing."

With a growl, Girbindon stood. "Must you be so rude? I've just given you a burst of immense power, and you thank me like that?" Girbindon snorted. "You can just stay down here. I'll have my fun up where all the other furs are." The bear rested a hand on the only door in the room. The door that led to freedom. Ecetal stared at it with fervent want, willing someone to come down the stairs and slam the door open, crushing Girbindon in the act.

Girbindon extinguished the torches in the room and locked the door behind him as he left. Ecetal listened to him clomp up the stairs.

The dragon scanned the dark room with his eyes that worked well in darkness. Everything was as usual.

The scent of food reached his bruised nose. He managed to sit up and retrieve it, but a heavy blanket of fatigue settled over him first. Ecetal succumbed to the exhaustion with little resistance and closed his eyes.

Forty-Three

Adamar urged Dakr on, pressing his legs to the horse's sides. Dakr pounded into the ground at a quick canter, Hmo and Ohanzee following. The horses were well rested from their stay in Hile, and had much more energy than they'd had on the mountains.

Branches blocked their paths, but Dakr jumped over them. The horse stretched his neck out as he ran forward.

The three hadn't greatly eased up on their horses since they left Hile behind, instead taking what remained of the afternoon and using it to their advantage.

Adamar focused on Miro as Dakr sped through the forest. He was getting closer to seeing Miro again. He ignored the ache in his leg. It would not deter him from his goal.

Relief flooded through him when they burst out of the forest. Dakr continued on, his hooves striking at the sparse grass and dodging around various trees placed in the plain. Another forest loomed across the way, but Adamar could see light jutting through gaps in the foliage, and had the faintest hope that the light was coming from a castle that held a bear and Miro inside.

Adamar knew it wasn't so. The light was sunlight. They were closer to Darvin than they had been, but at least another couple miles of riding awaited them before they were in the Darvin kingdom.

Adamar and Ohanzee smelled someone ahead of them before they saw the figure in between the trees. The fox was glad that Girbindon had not decided to come out and make a personal appearance. He wanted to catch the bear by surprise if he still could.

A marsupial stood in the path, hands on hips. Brown and tan fur made up the kangaroo's coat, while a muscular tail stretched out behind the kangaroo, its end resting on the ground. A simple brown cloak hung down over the fur's shoulders.

Adamar stopped Dakr, keeping one hand firmly around his bow while the quiver of enhanced arrows stayed slung across his back.

"Who're you?" The kangaroo asked. "What're you doing here?"

Adamar showed little expression. "I should ask the same of you."

The kangaroo smiled. "The name's Nachor. I'm searching for the Darvin kingdom. Do you happen to know where it is?"

Adamar searched the kangaroo's gaze for the a layer of innocence he might have been trying to wear, but the fox was unable to find anything. The kangaroo didn't smell like he was lying. "Why the Darvin kingdom?"

"Because I want to be a warrior. Where I come from, on the islands, our warriors are boring. I want to be part of a new branch of fighters. Going to the Darvin kingdom will let me do just that." Nachor watched the fox. "You didn't answer my question. Do you know where the Darvin kingdom is?"

Adamar shook his head; he didn't know the exact location of the place, only the direction in which it was located. And he wasn't about to help out a potential enemy. "When do you plan on arriving?"

The kangaroo shrugged. "Whenever I get there. I'm in no haste, and I hope the leader of the Darvin kingdom isn't either."

Adamar nodded slowly. Nachor turned and disappeared into the forest without another sound.

Ears alert and searching for any other travelers, Adamar had Dakr continue through the forest. Hmo and Ohanzee drew up beside the fox.

"That was strange." Ohanzee commented.

Adamar glanced at the trees ahead of him. "Why would he come here, though? Traveling from the islands takes a fortnight. Besides, the islands are prosperous and are known for their strong armies, if I remember correctly." Adamar said. "How did he even know of the Darvin kingdom?"

"Girbindon's influence has extended far." Hmo observed. "He has resources we do not know about. Remember that Thayn knew about it."

"Do you think he is focusing on the islands?" Adamar glanced at the bat. "It could be possible." How powerful was Girbindon, really? Was Adamar just ignorant?

"It could be. But let's not focus on such things right now. We have to reach Darvin as soon as possible. Walking won't be fast enough." Hmo said.

Adamar sighed and followed Hmo's lead as the bat pushed Olie into a running trot.

The kingdom of Darvin rose before them. They came to a halt on the edge of the forest. The sun set behind their backs, throwing beams through the forest and across the Darvin kingdom.

Emotions twisted inside Adamar as he gazed on where Miro was being held. His young kit was in there, waiting for him, but so was Girbindon, and Rowena's pup Chilo, who'd taken Miro from his home and sent this entire quest into motion.

Adamar recalled finding out that Miro had been stolen. The memory seemed like it had happened ages ago, while he guessed only a few weeks had passed since he, Ohanzee, Thayn, and Hmo had left in pursuit of his kit.

Adamar leveled his gaze on the building in front of him. As if sunken into the ground, a half-circle of land made up the Darvin kingdom. Dirt walls bordered the land on all sides, making it a challenge to climb down into Girbindon's realm on horseback. In the sunken half-circle stood a massive building.

Turrets danced up the sides of the rough rectangle. The building's sides extended almost to the edge of the sunken land, while its front retreated from the dirt walls. Large stones walked up the building, pausing only to stop and occasionally let a window filter sunlight into rooms. Two doors sat in the middle of the building's front wall. Tremendous windows stretched up one of the sides of the building.

The smell of the ocean rolled over the castle and brought the scent of salt to Adamar. He closed his eyes for a moment as he drew in the fresh, lung-expanding scent of the sea. Living in Eadageth never gave him a chance to come too near the ocean, and he'd only heard of its power. He was curious about the sea, and had an urge to go and visit the sea before night had fully set. Once he had Miro in his arms, of course.

Adamar glanced around the Darvin kingdom's land, searching for a way to climb down into the sunken ground and stay on his horse. He wasn't keen on entering on foot.

"You ready?" Ohanzee asked, pulling Galene up alongside Dakr.

Adamar nodded, keeping his gaze on the building before him. His voice was distant and scared. "I must admit; I'm a bit frightened. What if we don't find Miro?"

"We will." Ohanzee offered a supportive grin. But he also smelled of cold fear.

Adamar glanced at Ohanzee, and allowed a small smile to flash briefly over his muzzle.

Hmo spoke. "There's a staircase carved from the ground over there." He gestured to an end of the half circle. Adamar noticed the stairs jutting out from the dirt barriers.

The three guided their horses to the earthen staircase, going along the forest's edge. They stayed mostly behind the first layer of trees, letting their fur and cloaks blend them into the landscape. All three drew arrows and notched them to their bows, draping their horses' reins over the horns of the saddles.

Armored furs streamed out of the two front doors.

The warriors carried swords and spears in their grips, while a shield protected each one's opposing arm. Adamar saw muzzles and snouts poke out from beneath helmets that accommodated almost every type of facial structure. The warriors focused on the three on horseback.

Adamar aimed at the crowd before he let an arrow fly into the air. It hit its mark even as the ocean's wind protested against it, striking a warrior's helmet. The metal arrowhead dented the steel and the fur collapsed to the ground.

Hmo guided Olie between Galene and Dakr, and spoke in a whisper to the two furs on either side of him. "They are many in number, but weak in strength, it looks like. They look haphazardly put together. We just have to pick them off one by one. However, we shouldn't just stand here and do that, since it will give them a chance to surround us as we wait like idiotic prey."

Hmo then pulled an arrow from his quiver and loosed it onto Girbindon's soldiers.

Adamar had Dakr go down the staircase. He directed an arrow into a warrior to his side. Dakr reared as another warrior tried to spear him, but missed, the weapon sliding beneath the horse's belly.

Dakr's hooves crashed down onto the warrior, who yelped and collapsed to the ground. His armor was left full of horseshoe-shaped dents.

Ohanzee followed Adamar into the mass, shooting at close range. The coyote's arrows slid into the vulnerable ears of furs, and sometimes managed to lock two furs together by their furred ears. When they would be struggling to free themselves, Ohanzee would grab his arrow and quickly kick the furs out of his sight.

Adamar plunged into the mass, a mistake he regretted the moment a warrior smashed into his healing foot. Pain shot up his leg and the fox hesitated. He twisted in the saddle to return the blow, only to see that the warrior had disappeared.

With the amount of bodies writhing around making him nervous, Dakr kicked out, his hooves smashing in helmets and striking down furs. More of the warriors bled out from the doors, replacing those that they had lost. A couple horses followed, their riders holding on desperately. Both horses were white as newfallen snow.

Adamar kept shooting his arrows into the crowd, but he made sure he kept a few in his quiver, saving them for the monster that had stolen his pup. The fox lashed out with his bow, smacking it on heads as rage burned within him. He let his anger feed his energy. He stopped feeling the pain in his leg.

Girbindon's warriors clawed at Adamar and Ohanzee. The warriors tried to wound their horses.

Hmo remained above the sunken land, firing his arrows at the furs that attempted to sneak up behind his comrades. The bat protected the delicate membrane between his arms and chest by staying away from the fighters. He shot down anyone who attempted to climb up the staircase, while Olie grazed passively, as if the horse was in the middle of a peaceful pasture instead of on the edge of a battleground.

Adamar watched the edge of a sword swing and open a gash along Ohanzee's ribcage. The coyote snarled and grabbed the muzzle of the fur who had cut him.

The fox focused on the couple magical horses that had followed the warriors out. The horses ran at him and Ohanzee, until one, seeing Hmo, charged at the bat. Adamar tried to dodge the horses, but soon found Dakr himself rearing again and fighting the horses.

Adamar noticed that there were fewer soldiers around. While Dakr fought, the fox slid off the saddle and attacked any remaining furs. He watched Ohanzee with sadness, seeing the coyote have to kill a horse. The coyote loved ancestor horses, and his anguish was thick in the air.

While Adamar fought close to Hmo, the bat told him that his limited sight was getting in the way of fighting Girbindon's soldiers. He assured he'd return, and disappeared back into the trees.

When Adamar saw no more soldiers waiting to attack, he stopped and turned around slowly, checking to make sure every soldier was down.

The fox jumped at the sound of thunder. A whinny followed the boom.

A hand came up from the ground and wrapped around his ankle, startling him. Adamar jumped and tried to twist free. The hand tightened its grip.

An arm extended from the hand's wrist, and

turned as it knocked Adamar off balance, sending him crashing to the ground onto different bodies.

Other hands reached up from warriors only mildly injured, and gripped his limbs. The fox struggled, snarling. As he managed to bite someone's arm, others warriors rose. They surrounded Galene and pulled Ohanzee off of her.

Adamar thrashed against the warriors' grips, intent on being free and killing them. His quiver dug awkwardly into his back, and the fox rolled onto his side. The warriors followed him. He scolded himself for not recognizing the smell of the wariors just waiting to get him.

They took hold of his arms and wrenched them behind his back. Agony ripped through his leg.

Adamar rode out the wave of pain as still as could be. Girbindon's warriors took advantage of the opportunity and dragged the fox toward the doors. When they grew closer to the threshold, Adamar tried to bite them. The thought that Miro was just inside urged him on.

"Stop that," A warrior growled and kicked him in the stomach.

Adamar noticed that Ohanzee was also being hauled across the bloody ground. The coyote fought his captors, though his attempts were futile. The front of his cloak was soaked with blood, and Adamar hoped that the red wasn't Ohanzee's.

When the pain in his stomach had faded, the fox bared his teeth, ears pressed back against his head. Girbindon's warriors merely laughed and dragged him deeper into the bear's kingdom.

Forty-Four

Girbindon's warriors took Adamar and Ohanzee through an entryway that smelled of the terror and eagerness of the furs that had gone through it. Lit torches ambled up and down the tunnel, throwing shadows onto anyone who passed by.

Adamar twisted against the grips of Girbindon's warriors, but his attempts failed as they continued hauling him down the hallway. A path of blood from the torn-open wound on his ankle marked where he had been.

Ohanzee snarled he tried to squirm out of the warriors that held him. When the coyote eventually figured out that he wouldn't be able to get free, he went limp and became deadweight.

A large doorway stood close. Light bathed Adamar. As his quiver of arrows dug into his back, his thoughts focused on Miro hopefully being in the room they were just about to enter. Hope filled him when he caught Miro's scent. His kit had been here, and recently.

The fox had his un-injured foot catch on a piece of stone, and jolted as his captors looked to see what was stopping them. Adamar opened his jaws and caught one of the fur's wrists. He sank his teeth into the flesh and shook his head.

The warrior tried to tear his arm away. Blood ran into Adamar's mouth. He tightened his grip, shredding flesh.

His name being shouted made Adamar let go.

"Adamar." A low voice said. "Welcome to my kingdom."

The fox was pulled to his feet and forced to meet the gaze of the fur that had ordered the stealing of his kit.

Sitting in the center of a wall was a lavishly decorated throne, lit torches in stands on either side of it. The room smelled strongly of bear, jackal, and other smells... including Miro's. It seemed almost like Badr's and Avaha's scents were present, but that couldn't be. Tapestries covered the walls around the room, trying to draw one's attention away from the fur who ruled the place.

A bear stood on the steps of his throne, dressed in lavish, thick robes.

"It is a pleasure to finally greet you." Girbindon said, a grin plastered on his muzzle as he looked at the glaring fox. He smelled of victory, smugness, and joy. His gaze shifted to Ohanzee. "And it appears you've brought your friend. How wonderful. Two of you." The monster glared at Adamar. "No one greets me without a kneel or a bow."

The warriors pushed Adamar and Ohanzee to their knees.

Girbindon smiled as he stepped down the first of the stairs that led to his throne. "Are you ready to give me what I want?"

Adamar stared at the bear. He couldn't remember what the monster was talking about, if he'd ever mentioned something that he was after. The fox growled. "Where is my kit?"

"Within my grasp." The bear responded. "You should be glad; the time for you to retrieve him has passed, and yet I can say that his heart is still beating. Yours, however, may not be for much longer. It depends on how it goes, how you decide to give it to me."

Great relief stained part of Adamar's mind at his kit's survival, but he glanced around the room, searching for Miro. "Where is my kit, then?" He could smell Miro's scent trail disappearing behind one of the tapestries to his right.

Girbindon shook his head and stepped closer to Adamar. "You have to tell me that you are willing to give me what I want. This thing can only be given willingly. But I can trick you into doing so."

"I do not know what you're talking about." The fox snarled as one of Girbindon's warriors stepped on his foot. Pain squealed in his voice. "Just give me my pup back, and there will be fewer problems."

Girbindon stood before Adamar, glaring down at him. "You travel all this way, and yet you cannot be moved to give it to me." The bear continued watching Adamar. "Bring Miro."

Adamar turned his head toward the tapestry that had hid Miro's scent, and as if they had emerged from the wall, two furs fell out from behind the wall hanging. A deer went to stand at the base of Girbindon's throne, holding a brown mass.

Adamar's tail thumped against the ground at the sight of his pup. Relief relaxed his muscles. Miro was cradled against the deer's chest, looking around the room curiously. Adamar noticed how the young fox didn't squirm, and barely glanced at Adamar at first.

Then Miro moved his gaze back to Adamar. The kit cocked his head. Adamar breathed in Miro's sweet scent, but worried at the smell of blood and pain on him.

"Look at me." Girbindon growled. Only when he spoke a second time did Adamar do as asked, tearing his gaze away from Miro.

"Give what I ask without trouble, and there is a greater chance of him being yours." The bear repeated. Adamar didn't respond, instead choosing to glare at the monster.

Girbindon snarled. "How can you be so stupid? Do I have to say it out loud? Give it to me, or your cub will die!"

"I believe that I do not have what you want," Adamar said, baring his teeth. "I do not know what it is that you desire, you monster." He let the smell of hatred sit heavy in the air.

Girbindon's fists clenched. "How can you not be aware of your own power?" he shouted, voice reverberating around the room. "You have strength, and yet you cannot harness it, and for that you're an ignorant idiot."

The bear glanced at Ohanzee, and his expression eased into a sordid smile. "Did you enjoy my message?"

"You like causing pain, don't you?" The coyote returned with a growl, straining against his captors. He looked and smelled ready to kill the bear. Adamar could agree with that.

Girbindon laughed and looked back at Adamar. "You really have no idea what you are capable of? I was told that, but I didn't believe it." Girbindon narrowed his eyes. "Quit looking at your cub and watch me. I am the important one here."

"No." Adamar responded. "You're just the heartless fiend."

The bear seemed to contemplate things for a moment. "If you would allow me to explain, I can say what you're capable of. That might be easier, for both of us." When Adamar was silent, Girbindon went on. "There is something called magic, fox. I've already had to teach your kit about it, but I'll do the same for you, out of my generosity.

"Magic stems from something usually located near the body's heart, and is called a Magician's Lev. Most furs don't have it, since it died out during the Far-reaching War, when everyone was taking strong sorcerers for their own use. Some furs, though, are still born with it. You and Miro are two of those furs, Adamar.

"And that makes you both extremely powerful. It gives you power that you didn't know of until now." Girbindon paused and glanced at the furs holding Adamar. "Make sure that the possum wasn't lying." he growled.

Adamar snapped at the furs as they tore at a hole in his robe and shirt and pulled the fabric away from his chest. One of Girbindon's furs grabbed the scruff on the back of Adamar's neck and tugged, forcing his head up. Girbindon went close to Adamar and bent his head. The bear inspected the brown splotch of fur marring Adamar's white chest.

"You know all those outbursts you had, Adamar?" Girbindon teased. "That was me. I could control you through your Magician's Lev. I am that skilled in darker magic. And even you, coyote, I could mess with your mind a little bit, because you were close to Adamar. You're welcome for those doubtful feelings."

Ohanzee's scent changed into one of surprise that was soon overridden by more anger.

A growl sounded from Adamar's throat, but for once he didn't try to struggle. His worry about Miro's safety was greater than the pain the furs were causing him.

Girbindon strode away, apparently satisfied. "Release him."

Adamar caught himself before he smashed into the floor. He got to his feet, ears flattened back and teeth bared. The fox clenched his fists. "I don't care what you want. If you want that thing...the Magician's Lev. I know that I want my kit back."

The bear smirked. "This I'm aware of. Except, I won't do exactly as you request. You've to give me your Magician's Lev...something that you probably won't even notice is absent." Girbindon tipped his fingers together. "It'll only be a little pain, and then you can be off."

"With Miro?" Adamar asked, narrowed gaze tracking the bear.

"That, of course, I cannot confirm."

Adamar lunged at the bear. He barreled into Girbindon, taking him by surprise, and slammed him into the stairs that led to his throne. The bear snarled as Adamar dug his claws into him. The fox was grateful for those spars, for his bow had disappeared somewhere outside.

Hands gripped Adamar and pulled him off Girbindon. The fox squirmed, eager to get to the bear and rip his throat out. He purposely put his weight on only his good foot, forcing the warriors to be distracted with supporting him.

Girbindon stood and brushed himself off, glaring at Adamar. "You'll pay for that." Girbindon's expression softened. "Now. I will give you two options, and only two. You'll pick one of them. If you try to pick another, your comrade will die, and then you will pick the option I like."

Adamar stared at the bear with hatred in his eyes, but his body was displaying neutral curiosity. His ears were pricked, muscles mainly relaxed, while his tail hung still behind his back.

"Good. You've learned." The bear commented. "So you can either leave Miro with me, get back to your life and think about how your cub will grow to be a strong fur. Or, you can hand me your Magician's Lev, and you'll go free maybe with your cub."

Adamar glanced at the deer holding his kit. She didn't meet his gaze. "How could that happen?" The fox asked, slowly looking back at Girbindon.

"How could I retrieve your Magician's Lev? State your decision first."

Adamar mulled over the options for a brief moment. He wanted his kit more than anything, so the decision was easy to make. Miro would never get strong in this monster's grip. "You can have my...Magician's Lev."

The bear clapped his hands. "Wonderful, wonderful."

Adamar tried to twist his arms free. "So how will that happen?"

Girbindon grinned, as if proud of himself. "Chilo," he called. "Their services are requested."

Adamar's gaze went to a tapestry close to the one Miro had emerged from. A jackal ducked out from behind the wall hanging, his tail slightly tucked between his legs. The fox noticed the jackal only had three fingers on one hand, including the thumb, and anger flooded through him once more. The jackal smelled of blood. He'd had four fingers not long ago. He really was the one who had left that mark above Miro's crib. A possum that Adamar recognized followed Chilo. The fox began to say Badr's name in shock, but another fur stepped out after him and flanked Girbindon before she turned toward Adamar

Wearing the same dress she'd had on in his nightmare, Avaha smoothed the fabric and looked at her mate.

Adamar glanced at Girbindon, dread growing. He felt his strength ebb as his mate stood before him. "Why is she here?" Adamar managed, uncertainty conquering his thoughts. "Why did you take her, too? Let her go."

Avaha answered Adamar, her sweet voice sounding almost too kind. "Adamar, you've got the wrong idea. Girbindon didn't take me like he did with our Miro."

A minute went by.

Understanding flooded through Adamar, and he sank to his knees. Agony ripped at him. He struggled to comprehend that his mate was with Girbindon...he didn't know if she was just working for him, or if she'd lied about loving Adamar all along. Her betrayal sliced a wound in Adamar's heart, and he swore he could feel emotions drifting out of the cut, replaced by numbness.

The fox's ears drooped, and anxiety took over. If Avaha was with Girbindon, what would become of Miro? Would she kill him? But she wouldn't do that...he panted out of nervousness for a moment, before he caught himself.

So this is where she was educated...

Avaha spoke to Girbindon, and then went over to Adamar. She crouched beside him, lifting his muzzle in her gentle, betraying touch. She smiled sadly as their gazes met each other. "I know you're unhappy about this, but it was good." She laughed. "It was really good. You were so easy to trick...oh, Adamar, that was what I loved about you."

Adamar weakly pulled his snout back. "Get away from me," he warned, no threat left in his voice.

Avaha sighed and placed her hands in her lap, watching her mate. "Adamar," she said.

The fox bared his teeth at her, but couldn't express his anger more than that; his energy was gone. The furs holding him back were also holding him up.

He thought of Avaha's hysterics when he'd left, and wondered if those had been faked. He was certain now that she hadn't gone ballistic out of her passion for him, but more for how she didn't want him to leave and encounter Girbindon, therefore nearly ruining the bear's plan.

Adamar glanced at Avaha. "It really was you in the inn."

Avaha nodded. "It was. But that was then, and this is now. And now you're going to hear just how we can complete this extraction, so you do everything exactly as the Great King Girbindon wants."

Adamar watched his former mate rise and go back to standing beside the bear, a pleased expression on her face and in her scent.

"Badr, Avaha, if you will." Girbindon retreated to his throne, where oversaw the scenes unfolding before him.

The possum glanced at Adamar. "Your Magician's Lev is a delicate piece of your body that takes great work and great skill to master or to take from one's body. The Great King Girbindon has power of his own, but he would like more power, so he can rule his expanding kingdom even better. Since you're not using the piece of you that can perform magic, King Girbindon will take it from you and use the power stored in it.

"This will be done by a minor bit of surgery. King Girbindon will use his strength of sorcery to aid in the extraction."

Avaha spoke. "Using this amount of power will be very tiring for King Girbindon. This has not often been done before. I'm sure, though, that My King will be able to handle it.

"There's already a room set up for the task. We've been awaiting your arrival, Adamar." Avaha smiled.

Glass shattered.

Forty-Five

Adamar looked over to where a window had cracked, panes of glass falling from it as a spider web spread across the surface. Everyone watched a form punch the remaining shards from the bottom of the broken window. Hmo tumbled inside, and came up on one knee, arrow drawn.

Girbindon growled, his warriors just standing in their spots, staring at the bat. Attack!" The bear yelled, and began chanting beneath his breath.

As Girbindon's furs stumbled into action, Hmo feigned aiming an arrow at the bear, and instead sent the arrow flying toward Badr.

The possum squealed and collapsed to the ground, an arrow sticking out of his reddening side. Badr writhed, the arrowhead twisting into his internal organs as he squirmed and managed to bury the weapon deeper into his flesh. When had Hmo taken one of Adamar's arrows?

The fox decided that wasn't important now.

Warriors attacked Hmo, but the bat rolled out of their grasp and trained an arrow on them. He backed the warriors against a wall.

The fox was hauled to his feet. He struggled against those that held him, but his energy had yet to fully return, even though Hmo's arrival had sent adrenaline through everyone in the room.

The fox was pulled to one of the tapestries that hung on the walls, and became aware of Avaha leading the way. Someone pushed Adamar into the tapestry. He fell through it, landing on the rough ground of a tunnel hidden behind the wall hanging.

Before Adamar could stand, Avaha was at his side, her hand holding Adamar's muzzle shut. Her gaze was the opposite of its usual gentle calm, and her voice echoed the harsh expression crawling across her snout.

Adamar glared as she spoke.

"If you run back out there, I will make sure King Girbindon kills Miro. We can still use Miro when he's dead." Avaha glanced up and smiled as the tapestry blew in once again. Out of the corner of his eye, Adamar saw the deer and his kit standing just inside the tunnel's entrance.

Avaha's alert ears swiveled toward Miro. "Maybe I'll kill him myself." She smiled. "Wouldn't be hard. Just a quick choke hold and—"

Adamar bared his teeth and growled, daring her to go on about how she'd take the life from Miro. He raised a hand to claw her.

With a roll of her eyes, Avaha stood once again and waited until Adamar was on his feet before she moved down the tunnel, ordering him to follow. The deer holding Miro stayed where she was. Adamar wished the deer would just give Miro to him, and he could run off, take him somewhere safe, get Ohanzee and Hmo on the way.

Adamar felt half dead as he trailed Avaha, her betrayal still echoing in the numb, confused, angry, and lost fox.

Avaha led the way through hallways, up a flight of stairs, until they came to a camouflaged door. His former mate tugged on the door handle and pulled outward. With a smile, she disappeared inside the room.

Adamar glanced at Miro before he stepped inside. His kit watched him intently.

With fear beginning to slip into his blood, Adamar entered the room, and immediately felt trapped in its small space.

The place was built in a rough circle, stones running up the walls until they disappeared into a high-beamed ceiling. A table rested against a corner, a book propped open on it and nearly taking up the entirety of the wood. Piles of cloth—what Adamar realized were bandages—were standing against one of the table's legs, while beneath the piece of furniture rested metal tools that looked like they'd be in a blacksmith's shop.

Dominating the center of the room was a wooden structure. A square frame extended over a long, wooden table. Twisted metal hung down from the middle of the frame, narrowing into a point while helixes of the same element twisted around sides in the frame, allowing for the top of the structure to move down.

"Ready?" Avaha asked. She spread a cloth out on the long table. "You won't feel that much for long."

Adamar's ears turned out in worry. She had betrayed him once, could she do so again, and kill him instead of doing the sort of extraction Girbindon had commissioned? Would she? Adamar stared at the machine. His kit was just behind him. He'd be able to see Miro when the process was all over. But if Adamar didn't do as he'd decided, Miro would die.

Nevertheless, the fox took an anxious step back. "Avaha, I don't know about this." he said. "There has to be some other way."

Avaha curled her upper lip back in a snarl. "It's death for Miro. I can easily arrange that, if you like. Though I'm not sure you do."

Adamar shook his head, terrified, and went over to the machine. He followed Avaha's instruction as she commanded him to lie down onto the cloth, despite how he was trembling in fear. His tail was tucked between his legs.

Avaha moved around the table, making sure that things were in order before she began the surgery. "If Hmo hadn't killed Badr, this would be a lot easier." She grunted as she tightened straps around Adamar to keep him from jumping away.

Adamar didn't respond. He stared up at the metal drill hanging down above him, waiting to slice into his flesh and do whatever it exactly was going to do. Terror consumed the fox, sending thoughts of flight into his mind. He fought against them, struggling to console himself with how he was doing this for Miro. The fox whimpered, battling against instinct.

"Shush, it's going to be all right." Avaha leaned over him and gently stroked the fur on his forehead. "You won't even notice its absence." she smiled when Adamar flinched.

"Just so you know, Miro was born out of a gamble. Even though you have a Magician's Lev, Adamar, I and Girbindon couldn't know if Miro would. But he does, and Miro will help Darvin grow stronger, as your own Magician's Lev will. Girbindon will make Miro help."

"No, he won't." Adamar returned. "Because you will never have Miro." He met Avaha's gaze. "Never again." He was ready to rip Avaha's throat out. "So you had Miro just so you could use him. You didn't love him. You never did."

Avaha didn't say anything.

"Why did you do it?" Adamar asked, his terrified gaze tracking Avaha's every move. "What could you gain out of this?"

Avaha paused for a moment, her hands on a crank that let the drill drop. "Power." she murmured, and then twisted the handle.

The metal drill spun as it lowered towered Adamar's chest. Avaha had torn open the rest of his cloak to make the process less messy, and had then arranged the fabric around the brown spot of fur marking where Adamar's Magician's Lev rested.

Adamar trembled out of trepidation.

The twisted metal came down and struck Adamar's flesh.

Pain erupted. The world vanished.

Forty-Six

Time passed slowly in physical existence. Disputes between furs raged, and armies grew. Furs trained for challenges that would eventually kill them all, while others struggled with their own personal demons.

Injuries healed, while new wounds opened and bled onto the streets. Furs learned, experimented with agony and erudition. Leaders guided their realms, and ships sailed across open waters. Plans were born.

Life carried on as usual for most, and for others it became a strange thing that they couldn't fathom was occurring. The crops of farms were cultivated. The crops of minds died and didn't.

War began.

War full of eccentric weapons that hadn't been seen in ages. Furs once thought to be dead, long gone, reappeared and aided in the fighting. They lent their skills to the battles, but the sides in conflict never wavered in who had the advantage. Always one side had the upper hand, even though it had first been small, minor enough that few were aware of its existence.

Yet its influence had reached far. It had crossed the land, traveled the seas, carried by faithful disciples while leaders never took notice of the growing belief in it. Its influence appeared everywhere, for it was everywhere, but nowhere as well. For it to be everywhere, it had to be at the center, and it was only at the edges. It tried to close in, but battles pushed it back.

Furs changed their places while the side tried to grow stronger. Unwanted furs slipped into places where *they were celebrated, and found comfort and a home in these places as time went by.*

Furs matured together, exploring things that many had never seen before. Some died.

And some lived.

Those that survived did well in life, and rose to see new days, new worlds open up before them. The survivors, the furs watched in awe, but pain rested in them, agony that would never leave. They'd been changed, and change was inventible. Change always had eventual virtuous endings, though everything had an opposite.

Forty-Seven

A nightmare woke Adamar, filling his mind with such darkness that insanity would overwhelm him if he didn't rouse himself from the damaging dream.

The fox groaned and turned over, his whimpers cracking in his throat. Adamar slid to lying on his back as muted pain started in his chest. With each slow beat of his heart, the pain increased, until he desperately wanted to be rid of it.

Adamar opened his eyes, and light flooded them. He whined and shut his eyes, waiting for a few seconds to pass until the light didn't cause as much pain.

When Adamar looked blearily at his surroundings, he was comforted by that he was lying in his bed, at home, in Eadageth. The faded smell of Avaha and the stronger one of his kit danced around the room, penetrating his black nose.

The fox barely questioned how he'd gotten home, instead becoming curious by the bandages that wrapped around his chest, starting at halfway down his pectoral muscles and ending just below the bottom of his ribcage. The bandages looked freshly washed.

Adamar drew in a breath, his lungs filling with air, and agony tore through his torso. The fox whimpered and closed his eyes, willing the pain to leave and never come back.

A fur appeared in the doorway that led into the room. Soft, light brown ears stood above the deer's same-colored head, while a simple dress flowed down from the fur's shoulders.

Adamar struggled to connect the fur to a name, but his memory remained foggy. In pain, he tensed and growled the unknown fur.

The deer didn't appear disturbed by his threat. "Adamar, relax." The deer moved into the room, walking quietly over to Adamar's bedside. She pulled up a chair and sat next to him, ignoring his continuous low growl. "You're okay."

Adamar grimaced as a wave of pain washed over him. "Who're you? Where's Miro?"

"My name's Isun. Do you remember what happened?" The deer watched him carefully, analyzing his expression and smell for a hint to his actual thoughts.

"No." Adamar struggled to sit up, pushing up on his elbows. When Isun gently had him lie down again, he glared at her, but didn't resist. Weakness and pain walked around his body, leaving him vulnerable.

"Does the name Girbindon sound familiar?"

Adamar nodded. A foggy image of a massive bear standing before him appeared, but as soon as the fox tried to focus on the image, a headache crushed his skull. He whined and pulled the blankets up over his head, as if hiding beneath cloth would dispel any monsters.

"Don't be a fawn, Adamar." Isun chided gently. "Your memory should come back. Azoth said it might hurt."

"Azoth?" Adamar repeated and glanced at her. "What does he have to do with this?"

The deer shifted her weight. "Azoth, as crazy as this town claims him to be, is knowledgeable when it comes to magic."

"Magic?" Adamar repeated. He began to recognize things following the mention of the word. "Where's Avaha?"

The deer's expression saddened. "She betrayed you, remember?"

Adamar growled unhappily, memories returning. "I do." His gaze moved to Isun. If Avaha had betrayed him, if the fur he loved the most had done that, then he couldn't trust anyone. He couldn't trust Isun, even though she appeared to hold no jarring secrets.

Isun pulled a few leaves from a box beneath the bed, and began stirring them into a jar of water she'd been holding. "You're probably in a lot of pain. This should help."

When she held out the mixture, Adamar shied away, thinking that the liquid could be poison.

"Adamar, we're not going to hurt you. You're safe. Girbindon isn't after you." Isun said again. When the fox continued to refuse the mixture, the deer withdrew the mixture and stood. "I'll be back with your fawn and your friends. They've been waiting a long time to see you."

Adamar's ears pricked, alert. "How long?"

"Two months." Isun disappeared, leaving Adamar to his wound and his thoughts.

The fox closed his eyes. Though he was awake, sadness was taking his energy away from him. He guessed that some of the fatigue was also because of what lay beneath his chest, a memory that slowly was returning to him.

He remembered Badr and Avaha's presence in Darvin. At first it had appeared that Avaha had been taken by Girbindon, like the bear had done with Miro, but then Avaha had wounded Adamar emotionally. As soon as she'd been finished with harming him, she'd taken some organ out of him.

Adamar was staring at the ceiling, lost in thought, when Ohanzee and Hmo came in. The coyote sat in the chair beside Adamar's bed, Hmo choosing to lean against the wall.

Ohanzee looked as if he'd been half-starved, and was regaining weight. Nevertheless, a smile lit up the coyote's muzzle. "How're you doing?" he asked.

"Okay." Adamar pushed himself to his elbows, grimaced, and fell back down. "What happened at the end of everything? I remember getting to Girbindon, meeting him and seeing Avaha, but nothing else."

Ohanzee leaned against the back of the chair. "There was blood everywhere."

Together, Hmo and Ohanzee recounted the events following Hmo killing Badr. They spoke of how, while Avaha had been taking out Adamar's Magician's Lev, battle had raged inside the throne room. Hmo had managed to disarm the furs that attacked him, using Adamar's quiver, which Girbindon's soldiers had grabbed off the fox while Girbindon had been taunting him. The bat also admitted that he'd taken a few of the fox's magical arrows before leaving Hile.

Once Hmo had dealt with Girbindon's warriors, he'd turned to the bear himself. Girbindon had been furious, and used magic against Hmo. The bat entered into a brief battle with Girbindon, eventually emerging with an unconscious bear and a burn on the skin of his membrane.

Once the battle had finished, Hmo had gone over to Ohanzee and helped him to his feet. The coyote had been wounded badly enough that he'd been semi-conscious when Hmo went over to him. Still, however, the two followed the scent trail and found a tunnel sloping upward.

Ohanzee and Hmo traveled along the tunnels

after Adamar's scent. When they found him, Ohanzee described vividly, the room was soaked in Adamar's blood, and the fox was lying unconscious with his chest torn open. Avaha had fled. Isun came in from where she'd been hiding Miro when she heard the coyote and bat talking about what to do. She carried out the task of sewing together Adamar's flesh.

Hmo grabbed Adamar while Isun took Miro, and together they began to leave, Ohanzee covering their backs. They ran, and were nearly at the entrance when an awake Girbindon and Chilo showed up. The two tried to stop them. They were unsuccessful, with the lackey accidentally making his king trip and smash into the floor.

The four ran outside, where Hmo recovered the horses. Isun led the way to Hile with Adamar draped over Galene's back. The mare didn't mind carrying an unconscious body, and did so when the group crossed the Jdr Mountains, after visiting Hile and getting wounds tended to. Some of Hile's warriors guarded the group as they made their way across the mountains.

When they arrived at Eadageth a month later, they were half-starved from a shortage of food, but all were alive. Their arrival made a town happy to know that all well-loved inhabitants had returned.

Isun had then offered to tend to Adamar, an offer that Hmo and Ohanzee accepted while they started to practice their skills with the rest of the archers and recuperate. The deer had proved trustworthy since she'd sewn Adamar's flesh together.

Sometime during their first week back home, Azoth approached the group and explained about his familiarity with magic, as well as the healing associated with wounds caused by it.

When Ohanzee and Hmo finished, Adamar stared at them, and asked a short question. "Two months?"

The coyote gravely nodded. "Two months. Azoth said that it was normal for such a long time to pass, but that didn't ease Eadageth's worrying. When you live in a small place, everyone knows everything." Ohanzee absentmindedly rubbed his wrist, where the mountain clan had hurt him so long ago. "The archers have been especially anxious."

Adamar smiled weakly. Fatigue began to drape over him, but he tried to shake the exhaustion off; he wanted to speak to his friends for a little longer. "I think I'll be able to start training again, probably tomorrow." He was eager to get back into practicing after he'd heard how long he'd been out.

Ohanzee shook his head. "You're too weak. Both Isun and Azoth agree on that, and Azoth said that you wouldn't be able to do much for a while. The recovery from what Avaha did will take a long time. Even though Girbindon said opposite. Not that you should ever trust a word of that bear."

Adamar's expression fell. Then he asked a seemingly obscure question. "I can hold Miro, right?"

The coyote was quiet. "No." He said, unable to meet Adamar's eyes. "It might damage your wound."

Adamar opened his mouth to protest, but pain racked his chest, making him whimper and curl into a ball. The fox shut his eyes, struggling to stay conscious as agony attacked him. When the strongest wave passed, Adamar looked up to see that Ohanzee had pulled the blanket over him, and then left him to rest.

The fox stretched out along the bed, grimacing. His wound hurt, but he wasn't sure if it was worse than what he'd just been told.

Adamar whimpered and succumbed to sleep.

When Adamar woke, Isun was sitting near him, preparing food that didn't look in the least bit appetizing to the fox. Nevertheless, when it was offered to him, Adamar sank his teeth into a piece of bread, his stomach enjoying solid substance for the first in a long time.

He craned his neck to view the wound as Isun gently unwrapped his chest.

No fur covered the spot where a large, ragged line tracked down his ribcage, revealing pale white skin struggling to heal. The wound itself was large in width, while the center held a mass of messy black scabs. Green circled the dark middle, and Adamar thought he saw blue pulsing softly beneath the skin.

"What is that?" Adamar asked, looking at the blue as Isun cleaned the wound.

"That's your blood. When the Magician's Lev was taken out, it left a gaping hole in your flesh. Azoth says that your blood, your body, is working to close that gap. For now, though, you can't do much of anything, because if something hits your chest, it could disturb the healing, and kill you." Isun had Adamar sit up as she wrapped the cloth around his torso.

"How wonderful." Adamar remarked. "Can I go outside, or leave this room?" Could he see Miro?

Isun paused for a moment, churning over the idea. "If you fall when you stand up, you're staying where you are."

The fox nodded. He wasn't able to trust if Isun was telling the truth, and keeping him inside for his health, or because she had something to hide. Maybe, Adamar briefly wondered, she was keeping him from being teased, like he'd been in Hile.

Weakness swamped Adamar when he tried to put his weight on his feet. He fell heavily back onto the edge of the bed, and barely noticed that he'd sat on his tail. The fox put his head in his hands.

Isun watched as Adamar's chest heaved with tears. The deer's alert ears heard the cries of Miro from the young fox's room, but she stayed for a moment, watching to see if his father would be okay.

Isun pulled a table over, leaving a pitcher of water and scraps of food, thinly sliced so Adamar could eat without upsetting his stomach. Then the deer turned and left, going to tend to Miro.

The black fur on Adamar's hands was quickly soaked as he cried. He'd woken up to a nightmare, and was sure that it would stay for what appeared to be forever. He was trapped, his mind free to wander into dangerous places, but his body was stuck at home, stuck in bed, which he wasn't able to travel far from. He wasn't even capable of standing. It was pathetic.

Adamar wept for a while, and when his cries began to stifle and end in short hiccups, Isun appeared in the doorway, carrying a brown ball of fur.

Adamar looked up with red eyes. When he saw Miro, a sad smile briefly flitted over his face. He imagined being able to hold his pup, instead of just viewing him from a distance. Miro squirmed with the same thought, his small tail wagging.

Isun brought his kit over and set him on the bed beside Adamar. The fox shifted his weight, and his tail thumped against the bed in time with his kit's. Miro reached for Adamar to hold him, and crawled to the fox's leg. Adamar wrapped an arm around his kit and pulled him to his side. That didn't hurt, so it was okay. But when Miro attempted to climb into Adamar's lap, Isun pulled him back.

Miro whined, not understanding why he couldn't be with his father. "Father," the fox kit said.

With widening eyes, Adamar glanced at Isun.

"Don't tell me that that isn't his first word."

The deer sorrowfully shook her head. "You've missed a few events."

Adamar sighed, anguished. Lost.

"Azoth would like to talk to you, though." Isun picked Miro up and cradled the unhappy fox kit. Adamar watched with longing as she left. When Azoth came in, the fox had closed his eyes and hung his head.

"Now that's no way to enjoy life," the wolf chided. "Wake, Adamar. Come on, up to life."

"I don't have a life now."

"You have as much life as a donkey." Azoth knocked on Adamar's skull. "Anyone in there?"

The fox shied away from the friendly blow. "Not now, Azoth."

Azoth shook his head. "Now? Now is nothing. I'm to teach you how to use magic. Magic never waits for time."

Adamar glanced at the wolf. "You know I can't perform magic. I just lost the organ that could let me do so."

Azoth grinned. "Mysteries. When your Miro grows up, and your strength returns, I'll teach you. There's always a way around everything." Azoth's yellow eyes glanced at the food near Adamar. "Eat something. You'll feel better, you chicken's tail."

The fox smiled lightly at Azoth's insanity, and did as asked. He looked up at   the wolf, head tilted curiously. "How do you know about magic?"

"You know few and you know all, and then you understand." Azoth shrugged. "My past isn't heard, so therefore none can question it."

His answers puzzled Adamar. "Did you apprentice with a sorcerer?" The fox asked. He realized that his foot wasn't hurting, and from closer inspection of it, saw that the gash from the mountains had healed. At least something of him wasn't broken.

Azoth eyed him. "And who would take me, he with yellow eyes?" The wolf laughed. "Differences! How they separate and join us."

Adamar nodded. Pain crossed his expression as the gap near his heart throbbed, slowly putting itself back together. "So," he said, and paused to ride out a wave of stabbing hurt. "How long, exactly, till I can get back to archery?"

The wolf shook his head. "Not for a while. I know you're really in love with archery and all that lovely news, but it's too dangerous for you outside. The extraction of the Magician's Lev is something that many do not survive, and those that do are left as you are. It's going to be a long healing process. Girbindon will grow stronger. Maybe you'll be able to go to a trial by the time Miro is fifteen, give or take."

Adamar's ears dropped back. "Fifteen?" He repeated. "That's years away! How could something take so long to heal?"

"The workings of ways are strange." Azoth said. "Though there is a trick that isn't really known to help your healing." The wolf glanced behind him, then back at Adamar. "If your mental health is good, then so shall be your physical health. You're in pain from what Avaha did to you. Yet wheels turned to another, and someone instead followed you home." The wolf smiled and shouted over his shoulder. "Blank! In here!"

Adamar's eyes widened as Skyor ran into the room. He was followed by a stumbling Miro, who was in turn followed by Isun as she tried to catch the runaway fox kit.

The wolf smiled, a little taller than before. His grin grew at the smell of Adamar's utter confusion that turned into happy surprise. "I'm here to help you grow big and strong! We can defeat that bear together."

Jenna O'del

Acknowledgements

Thank you, Carmen Agra Deedy, wonderful children's author, wonderful editor. You helped make this manuscript much better than it was, and I will be eternally grateful for your willingness to read it as it first was. A million thank yous.

Zach: Thanks for putting up with me vaguely talking about this for a couple years.

And Mom. Thank you for bravely putting up with me not letting you read it until publication.

Daddy, thank you for managing to read part of the first draft. It's better now, I'm telling you.

From the Author

Hello, reader. Thank you for picking this up and daring to read this debut novel.

Do you mind daring a little more, and writing an honest review? If you enjoyed this book, please share it with those around you, so the enjoyment can be spread.

Thank you for everything.

—Jenna

Jenna O'del is a seventeen-year-old writer from Rhode Island. She has been actively writing since fifteen, and when not writing, enjoys sailing, being with horses, and a good story. This is her first published novel.

Contact Jenna: jennaodelauthor@aol.com
Website: jennaodel.wordpress.com
Tumblr: jennaodel.tumblr.com
Facebook: facebook.com/TheHiddenStrengthSeries

Made in the USA
Middletown, DE
04 March 2016